"Sword-wielding rats, feline p——— ———, and ———
fill this adventure with in————————
Fiedler thorough——————
—Publisher ————

"Riddled with surprises, the fast-paced, complex plot features a
host of vivid, memorable rodent and feline characters."
—*Kirkus Reviews*

"[A] captivating animal fantasy set in the subway tunnels of
modern-day Brooklyn, NY. . . . *Mouseheart* will please fans of
novels by Erin Hunter, Brian Jacques, and Kathryn Lasky."
—*School Library Journal*

"The underground world and mix of intrigue, prophecy, and
betrayal bring to mind Suzanne Collins's Gregor the Overlander
series. . . . Fans of Brian Jacques's Redwall Abbey series may
enjoy this modern adaptation of rodent politics and warfare."
—*Booklist*

"Students who appreciate a tale where animals take on human
characteristics and engage in action-packed battles will be drawn
to this first in a series. Several plot twists require keen attention."
—*Library Media Connection*

"A tiny, new hero has arrived!. . . . [A] *Braveheart*-style epic
adventure. . . . The story also emphasizes love and loyalty, and
provides clear examples of mercy and restraint."
—*Christian Library Journal*

"Captivating and cunning, *Mouseheart* is the next great
adventure. . . . the first in the series, which promises to deliver grand
adventure and great storytelling. Hopper is one little mouse who
roars! Readers who loved Jacques's Redwall series
and Hunter's Warrior series will love this new series."
—*ABookandAHug.com*

# MOUSE

Also by Lisa Fiedler

· · · · · · · · · · · · · · · · · ·

Mouseheart Vol. 2: *Hopper's Destiny*

Margaret K. McElderry Books

# HEART

VOL. 1

LISA FIEDLER

With illustrations by VIVIENNE TO

New York  London  Toronto  Sydney  New Delhi

To the kids on "The Grit,"
who make summer feel more like magic:
Will and Julia Erickson,
and Matthew, Christopher, A. J., and Brian Carbone.

*Hey, A. J. . . . here's your story!*

MARGARET K. McELDERRY BOOKS

An imprint of Simon & Schuster Children's Publishing Division

1230 Avenue of the Americas, New York, New York 10020

This book is a work of fiction. Any references to historical events, real people, or real places are used fictitiously. Other names, characters, places, and events are products of the author's imagination, and any resemblance to actual events or places or persons, living or dead, is entirely coincidental.

Text copyright © 2014 by Simon & Schuster, Inc.

All rights reserved, including the right of reproduction in whole or in part in any form.

Margaret K. McElderry Books is a trademark of Simon & Schuster, Inc.

For information about special discounts for bulk purchases, please contact Simon & Schuster Special Sales at 1-866-506-1949 or business@simonandschuster.com.

The Simon & Schuster Speakers Bureau can bring authors to your live event. For more information or to book an event, contact the Simon & Schuster Speakers Bureau at 1-866-248-3049 or visit our website at www.simonspeakers.com.

Also available in a Margaret K. McElderry Books hardcover edition

Book design by Lauren Rille

The text for this book is set in Absara.

The illustrations for this book are rendered digitally.

Manufactured in the United States of America

0415 OFF

10 9 8 7 6 5 4 3 2 1

The Library of Congress has cataloged the hardcover edition as follows:

Fiedler, Lisa.

Mouseheart / Lisa Fiedler ; with illustrations by Vivienne To.—1st edition.

p. cm.

Summary: Hopper escapes a pet shop and soon finds himself in the tangle of Brooklyn's transit tunnels in Atlantia, a utopian rat civilization where Hopper is treated as a royal guest until a multi-generational and multi-species battle breaks out and Hopper learns terrible, extraordinary secrets, including one about his destiny.

ISBN 978-1-4424-8781-9 (hardcover)

ISBN 978-1-4424-8784-0 (eBook)

[1. Adventure and adventurers—Fiction. 2. Mice—Fiction. 3. Rats—Fiction. 4. Cats—Fiction. 5. Utopias—Fiction. 6. Secrets—Fiction. 7. Fate and fatalism—Fiction.] I. To, Vivienne, illustrator. II. Title.

PZ7.F457Mou 2015

[Fic]—dc23

2014026207

ISBN 978-1-4424-8783-3 (pbk)

# PROLOGUE

**The young rat prince** knew he was taking a monumental risk. He knew that his father, the emperor, would be livid should he ever learn that he had ventured out into the Great Beyond.

But he did not care. The morning began with the usual pomp and circumstance: a formal breakfast with His Majesty the Emperor Titus, in which the emperor, Zucker's father, ignored both Zucker and Zucker's mother, the beautiful empress Conselyea. After the silent meal the young prince accompanied Titus to a meeting of his royal advisors, and then they went directly to the armory, where his father, with a critical eye, watched him at fencing practice.

The prince was, as always, lithe and lethal. His instructor was pleased and complimentary, but Titus could not be bothered to praise his son's talent.

After fencing Zucker was ushered off to the schoolroom.

Ordinarily he would have complained, but today he didn't mind. This was the crux of his plan of escape.

As expected, the prince's elderly tutor only managed

to drone on for about three minutes before the old rat dozed off into a deep sleep.

This gave the prince the opportunity he needed. He quickly changed out of his elegant vest and breeches and slipped into a shirt made of coarse fabric, which he'd borrowed from one of the servants the day before and hid in the corner of the schoolroom. Then he grabbed his rapier and tiptoed out of the classroom, through the royal apartments, and out into Atlantia.

He kept his head low so as not to be recognized as he darted through the market square to the main gate; with a little luck he'd be able to sweet-talk whichever cat was guarding the gate that morning into letting him through.

Make that a lot of luck.

He stopped short at the sight of a young feral he'd never seen before. The big orange beast looked as though he'd recently been in a fight . . . and lost. His gashes were crusting over to scabs, and there was a festering wound on his tail that looked like a bite mark.

The unfamiliar guard hissed. "What do you want?"

"My father has sent me to roam the tunnels and scavenge for wares to sell at market," Zucker lied.

The cat smirked. "What if I decide not to let you out?"

"I think that's a bad idea," Zucker said, his hand

instinctively moving to the handle of his sword. "You're new. Who are you?"

The cat answered with a cocky toss of his head. "The name's Cyclone. I was named after the roller coaster at Coney Island. 'Cause I'm fast and scary."

"Never heard of Coney Island," the prince shot back, matching Cyclone's attitude.

"You tunnel rats don't know nothin,'" scoffed Cyclone. "I used to live upland, but my humans had a problem with me clawing stuff."

"Like their furniture?"

"Like their legs. And arms, and the occasional cheek and forehead." Cyclone laughed.

Without warning, the cat swung one plump orange paw, smacking the prince hard into the wall and knocking the wind out of him.

Dazed, the prince reached for his sword, but before he could draw it, the cat had snatched him up, holding him so that they were nose to nose.

"I don't particularly enjoy rat flesh," said Cyclone, his reeking breath hot in the prince's face. "But in your case, I might make an exception."

The prince writhed in Cyclone's grip, but the cat held fast. His teeth were slick with drool, and those stagnant-green eyes glowed.

And then . . .

*Thwap!*

The stone flew from the darkness and smashed

into the cat's cheekbone, immediately raising a welt. As Cyclone wobbled, the prince wriggled free and jumped to the ground.

"Hurry up!" came a voice from outside the gate. "While he's dizzy. Run!"

The prince didn't bother to question the logic of running toward an unknown voice beyond the safety of the wall—he just did it.

One razor-sharp claw came down upon his tail, pinning him to the spot; the prince fell forward and landed hard on his face. He struggled, hind paws scraping up clouds of dust, front ones reaching, reaching . . .

The prince looked back and his heart lurched as he saw the cat's open mouth, pink tongue, and jagged teeth coming straight for him.

Unable to watch, he whipped his head away, and to his shock, standing before him was a little brown mouse.

A little brown mouse . . . with a very big sword!

The mouse reached over the prince's head to plunge his blade into the cat's paw. The cat let out a shriek, and the prince was free. He ran for the gate with the mouse right behind him.

"When I shout, 'Now,'" cried the mouse, panting as he ran, "we slam the gate closed! Together. You got me?"

"Gotcha!"

They cleared the gate just as the hissing feline went

into his crouch. The prince and his unknown rescuer took hold of the bars.

Spitting, sputtering, eyes flashing, the cat launched himself into the air.

"Now!"

The prince heaved.

The gate closed just as Cyclone began his descent, his face connecting with the knifelike point of one of the iron bars—piercing, puncturing.

Cyclone jerked his head back and let out a sickening wail.

The prince and the mouse gaped in revulsion as blood spurted from the cat's eye socket.

"I didn't mean for that to happen," breathed the mouse. "Honest!"

As the cat continued to howl in agony, the young prince thought he might be ill, but he managed to collect himself.

"*You* didn't do it," the prince corrected. "*He* did. And besides, you heard him—he would have eaten me. This was self-defense, plain and simple!"

The prince pressed his face to the iron bars and shouted, "Hey, Cyclone! I think from now on you're gonna be called Cy*clops*!"

The cat moaned in pain, pressing both his front paws to his ruined eye. "And if yer thinkin' about getting even, think twice. You picked the wrong rat to mess with!"

Cyclone opened his remaining eye and hissed.

The prince lifted his chin. "I'm His Royal Highness the Crown Prince of the House of Romanus! And if you ever so much as attempt to pluck one whisker from my royal face, you can kiss all nine of your pathetic lives good-bye!"

Cyclone grunted.

The mouse stepped forward and addressed the wounded cat.

"I believe what you've just done is a violation of the Accord between Queen Felina and Emperor Titus," he said calmly. "All the prince has to do is tell one of his father's soldiers, and you'll be swinging from your tail in the town square before lunchtime. However . . . I believe we might be willing to make a deal with you."

The prince grinned. This mouse had guts.

Cyclone brought his bloody face closer to the bars. "What kind of deal?"

"From now on the prince can come and go as he pleases. Any time of the day or night. And you don't say a word. To anyone. Ever. Now, if you'll agree to that one simple condition, we'll agree not to go running back to the palace right now to, if you'll pardon the expression"—he glanced at the prince—"*rat* you out!"

Cyclone let out another miserable meow, but he nodded.

With that, the rat and the mouse took off into the tunnel.

When they reached the first bend and Atlantia was out of sight, the prince turned to his new friend.

"Thanks for saving my life," he said.

The mouse shrugged. "All in a day's work." Then he held out his tiny paw to shake. "By the way, I'm Dodger."

# CHAPTER ONE

THE CAGE LID CLOSED with a hollow *clang*.

It was followed by the metallic zip of the lock sliding into place.

Hopper pressed his soft muzzle to the bars. The shopkeeper had just filled their bowl with a meal of pellets and lined the cage with a fresh sprinkle of aspen shavings and a handful of shredded paper; now the space was clean and almost cozy. Hopper listened as his brother, Pup, burrowed happily into the crisp, new wood curls. Pinkie, their sister, found no such comfort as she clawed at the shiny metal clasp that held the cage lid in place.

Pinkie clawed whenever she could. Pinkie was like that.

"Closing time," Keep muttered, humming off-key as he went about his chores. Hopper watched sleepily as beyond the big window, Brooklyn had begun to fade into twilight and shadows.

The other mice who shared their cage were already piled into a white-and-brown heap in the corner. Young, and new to the shop, they tired easily. In seconds Hopper could hear the gentle snuffles and sighs of their collective slumber.

Keep's gravelly voice rumbled from the back of the shop. "Birds . . . check. Felines . . . check. Reptiles and amphibians . . . check, check."

This was Keep's end-of-the-day litany—checks and reminders and grumbled complaints about ill-smelling feed and dirty cage bottoms. Hopper knew the routine by heart, but he took little joy in the familiarity of it. He hated the darkling hours.

Their mother had disappeared at dusk.

Now Keep returned to the mouse cage. He gave the clasp a tug to see that it was secure.

"Rodents . . . check."

Lucky for Keep, he pulled his chubby thumb away just before Pinkie could sink her teeth into it.

And that was the last of it. Hopper knew all that remained was for Keep to turn the sign from OPEN to CLOSED. This would inform the patrons on the other side of the big window that there would be no more adoptions today; it was time for the animals to rest. Keep would take his leave, sweeping a chill blast of air into the shop as he opened the door. The bell on the handle would jangle fitfully as the door swung wide; then it would close with a loud, metallic *clack* as Keep locked it with his key. After that, the shop would fall silent but for the bubbling of the aquariums and the sleepy chirping sounds of animals dreaming of a far-off future in a place called home.

But not Hopper. He only ever dreamed one dream. And it was not so much a dream but a memory of his mother on the last day he had ever seen her. It was vague and hazy, but buried deep inside it was the image of her lovely brown face and her twinkling eyes, filled with love.

In the memory Hopper and Pinkie and Pup had been no larger than pebbles, pressed against their mother's warm, silken fur. The sun outside the big window had been setting when Keep had approached the cage. And something in Hopper's mother's eyes had turned to ice.

*She knew. Somehow she knew.*

"What's wrong, Mama?" Hopper had asked.

Pinkie had been curled around Pup, sound asleep.

*A creaking sound . . . The cage lid being lifted . . .*

His mother's heartbeat against him, her eyes glittering with tears as they'd darted back and forth between Hopper and Keep. "Find the Mews," she'd whispered. Her voice, ordinarily sweet and calm and wise, had been frantic. "Find the Mews, Hopper. You must."

But Keep had had her by the tail, and in the next moment Hopper's mother had been dangling above him, her arms stretching out to him desperately.

Hopper had heard her utter a word that might have been "below." But he had been too terrified to comprehend. Then she was gone.

He had watched from sun to sun, seeing the light change the sky outside the big glass, but his mother had not come back.

When at last Pinkie had been certain that their mother was lost to them forever, she had turned on him.

"You didn't do anything to stop it!" she had seethed.

"What could I have done?" he'd asked in a small voice.

"Woken me, for starters! I would have known what to do. I would have *fought* for her."

The disdain in her eyes, the scorn in her voice, had caused Hopper to burrow into the aspen shavings in shame.

Pup had come and cuddled beside him. Pup had been even tinier then . . . so delicate and fragile. His ears had been smaller and pinker than Hopper's, nearly transparent.

"Maybe Mama went home," he'd said in his hopeful way. "Maybe that's what happened, Hopper."

Hopper had nodded, but there was a lump in his throat. "Yes, Pup. That's probably it."

"So we should be happy for her, then."

Hopper had smiled at his brother but hadn't replied. He had seen his mother's eyes when Keep pinched her tail and jerked her out of their cage. She had not been adopted, brought to a better life. She had been violently stolen. Hopper knew it in his gut. *Find the Mews*. The phrase haunted him as much as the image did. He still couldn't be certain that's what she'd said as she'd bobbed above him, her paws reaching for her babies even as the hand pulled her from their lives. But he would never forget the tone of her voice. It was a promise, a warning, a plea . . .

*Find the Mews.*

Sometimes in the memory Hopper could almost feel the warmth she'd left behind in the nest of paper and wood. She was there and she was gone. And in the dream he could do nothing but watch her go.

And always Hopper would awaken with his eyes damp and his heart aching.


Hopper closed his eyes and listened, first for the whine of the money machine being put to bed, then for the bell on the door that would signal Keep's departure.

But the sounds didn't come.

Hopper waited.

Still no machine. Still no bell.

He opened his eyes, his pink nose twitching with awareness. What was Keep waiting for?

Suddenly Keep's booted feet stomped across the shop to the counter, and he angrily muttered something under his breath.

Curious, Hopper peered through the bars, but all he saw was his own reflection in the glass tank next to his cage.

Same old Hopper: small and brown, with a white ring around his right eye; slender paws and long, smooth tail, tapered to a point at the end like a whip. Bright black eyes, and dainty, oval ears, flickering now as he listened to Keep's movements.

Coins rattled as the money drawer banged open, then closed again. The machine let out one last long beep and the shop went still.

But then the door flung wide—the bell jingled madly as the shop was assaulted with a rush of cold wind. A lanky boy wearing a snug woolen cap and a black jacket stood in the doorway. His face was thin and pale, and his eyes narrowed as he locked his gaze on Keep.

Worst of all was the long, slithering horrible thing he carried, draped around his neck.

Hopper's heart thudded and his blood went cold as one word and one word only trembled on his tongue.

*Snake!*

# CHAPTER TWO

HOPPER DID NOT KNOW how he knew that word—perhaps he wasn't even saying it properly, but he *knew* it . . . knew it in his bones, from the tips of his whiskers to the point of his tail. It was a knowledge born of instinct.

Without thinking, Hopper scampered across the papery floor of the cage and threw himself in front of Pup and Pinkie.

"What are you doing?" Pinkie hissed.

"Shhh," said Hopper. He was quivering now, watching with wide eyes as the skinny boy marched himself across the shop to Keep's counter. The snake clung to his bony shoulders, moving like something from another world. Its flattened, diamond-shaped head darted from side to side, a forked sliver of tongue flicking in and out between long, curved fangs.

"What is that?" Pup whispered from behind Hopper. His wispy little voice was filled with terror.

"It's a snake, you runt!" snapped Pinkie.

A jolt of anger shot through Hopper. He had asked Pinkie a hundred times not to call Pup "runt." But now was certainly not a time for reprimands.

"Where's my feeders?" the boy demanded.

"You're too late," said Keep, shrugging his stooped shoulders. "I told ya, I close at five—I already rung out."

The boy frowned. "It ain't my fault the trains were late tonight."

Keep laughed. "You took that monster on the subway? Boy, I bet you gave a lotta folks the fright of their life!" He shook his head, still chuckling. "Imagine that! A boa on the Brighton line!"

*Boa.*

Hopper had heard that word before, and it shot into his ear like a poison dart.

*Boa.* As in *boa constrictor.*

Keep had had one once. It lived in a heavy glass tank on a sturdy shelf in an area of the shop Hopper and the other mice could not see from their cage. But he'd heard people talking about it, describing it—they'd called it "a hideous slithering rope of a thing, with scales and sharp teeth." They called it "fierce" and "frightening."

Now that Hopper was seeing one with his own eyes, he knew they'd been right.

He turned his attention to the counter, where the boy was tapping his foot, ignoring Keep's laughter. He stroked the snake's scaly neck. "I need feeders *now.*"

Pup turned to Pinkie. "What's a feeder?" he asked quietly.

Pinkie's answer was a grim look.

"I told ya," Keep said, "I'm closed. The register's computerized, so I can't open it again till tomorrow morning. Come back then."

Then Keep smiled.

"But you can have a peek at 'em," he told the boy. "Whet the beast's appetite, so to speak." With a pudgy finger he pointed across the shop.

Directly at Hopper.

The boy gave a little grunt. With his snake writhing on his shoulders, he crossed the floor to the mouse cage.

Drawing himself up to his full stature, Hopper spread his arms wide to shield his family, pressing Pinkie and Pup against the back bars of the cage, shivering as boy and snake moved closer. And closer.

"Jeesh," the boy huffed. "No aquarium?" He poked a scrawny finger between the bars of Hopper's cage and tugged. "This thing's practically an antique!"

"I like to keep my costs down," Keep muttered. "So sue me. Why waste money on first-class accommodations for vermin?"

Suddenly the angular face of the boa constrictor popped up against the bars, and the creature let out a sickening hiss. With a terrified yelp Hopper dove beneath the tattered paper scraps and aspen wood flakes, curling himself into a trembling ball of panic.

"Easy, Bo," the boy said, chuckling. He ran a bony finger along the bars, causing the cage to shake. With an ear-splitting cackle the boy turned on the heel of his black sneaker and sauntered out of the shop.

The bell jangled itself to silence, and minutes later the place went dark.

*Jingle. Slam. Clack. Quiet.*

A parakeet whistled, almost as though it were bidding Keep good riddance.

Pinkie poked Hopper hard. "You can come out now," she said with disgust. "They're gone."

Cautiously Hopper stuck his nose out from where he was huddled beneath the shavings and paper shreds.

"What a family I've got," Pinkie spat. "A coward and a runt."

Hopper opened his mouth to scold Pinkie but stopped himself. He felt his heart sink because he knew she was right. He *was* a coward.

And Pup was smaller than even the youngest mice in the cage. He was weaker, too. Still, Hopper loved him dearly. Pup was sweet and gentle and looked up to his big brother and sister with utter confidence and admiration.

Hopper had to admit, Pinkie deserved that admiration. She was brave and bold and tough. She and Hopper may have looked exactly alike—same gray-brown pelt, same white marking (although Pinkie's ring circled her left eye), but inside they couldn't be more different.

Hopper loved to pore over the paper scraps that lined their cage, trying to make sense of the print and symbols on them. He found the squiggles and colors fascinating, even though he didn't quite understand their messages.

Pinkie, on the other hand, was all energy. She rarely sat still long enough to read or even think. She was spunky and courageous, and always ready for a challenge. Or a fight.

Hopper often wondered if Pinkie hadn't been sleeping so soundly when his mother was taken . . . if *she* had been the one who was awake, would she have done something, like she said she would have? Would she have been able to save their mother from whatever fate awaited her outside their cage?

He couldn't say for sure. But in his heart he knew that at the very least Pinkie would have tried.

He was exactly what his sister said he was. A coward.

Maybe it was time to change that.

If only he could.

# CHAPTER THREE

HOPPER DIDN'T KNOW WHEN he had dozed off, but he awoke with a start the next morning. Scraps of paper clung to his sweat-dampened fur, and his whole body shook with horror.

He nudged his sister. She snarled in her sleep. He nudged her again.

"What do you want?"

"That boy wants to feed us to his snake."

Pinkie sat up, carefully moving Pup from under her arm where he was curled up asleep. "Say that again . . ."

"*We're* feeders," Hopper confirmed. "Not to be taken home as pets, but—"

"To be taken home for dinner," Pinkie finished, horrified.

"Correction," Hopper said with a sigh. "Breakfast." He turned toward the big window, where the first smudges of morning light had begun to brighten the sky behind the tall buildings.

Pinkie wriggled away from Pup and began to pace. For a moment Hopper just watched her. When her narrow rear paw caught on a long, glossy paper scrap, she shook it off. It billowed into the air, then landed in front of Hopper. He glanced at it, noting a round marking—bright red with some kind of hieroglyph inside. And more symbols: S-U-B-W and 14.

He had no idea what to make of the markings, and now was not the time to dwell on them. He brushed the crinkled scrap aside.

"The boy will be back soon after Keep opens," Hopper said, willing his voice to stay calm. "We have to be gone by then."

Pinkie whirled to glare at him. "Oh, really?" She slapped her tail against the bars; the noise caused one of the mice in the corner to stir in his sleep. "And how do you intend to do that?"

"Keep has to feed us," Hopper reasoned.

"When Keep puts the food in our bowl, we can climb up his arm and out of the cage. Then we can jump down and escape."

Pinkie frowned. "And by 'we' you mean . . . ?"

Hopper motioned to the sleeping pile of mice in the corner. "All of us. We can't leave them behind."

Pinkie sighed heavily. "I suppose not." Her whiskers twitched once, twice. "I say we bite him."

Hopper shook his head. "Absolutely not. We run up and we run out. No need for more trouble."

"The man is planning to feed us to a boa constrictor, Hopper. I don't think this is any time to concern ourselves with manners. Now, if we all just get in one quick chomp—" She gnashed her sharp teeth in demonstration.

"What good will that do?" Hopper asked. "If we bite

his hand, he'll pull his arm out of the cage and we'll have nothing to climb!"

Pinkie didn't say so, but Hopper could tell she saw the logic in that.

"Satisfaction," she said at last. "We'd have the satisfaction of making him scream in pain."

Hopper's stomach turned over. Sometimes it was hard to believe that he and Pinkie were related.

"No," he said as firmly as he could. "We're going to do this my way."

Pinkie blinked at him. "Since when are you so bossy?"

*Since I don't want to find myself on the inside of that slithering beast,* Hopper thought with a gulp. But what he said was, "Wake the others. And tell them our plan."

Pinkie paused; for a moment Hopper thought she was going to argue. Instead she rolled her eyes and skulked across the shavings to awaken their cagemates.

Pinkie listening to Hopper—the thought exhilarated him. Maybe he'd be able to pull off leading this escape after all.

Across the cage he could hear Pinkie murmuring and the others protesting, then finally agreeing to the plan.

Hopper looked at Pup, a small lump still asleep in a pile of curled wood shavings, and a surge of big-brotherly responsibility flooded his veins. He decided there and then that he would see to Pup's safety himself. No harm would come to that tiny ball of fluff, not if he could help it.

Feeling bolstered and determined, he turned to watch the morning sun brighten the Brooklyn sky. Keep would be arriving soon, pushing open the door, bringing the cold in with him.

And then they would make their escape—to where, Hopper did not know.

But he did know this:

Bo, the hideous snake creature, would go hungry this morning. With any luck the beast might even starve to death.

Pushing the memory of those bladelike fangs from his mind's eye, Hopper fixed his gaze on the big glass to await the daylight and to watch for Keep's imminent arrival.

His heart frantically drummed against his ribs.

Just once, he wished his mouse heart could beat with the thrill of bravery, of courage—and not fear.

But for now all he could do was press his nose against the bars.

And wait.

# CHAPTER FOUR

HOPPER DID NOT FLINCH. He didn't even blink when, finally, he heard the sound of Keep's key in the lock. Sometime during Hopper's watch the pale sun had disappeared and it had begun to rain, turning the outdoor world a dull gray.

The bell rattled and Keep bustled in, shaking water from his coat. Hopper knew that on wet days patrons were few and far between, and this always made Keep cross. On rainy days he would grumble that the shop smelled of mildew and damp fur, and this kept the patrons away.

A prickle of hope tingled in Hopper—perhaps the wet would prevent boy and boa from venturing out. Still, he did not take his eyes off the door.

Pup was sleeping, snuggled beside the water bowl in the corner. After a moment Hopper felt Pinkie sidle up. Her whole body was tensed, like a coil of fury, ready to pounce. She flicked her pinkish tail in the direction of their cagemates. "They want to know where to go . . . you know . . . *after* we get out."

Hopper gulped. It was a good question. His plan only got as far as up Keep's arm and out of the cage. Following that . . . there was nothing but mystery.

Suddenly the shop door slammed open; it hit the wall so hard that the bell loosened from its chain and fell to the floor with a hollow clunk. Silhouetted in the doorway with the rain pouring down behind them loomed the skinny boy and his wicked reptile, curled around his shoulders.

"He's here earlier than I thought," Hopper said to Pinkie.

"Is that thing a pet or a scarf?" Pinkie huffed, but beneath her wisecrack Hopper heard concern.

"Go wake Pup," he whispered. "Tell him it's time."

"I still think we should fight," Pinkie complained. "Don't you think our lives are worth a little scuffle?"

"Go wake Pup," Hopper repeated.

Hopper turned to signal the others. They were ready. Frightened. Panicked. Petrified. But ready. He gave them a quick nod.

One of the cagemates let out a determined squeak.

"Look, Bo," said the boy in his screechy voice. "Breakfast." He came toward the cage, his wet sneakers slapping the floor. "So how would you like your mice this morning, pal? Over easy? Scrambled?" He gave a snort of laughter. "Or maybe just raw?"

The snake hissed, weaving from side to side, his tongue darting madly in anticipation of his meal.

The boy's scrawny fingers reached for the lock on the cage lid.

But Keep hustled over to brush the boy's hand away. "This ain't no self-serve establishment, kid. Now, how many do you want?"

"Well, Bo here's a growing boy, ain'tcha, buddy?" The boy stroked the snake's neck. "So how about the whole bunch?"

"Fine by me," said Keep. "There's more where these came from." He slid open the lock.

"Ready . . ." Hopper whispered.

Keep opened the lid.

"Set . . ."

Keep reached into the cage, his hand ready to scoop them out.

"Go!"

Pinkie let out a piercing squeal, a crazed war whoop. The cagemates moved as one, scrambling into Keep's cupped palm, then surprising him by leaping to his wrist and scampering up his arm.

"Run!" cried Hopper, boosting Pup out of the wood curls and onto Keep's plump forearm.

"Hopper," Pup cried, "I'm scared!"

"I know, Pup . . . just run!"

Pinkie was already as far as Keep's elbow. She stopped, midscurry, to look back toward Pup, who was struggling to get a foothold. His paws clawed at the pudgy flesh, desperate to grasp the springy hairs to keep from falling off.

"Come on!" Pinkie cried, unfurling her tail. "Grab hold!"

Hopper watched, heart racing, as Pup reached a paw for Pinkie's wiry tail. He missed.

Pinkie whipped it toward him a second time.

He caught it.

"Hopper!" Pup's voice was a faint cry as Pinkie jerked him upward along Keep's chubby arm. "Hurry!"

Hopper made a great leap, which landed him halfway up Keep's forearm. Most of the cagemates had reached the top and were bravely jumping off, diving from Keep's stooped shoulders to the relative safety of the shelf below. One mouse bit into the edge of the pocket on Keep's shirt, and as Keep squirmed, the seam split, tearing the pocket away and taking the cagemate with it.

Keep's shock had given way to anger now; he was shaking his arm wildly in an effort to dislodge the swarm of mice.

The boy was laughing, and Bo's head darted back and forth in a frenzy, a blur of flickering tongue and gnashing teeth, watching frantically as his morning meal escaped before his beady eyes.

Pinkie and Pup were nearing Keep's shoulder now, and Hopper was bringing up the rear. He couldn't believe their luck—they were *this close* to freedom. Keep was so flustered and confused by the commotion that they might just make it.

But Pinkie had suddenly stopped short. Hopper gasped as Pup, still clinging to her tail, whipped sideways. Now he was dangling over the side of Keep's arm, several feet above the hard cement floor.

Pinkie's eyes flashed like fire. She couldn't help herself. . . .

Hopper's own eyes went wide when he realized what she was going to do.

"Pinkie!" he shrieked. *"Nooooo!"*

But it was too late. Her pointy little teeth were bared, and she was sinking them into the pale, spotty flesh of Keep's limb.

Hopper felt the world lurch as Keep, howling in pain, gave his arm a powerful shake. Hopper scrambled to grab hold of a large brown mole on Keep's inner arm and held on for dear life. Pinkie was still attached by her teeth; she'd clamped down and was not letting go for anything.

But Pup . . .

Pup swung like a pendulum from Pinkie's long tail. One of his paws had lost its grip; he was clutching desperately with the other, but Hopper could see that his grasp was slipping.

"Hold on, Pup!" But even as Hopper screamed the words, he watched in horror as Pup's tiny paw gave way.

He was falling . . .

Toppling in midair . . .

*Falling!*

# CHAPTER FIVE

HOPPER'S STOMACH TURNED OVER at the sound of the small, dull thump. All he could see was a tiny puff of beige-brown fur lying perfectly still on the concrete floor.

Anger exploded. Anger, and grief. Without thinking, he opened his jaws and sunk his teeth ferociously into Keep's skin.

Another jolt of Keep's arm! Pinkie, who had released her bite hold and was watching Hopper, was caught unawares. She lost her balance and tumbled, head-over-hind-haunches until she, too, was falling through space, dropping toward the hard, deadly surface of the floor.

Hopper released his hold on the stubby birthmark and reached out . . . out . . . stretching . . . grasping . . .

Just as Pinkie came spiraling within reach, Hopper made a mad grab. The tips of his claws connected with her tail and he grabbed hold, clutching for all he was worth, gripping her tail against the force of gravity.

Now Pinkie dangled in space, teeth bared, whiskers quivering, arms flailing.

But safe.

Well, sort of.

Keep's fleshy hand closed around the two of them and squeezed.

In the darkness of the fist Hopper could barely breathe. He was sure they were done for when . . .

Light!

Keep's hand unfolded. Hopper felt himself dropping but not far. He and Pinkie went skidding across a smooth, papery surface, colliding with a shallow wall of the same material.

Cardboard?

Box!

Hopper had seen these contraptions a thousand times. The cardboard box was the vehicle in which hamsters and gerbils and guinea pigs went home.

And, apparently, how feeder mice traveled to their snakes.

Gasping for breath, Hopper disentangled himself from Pinkie just as the box closed. Streams of pale light sliced into this new darkness through several tiny holes in the lid.

"I don't think this is an improvement," Pinkie said with a sneer.

Hopper ignored her. He had to think!

His mind was muddy, and his thoughts came in hazy waves. His memory called up that familiar, dark recollection—his mother ascending from the wood shavings, disappearing upward into the unknown as if by some evil magic. The recollection blurred, splintered, blending itself with the more recent horror of watching Pup, not rising but falling—in his memory it was as if they passed each other in slow motion—his mother rising . . . rising; his brother falling . . . falling . . . and then there was Pup sprawled on the pet-shop floor, silent, still.

Hopper tamped down the despair. Perhaps it had looked worse than it was; perhaps the impact had merely stunned Pup. And in that case, maybe the cagemates had rallied and rushed to his aid. Maybe they'd roused him from his stupor or carried him to shelter, out of the path of Keep's enormous tromping feet.

Maybe.

But in his heart Hopper knew the chances of that were slim.

"This is your fault," came Pinkie's voice from the shadows of the box. "You're weak. And stupid! Pup is gone and here we are, trapped, awaiting our own death sentence."

The words were worse than any gnashing she could have given him.

Hopper shook off the heartache and forced himself to think.

In the corner of the box was a slim gap where the cardboard came together. Hopper scurried over and peered out.

The skinny boy was hobbling about to avoid stepping on the cagemates who, with nowhere else to go, were dashing back and forth across the floor in a crazed rush. The boy wasn't laughing anymore. Now he looked mad.

"You can keep your stinkin' cage mice," he barked at Keep. "I can catch better ones in the subway anyway!" Bo, jabbing his head in Keep's direction and hissing angrily, seemed to be in agreement. With one last menacing hiss, boy and snake stormed out of the shop.

Keep muttered something nasty-sounding about "kids today" and clomped off toward the back room, closing the door behind him.

Then things became very, very quiet.

Hopper peeked through the slit in the corner and listened. There was a faint noise, a sound he thought he'd heard before—a spattering sound, a splashing sound.

The rain.

Not the dull, muffled sound of the drops hitting the roof or the windows of the shop. This sound was clear and close, louder and more immediate. Hopper had heard it before but only in quick little spurts when the shop door opened on a stormy day; in the few seconds it would take for the door to swing closed, he would hear the rain clearly, its noisy patter as it hit the sidewalk. Then the door would close and the sound would soften again.

But this time the sound wasn't softening.

The door was open! The angry boy had left the door open when he left.

"Pinkie, come here. Look!"

Pinkie pressed in beside him and looked out. When she spotted the open door, she knew instantly what he was thinking.

Hopper pressed his mouth to the gap in the corner joint and called out to his scurrying cagemates.

"The door!" he cried. "Run for the door!"

They all stopped running at once. Five pairs of pink eyes blinked as they stared in awe. They didn't seem to know what to make of this command. It was Hopper's voice coming from somewhere high above them, but they could not see him.

"Run!" he cried again.

But the mice remained frozen. Hopper's word echoed from inside the box, reaching their tiny ears in a hollow, ghostly howl. Even to him it sounded like the voice of some unseen being, some magical force.

"Idiots," Pinkie growled. "They think you're some kind of all-seeing rodent spirit." She began backing up toward the far wall of the box.

"What are you doing?" Hopper asked.

Pinkie took a deep breath. "When I give the signal, we run as fast and hard as we can and throw ourselves at the opposite wall, got it?"

Hopper nodded.

"Ready? *Go!*"

Hopper bolted with all his might; Pinkie was like a flash of lightning. The brother and sister hurled themselves across the box and slammed into the cardboard wall at the exact same moment.

The box tottered, then tipped, landing on its side and knocking the lid askew.

"Push!" cried Hopper, pounding his tiny paws against the cover.

Pinkie did the same and the lid came away! Hopper and Pinkie leaped out of the darkness and found themselves on the counter near the money machine. All they had to do now was shinny down the machine's cord and . . .

The door to the back room flew open, and Keep returned.

He was wielding a broom.

The straw weapon was kicking up a small tornado of dust and grime. The cagemates scurried madly in the dirty cloud, darting to and fro to avoid being swept into oblivion.

"Mangy little beasts!" Keep snarled.

The broom swung like a bristled gauntlet. Hopper gaped in terror as its angled edge connected with an errant tail, sending the petrified cagemate skidding and squealing across the floor to crash headlong into the base of the counter.

Pinkie was edging toward the fat electrical cord; was she still considering crawling down?

"Have you lost your *mind*?" Hopper breathed.

"Maybe, but if I stay here, I'll lose my *life*!"

Hopper looked from his sister to the open door. The sharp claws of fear pricked his skin as doubt began to overtake him.

"It's too big a risk," he said, shaking his head.

But Pinkie was clearly done talking. She growled and lunged for Hopper, wild-eyed, sinking her pearly little fangs into the tip of his ear.

Hopper howled in agony as Pinkie jerked away, gripping a strip of tender skin in her clenched teeth.

The pain was blinding, and Hopper's fury ignited. He leaped toward his sister even as the piece of his flesh still dangled from her teeth. He attacked her exactly as she had him, biting down viciously on her ear and yanking hard, maiming her just as she had him. Hopper sputtered, already sick from the vile taste of blood and skin in his mouth and from the knowledge of what he had done.

Would he have apologized? Would he have blamed his violent act on the pain and fear and sorrow that was threatening to overwhelm him? Would he have begged his sister's forgiveness even as he spat the delicate pink fragment of her ear out of his mouth?

He would never know.

Because before he could speak, or move, or even think, the brittle yellow head of the broom slammed down on the counter, just inches from where he and Pinkie were crouched, panting and bleeding.

"Vermin!" Keep shouted. "Varmints! Get down from there!"

Hopper didn't have to be told twice. He took off at a run, his claws rasping against the smooth surface of the countertop. He sensed Pinkie at his heels. As one, they sprang for the thick electrical cable, half scampering, half sliding down to where it ended at a socket near the baseboard.

Hopper jumped the short distance from the cord to the floor. Now that the broom dust had settled, he had a clear view of the open door. Summoning his courage, he sprinted for it, only vaguely aware of the motionless bodies of the cagemates that littered his path. His eyes searched desperately for Pup, but he didn't spy him anywhere.

Pinkie was close, running just behind him. "Go!" she cried, her breath hot on his haunches.

Toward the door.

Toward the dark.

Toward the rain.

Toward the world.


Hopper ran, the only sound in his ruined ear the scraping of his claws on the cement floor. The only thought in his head:

*Escape!*

They were close, *so* close. . . . Hopper could feel the damp, cool air swirling in from the street.

Keep was right there, stomping toward the door, ready to slam it closed and lock them inside forever.

But Hopper kept that narrow opening in his sights; the now-silenced bell lay rusty and forgotten on the floor.

Heart racing, muscles burning, Hopper put his head down and aimed for the slice of gray daylight visible through the opening, the breach that separated in from out, confinement from freedom, living from . . .

"I'll teach you to run from me," Keep cried, his hand reaching for the door.

Behind Hopper, Pinkie wheezed and grunted but managed to keep up.

They were nearly through!

Keep let out a mighty groan; too late, he slammed the door. The force of it propelled Hopper and his sister forward into the rainstorm.

They were out. They had escaped into the world beyond.

And still, Hopper ran. He wanted as much distance between himself and that horrible prison as he could get.

Only once did he dare to look back over his shoulder.

Keep stood framed in the doorway, in that bright rectangle of light, looking angry and defeated. He was pounding one fist against the door, even as he used the other to flip the cardboard sign.

CLOSED.

But he couldn't hurt them now. He couldn't sweep them up and throw them in a box or sell them to a wicked human boy with a reptile writing around his shoulders.

Keep was the one who was trapped now. Keep was *in*.

And Hopper and Pinkie, for better or for worse, were *out*.

*Without Pup.*

# CHAPTER SIX

THEY WERE ON SOMETHING called a "sidewalk."

Hopper had heard Keep use the word many times; he'd rap on the big glass and scold the young human packs who lingered aimlessly in front of the shop: *"Hey, you punks, quit dropping those gum wrappers on my sidewalk!"*

Hopper had never wondered or even cared exactly what a sidewalk was. But now here he was, scrambling along a wet one with his sister, dodging the shoes and boots of what seemed to be an endless throng of quick-stepping human travelers.

Hopper was surprisingly agile for one who had spent his whole life in a cage, and the sensation of the raindrops hitting his fur was strange and wonderful. Air and noise and shadow and motion were everywhere. And the smells! The myriad, indescribable smells! More than just insect, rodent, feline, and fish. His nose twitched of its own accord as he breathed them all in.

One of the scents he could not name was an acrid one, an unpleasant smell that seemed to come from the strange, enormous rolling machines that roared on their own kind of sidewalk, wider than the one along which the humans were treading. These machines growled like wild animals, flashing lighted eyes into the rainy gloom.

It was becoming clear to Hopper that danger was everywhere.

When he was satisfied that the shop was a good ways behind them, he slowed down; Pinkie again took her cue from him.

"Look what you've done," she hissed, her eyes taking in the vastness of their new world. "You led us into the rain. And Pup. We've lost Pup."

Hopper curled his tail around his legs. *Pup. What happened to Pup?* "We'll find him," Hopper said. "Besides, you didn't have to follow me," he pointed out sharply.

He walked with his sister to the edge of the sidewalk, to the relative shelter of a large receptacle fashioned of metal mesh. Away from the foot traffic they crouched near the base of it, and despite their anger, they instinctively huddled together against the chill. Hopper looked upward at the tall, cagelike barrel and watched as passing humans dropped things into it: various items they seemed to regard as useless— crumpled paper, empty cups, and the remains of uneaten food. In fact, of all the smells that were assailing him out here in the universe, it seemed the best ones were coming from deep inside this strange cylindrical basket.

Hopper reached through one of the holes in the metal mesh and rummaged around gingerly. Finally he withdrew something that looked and smelled edible; he tentatively brought it to his nose.

His belly reacted instantly, tumbling with unbidden pangs of hunger.

*Twitch. Twitch.*

This was no pellet.

*This* was some human delicacy, to be sure. *Meat,* Hopper thought, examining it; it was narrow and rounded, shaped like a plump human finger smeared with thick yellow goop. Clinging to Hopper's aromatic find was a square of flimsy paper decorated with a series of markings like the ones he found emblazoned on the shreds of paper that lined his cage.

## WILBUR'S WEENIE WORLD
### 555 Atlantic Ave. Brooklyn
## BEST HOT DOGS IN NEW YORK

Of course, like the ones in his cage, these printed curves and slashes meant nothing to Hopper. The drawing showed a larger version of the half-eaten item he now clutched in his paws, which was still giving off a most tantalizing aroma.

Cautiously Hopper nibbled the end of it.

It was warm and succulent and spicy, and there were tiny chunks of something green and sweet mixed in with the yellow glop. As he chewed, the meat left a slight film of grease on his mouth.

His stomach quickly filled, and Hopper wondered if

he should share this culinary treasure with his sister. Then he remembered sourly that she'd already eaten a piece of his ear.

But she was eyeing his prize with a look of longing. "Give it," she demanded.

"No," said Hopper, his mouth full. "Find your own."

Pinkie narrowed her eyes and ground her paws into the sidewalk. She pounced, toppling Hopper backward and sending the mysterious and wonderful food morsel flying through the air.

The siblings tussled, pulling at fur, nipping at tails, unaware that all the while they were rolling closer and closer to the edge of the sidewalk, toward the wide black stripe upon the earth where those rolling, growling, light-eyed monsters zoomed past.

As Hopper and Pinkie struggled, punching and kicking, Hopper became aware of a droning sound— it was like rain but more than rain. It sounded like *all* the rain that had *ever* rained. But now it was not falling from the dark sky above; this sound was close by—just over the edge of the sidewalk. Rushing, splashing, moving—a watery torrent.

Panic clenched in Hopper's gut. "Stop!" he cried.

But, of course, Pinkie went right on pummeling him.

He nearly managed to right himself, but his sister would not release her hold. They continued to somersault toward the border of the sidewalk, closer to the sound of the rushing water.

Suddenly Hopper and Pinkie found themselves submerged. The water held them in an icy, airless stranglehold. The miniature rapids tossed and spun them, bearing them furiously forward while they clung to each other for dear life.

Just when it seemed to Hopper as if he could not hold his breath a single second longer, a small wave swelled from the bottom of the whipping river, lifting and thrusting him upward. He broke the surface, gasping, flailing, gulping in oxygen, blinking filthy droplets from his eyes and slapping at the water in a pitiful attempt to swim.

*Breathe*, he commanded himself. *Keep your head above water and be calm . . . drift . . . float. Relax and breathe, and help Pinkie . . .*

It was then that Hopper realized: Pinkie was no longer wrapped around him, sharing the terror of this wild ride.

She was gone.

His stomach clenched in a knot of anguish. How had he lost her? Why had she let go?

Hopper shouted, "Pinkie!" But his voice was lost to the whooshing noise of the raging water.

Ahead, a dip in the gutter had created a tiny whirlpool.

Tiny but deep.

And strong.

The water that ferociously pulled Hopper now

seemed to confuse its course, turning around on itself, chasing its own current in a swirling circle of speed.

Round and round.

Hopper began to stroke, frantically trying to steer himself back upstream. He kicked his legs, swished his tail in hopes of changing direction.

But the drag was unrelenting, reaching for him with liquid fingers, reaching for him as Keep had once reached for his mother . . . as Hopper should have reached for Pup, to save him from the fall.

And then the whirlpool caught him. Dizzy and weak, Hopper tried to tread water. But the spiral was sucking at his tail, his paws, pulling him, tugging him.

Down.

Down.

Deeper.

Farther.

The whirling gave way to plunging, and Hopper felt as if he were a part of the water itself—as though his mind, body, and soul had turned to fluid, spilling into some blackness that waited way below the world.

Lost in the waterfall, he surrendered to the deluge. . . . The water had become a rushing column, and Hopper toppled and tumbled within it, plummeting toward . . .

. . . nowhere.

And then the pouring sensation ceased and he landed hard, the back of his head colliding with some unforgiving ground. The pillar of water had deposited him in a vast but shallow, slimy puddle; the puddle trickled and seeped away from itself, edging outward into even more blackness, more nowhere. Dampness clung to the walls, the ceiling, the very air, though Hopper could see nothing in the gloom.

This new world into which he'd been so violently and helplessly dropped was a dank, sprawling cavern filled with echoes.

Hopper knew he should rise. And run. He should find his way out and head to higher ground. He had to get out of this godforsaken cave.

But the little visibility afforded to him was suddenly turning to haze; his eyes were going blurry. His stomach roiled.

"Pinkie . . . help me," he whispered, but it was only his own voice that came to him in a ghostly repeat. Down here, even the whispers echoed.

He was aware of an ache in the back of his head; it joined forces with the sting of his torn ear. When he tried to lift his shoulders, an exquisite pain thundered inside his skull, and he had to lower himself again into the slime.

Hopper felt his eyelids flutter; prickles of light broke behind them. It was better than the gloom, he decided, so he closed his eyes and kept them closed.

In the moment just before he yielded to the void, he called for his sister one last time.

"Pinkie . . . ," he rasped.

He was fading fast, but he heard himself speak her name as clearly as if he'd bellowed it.

# CHAPTER SEVEN

HOPPER CAME TO SLOWLY, his mind replaying the grisly scenes from the last several hours. His bruised body protested even the slightest movement, so he simply lay there. How far away those clean, crisp aspen curls, that tiny bowl of fresh, clear water, seemed now. And Pup . . . it hurt most to think of Pup.

He drew in a long, trembling breath; his ribs throbbed and his lungs felt sodden and sluggish. He was wetter than he'd ever been in his life, soaked all the way through his fur to the delicate pink skin beneath. His bones seemed chilled to the marrow.

The mere thought of opening his eyes nearly overwhelmed him with dread.

Because Hopper knew.

He was not a worldly mouse, nor an educated one, but he was wise enough to know that once he allowed himself a glimpse of this unexpected nightmare into which he'd fallen, his life would never be the same again.

No going back.

What had been before would be forever gone. All of it. All of *them*.

But there was no point in delaying the inevitable. If he were doomed to exist in this miserable hole in the world, he might as well see what it looked like.

Swallowing hard, he opened first one eye and then the other.

The place was still a vast, empty cavern. Still dark, still clammy.

His eyes began to adjust and shapes availed themselves—Hopper could make out the jagged stones of the walls that curved overhead in a towering arc of chipped tile. The pillar of water that had deposited him here had subsided, and now only the odd drip or trickle fell from above, landing on the surface of the puddle with a *plink* or a *ploink* or a *splat*, sending a dark shimmer of ripples across the black surface.

*Plink.*

*Ploink.*

*Splat.*

As though the ceiling were crying.

Hopper lifted himself from where he lay in the shallow pool. He was wobbly at first but eventually regained his equilibrium and set out to explore his immediate surroundings.

Taking cautious, mincing steps, he made his way out of the puddle, then up a slight slope, where he found himself standing on a long, rusted metal rail. His eyes followed its path, where it curved around a bend in the long arched tunnel and disappeared into the darkness. A similar rail lay parallel to the one on which Hopper perched, and between these two solid metal bars lay a series of narrow, evenly spaced wooden planks. These, too, continued into the darkness and out of sight. For all Hopper knew, the rail, the planks, and the tunnel stretched all the way to infinity.

Overhead he saw a web of heavy cables and frayed wires.

He spied a burned-out, naked lightbulb with a rusted pull chain mounted to an ancient fixture on a wall.

Mostly, though, he saw garbage.

Things abandoned, lost and long forgotten, littered the place, moldering and rotting before his black eyes. Bits of human artifacts like worn shoes, torn paper, items electrical in nature, and a scattering of the small, shiny discs—coins, like the ones he'd seen Keep drop into the money machine a hundred times a day. There were more empty cans and broken bottles than he could count.

*Home sweet home,* he thought bitterly.

When an objectionable odor wafted from some far-off corner, Hopper knew instantly that he was not the only living creature to inhabit this dungeonlike place.

Wonderful.

He tamped down his worry and continued to peer into the darkness.

Just beyond the puddle he was able to make out

a miniscule pile of twiglike objects; bleached and brittle-looking, they appeared to be of varying lengths, angles, and curvatures.

Could those be . . . ? Were they . . . ?

*Bones!* An entire skeleton, in fact.

Hopper's stomach turned. Something had *died* here.

It just was too much for the mouse to bear. Crushed by a wave of despair, he covered his face with his paws and wept. His sadness was utter and complete; so devoid of hope was Hopper that he thought he might just sit there and cry like this forever.

And then he heard it. A rumble—mild at first; a distant thrumming that grew louder and closer with every twitch of his whiskers.

The ground beneath him began to quake as the rumble grew to a roar. From nowhere a sparkling light sliced through the bleakness! It looked almost like the sun, but even a sheltered rodent like Hopper knew that the sun did not shine underground.

And the sun did not come barreling toward you in a shrieking, grinding blur. The metal rail beneath his paws was vibrating fiercely now, and Hopper was bouncing right along with it.

Once again, terror immobilized him, just as it had when he'd witnessed poor Pup suffer that fateful free fall.

The shrieking thing was charging right for Hopper. The ground shook violently as the great beast bore down on him; its screeches ricocheted off the walls as the light swelled, drawing nearer, nearer.

Hopper squeezed his eyes shut, awaiting impact. . . .

Then something slammed into him hard, knocking him off his feet and propelling him sideways into the atmosphere, away from the jaws of the ravenous metal monster. Hopper could not get a visual on his attacker, but he could feel that whatever—or whoever—had collided with him was large and muscular, agile and fast.

And . . . *furry?*

They landed in a tangled heap, a good yard clear of the rumbling rail.

"Keep your head down, kid!" the stranger shouted in a gravelly voice.

Obediently Hopper ducked just as the speeding metallic serpent rocketed past. It came and went in a deafening explosion of sound and a dazzling shower of sparks, bombing right over the spot where Hopper had sat shivering just seconds before. Even its echo was earsplitting; the light left nothing but shadows in its wake.

But thanks to the hefty ball of fur and sinew that had come out of nowhere and tackled him, Hopper was safe. Unharmed.

Alive.

It was a few seconds before Hopper realized the mysterious stranger was still pinning him to the ground.

"Get off!" Hopper squeaked, then immediately wished he'd said something more valiant—anything to make him sound a bit more threatening.

"Easy there, kid," said the voice. "In case you didn't notice, I just saved your life."

The assailant released his hold and stood. Then he reached down and offered Hopper a paw.

But all Hopper could do was stare in absolute shock.

The heroic stranger had a face similar to Hopper's own but narrower, with a much longer snout and (in Hopper's estimation) a lot less sweetness. His body had the same teardrop shape as Hopper's, but the stranger was a great deal larger and bulkier all around. In fact, compared to Hopper, this creature was enormous, with sharp claws and a bald, ropelike tail. He was scarred in several places, but powerful muscles rippled under his matted fur. He had a rugged way about him, but there was wisdom behind his glittering onyx eyes.

Hopper knew exactly what this animal was—Keep had occasionally complained about these shifty, bedraggled, unwelcome sorts who roamed the city through the gutters and sewers and alleyways, calling them filthy, disease-ridden, and vile.

This was a rat.

The rat brushed off his dirty pelt. "I'd ask if the cat's got your tongue, but around here we don't like to joke about stuff like that." He chuckled amiably, and the sound rolled away into the shadows. "The name's Zucker, kid. Zucker of the Romanus. Now, are you going to get up, or should I just scuttle off on my merry way and leave you here to rot?"

He extended his paw again, and this time, having no other choice, Hopper took it.

Zucker gave Hopper a firm, upward yank. "Now listen to me, and listen good. If you never learn anything else about these tunnels, you better learn *this*: Stay! Off! The Tracks!" Zucker accentuated his words with strong pokes to Hopper's chest. "Those screamers can come along anytime, and if you're not paying attention, you can wind up like"—he turned and motioned with his long nose in the direction of the bone pile—"well, like that guy."

Hopper thought he might be sick.

How had it come to pass that he was here, enveloped in this musty, unfamiliar darkness, taking life lessons from a *rat*?

And yet there didn't appear to be anything wicked or sinister about this particular rat. He was not only courageous but also friendly and funny, and he gave off an aura of bold, swaggering confidence.

Unfortunately he also gave off a nasty, swamplike stink.

Hopper wrinkled his nose and coughed.

"What now?" said Zucker. "Do I offend?"

The rat made a show of lifting his arm and sniffing beneath it. Then he gave Hopper a grin that showed his pointy teeth. "I live in a subway tunnel. It's not exactly the Botanical Gardens. But don't worry. You get used to it."

"I don't want to get used it," Hopper said. He much preferred the clean animal scents of the pet shop; sewer gas and rat sweat did not appeal to him at all.

And what *on earth*—or, more accurately, *under* it— was a subway tunnel?

Zucker ruffled the fur between Hopper's ears. "No need to treat me like I'm bubonic." He laughed again, but his laughter soon trailed off as he looked around. "Are there more of you?"

Hopper's throat tightened into a lump, and he looked away from Zucker's scrutinizing stare. There *were*, he wanted to say. There were Mother and Pup, and the cagemates. There was Pinkie. But not anymore. He managed to reply with a sad shake of his head.

"Ah." Zucker nodded as though he understood. "Well, then I guess you and me are gonna have to team up. For survival, I mean. *Yours*." He let out a loud burst of laughter. "I'm probably the only chance you've got down here."

Down. It was suddenly the most awful word Hopper had ever heard. He wanted to be *up* again; up was where the world was, with its pet shops and sunrises and harmless cagemates who didn't reek of stagnant water and perspiration.

"So tell me, kid, how'd you end up down here anyway?"

But before Hopper could utter a word, Zucker grabbed him, tucking the bewildered mouse behind his back. The rat's eyes darted anxiously around the dark cave.

"You hear something?"

Hopper shook his head and finally found his voice. "No, but I want to ask—"

"Shhhh!"

Hopper could feel the big rat's whole body tense in anticipation. Zucker sniffed the air, his whiskers quivering, his ears pricked up; he didn't seem afraid, but he was clearly on full alert.

They stood there, perfectly silent and perfectly still. Finally Zucker relaxed. Whatever intruder he thought he'd heard must have gone on its way.

With a sigh of relief he nudged Hopper out from behind him. "We better get moving, little one," he said. "And fast. The sooner we get you behind the gate, the better."

Hopper was aware of the concern in Zucker's voice. "Wait," he pleaded, tugging desperately on the ragged hem of Zucker's leathery tunic. "Where are you taking me? I want to know."

"More walkin', less talkin'," Zucker admonished, glancing around once more for good measure. Then he gave Hopper another gentle shove toward the gaping mouth of the dreary tunnel. "Follow me."

With that, Zucker of the Romanus took off at a sprint, away from the puddle and the rails and the decaying bone fragments.

What else could Hopper do?

He followed him.

# Chapter Eight

**THEY RAN.**

For miles they ran through the dank, twisting tunnel. Under rusting pipes, over fallen beams, through clouds of hanging smoke, and across dirty rivulets of slow-moving water. The ground was rough beneath Hopper's tender paws, and the air was almost too thick to breathe. He galloped along behind Zucker, operating on pure, blind trust—he had no idea where this stranger was leading him or what he'd find when they got there. Still, Zucker seemed to be the lesser of all the possible evils that might be encountered in this grim subterranean world.

So Hopper ran.

He struggled to keep up with his new companion for as long as he could, but at last his legs gave way to exhaustion. He collapsed in a panting heap. Zucker, immediately aware that Hopper was no longer behind him, doubled back to join him.

"You okay, kid?"

"Not really," Hopper said between gasps. "How much farther?"

"Not far now," Zucker promised. "There's a safe haven around that bend there."

"Can we rest? Just for a minute?"

Zucker threw an uneasy glance over his shoulder in

the direction from which they'd come. He didn't look entirely thrilled about stopping, but he nodded. "Not too long, though. This place is crawling with things that are hazardous to your health."

Hopper closed his eyes.

"Hey, look at this!" Zucker's tone was a mixture of surprise and delight. "A cricket! You don't see these fellas around much on account of they're pretty good at blendin' in. But legend has it they're good luck."

Hopper opened his eyes and found himself face-to-face with the most peculiar creature he'd ever seen. He let out a little yelp.

"He won't hurt you. He's just a bug."

Hopper cocked his head, further shocked when the cricket began to rub his legs together and suddenly the tunnel was filled with a cheerful, chirpy melody.

Zucker laughed. "I guess you could say that crickets are the fiddlers of the bug world."

"What's a bug?"

"You know . . . an insect."

That was a word Hopper did know. Back at the pet shop "insect" was another name for reptile food. But he'd never known that insects were so musically inclined. If he had, he might have felt worse about Keep feeding them to the lizards.

"The good thing about bugs," Zucker explained, "is they mostly keep to themselves. But if a whole bunch of 'em decide to get together, then you've got yourself a problem. You got what ya call a 'swarm,' which can be a pretty powerful force."

Hopper eyed the cricket, with his skinny, angular legs (six of them!) and flimsy antenna, and failed to see anything even remotely powerful about him. On the contrary, the metered twitter of his song was quite calming, and the cricket seemed happy to perform for them. He chirped contentedly while Hopper caught his breath and enjoyed the show.

But Zucker's apprehension soon got the better of him. "Look, kid, much as I hate to walk out on a free concert, we really need to cover some more ground."

The cricket stopped chirping so abruptly that for a moment Hopper thought the insect had taken umbrage at the thought of them leaving in the middle of his musical performance. But when Hopper saw the cricket dive beneath a nearby stone, he knew the bug's reaction had nothing to do with artistic ego.

Hopper felt Zucker's grip around his waist; before the mouse knew what was happening, the rat had them ensconced within a crumbling crevice in the old stone wall; the gap was just big enough to conceal them.

From what, Hopper had no idea.

But the alarm in Zucker's eyes was so great that when the rat pressed one slender claw to his mouth, warning Hopper to keep quiet, Hopper obeyed.

The voices seemed to erupt from nowhere—they

were so shrill and unearthly, it was as though they were coming out of a dream.

Or a nightmare.

*"Aye, aye, aye!"* The frenzied warbling pierced the murky silence in an unmistakable call to arms. It was half song, half battle cry, and it sent chills from the tip of Hopper's tail to the top of his ears.

*"Aye, aye, aye! Aye, aye, aye!"* This time the high-pitched cry was followed by the clattering noise of metal scraping stone.

"Weapons," Zucker mouthed. "Sharp ones."

Hopper nearly fainted.

He was aware of the sound of marching paws, treading just above where he and Zucker were hiding. They were close . . . so very close. Hopper might have moaned out loud if Zucker hadn't clapped a paw over his mouth.

"Not a sound." The words were a baritone whisper against Hopper's ear.

Hopper held his breath and willed his body to quit trembling for fear the unseen villains might hear the rattling of his bones. And then . . .

"Stop, brothers!" trilled a voice from above. "We've found him."

The march came to an immediate halt, and the voice spoke again, decisive and sure. A girl's voice!

"He's near," she proclaimed. "Zucker is close by."

Hopper's eyes flew open wide.

Zucker replied with a shrug and a sheepish grin.

"Are you sure, Firren?" asked a deeper voice.

"She can sense him," said another.

"No," the girl, Firren, corrected. "I can *smell* him."

Hopper shot Zucker a look that said, *I told you so.* But this was not the time to argue over personal hygiene, and Hopper knew it.

The weapon-wielding hunters were on the move again. There was the shuffle of running paws above Hopper's head, and then one of Firren's soldiers leaped down from the ledge. He landed adroitly on his hind legs just inches from where the mouse and rat were hidden.

Hopper bit back the scream of fear that threatened to rip from his throat as Zucker quickly wriggled them farther into the space inside the rock.

But not so far that Hopper couldn't see the enemy.

The one that had jumped down was kicking over stones in search of Zucker. His brothers-in-arms scampered down from the ledge and joined him in his quest.

Hopper was stunned—not because of the ferocity with which they approached their task, and not because of the deadly-looking blades they carried, slung across their backs.

But because they were *rats.*

Why would rats hunt one of their own kind?

There were three of them, all large and brown, but

none quite so big as Zucker. Clearly, these rodents were soldiers. Two had scarlet bands encircling their right arms; the third's armband was a royal blue color but with a white stripe emblazoned on it.

"I don't see him!" said the one with the blue band on his arm.

"Keep looking!"

They moved like the warriors they were—fearlessly, nimbly. Nearer and nearer they came to the shadowy nook where Zucker and Hopper hid.

Hopper knew they had to do something to throw them off the trail!

*Now!*

But *what?*

Slowly Zucker bent down and picked up a small pebble from the dirt. Carefully, quietly, he cocked his arm, then lobbed it toward the stone beneath which the cricket had taken cover. When the pebble hit the dirt beside the stone, the startled insect sprung out from under it, hopping madly into the darkness and kicking up a thick cloud of dust as he went.

"Zucker!" cried one of the soldier rats.

"There he goes," hollered another. "East!"

Blades shimmering, the rats dashed off after the cricket they believed was Zucker.

Hopper turned to his protector in amazement.

Zucker was actually grinning. "That was almost too easy," he whispered.

"But what about the girl—"

"*Sh!*"

Firren was in view now. Hopper could see her clearly on the far side of the tunnel. She was frowning, as though she knew that her brother warriors had made an enormous error in judgment.

Hopper studied her. To his surprise, she was exceptionally petite for a rat. He thought of Pup, and how much smaller he was than the rest of the family. However, this Firren was no runt. She was exquisitely formed, with a glossy gray-brown coat, a pert little nose, and lovely black eyes that were as big and as deep as the midnight sky. But there was something more, something strong and powerful that seemed to radiate from deep within. Intelligence. Guts.

Even from this distance Hopper could feel the fierceness of her.

Like her cohorts, she, too, carried a weapon—a lethal-looking sword with a long, elegant blade and a glittering handle. A delicate, shimmering cape of silver cloth floated behind her as she walked. Beneath that she wore a blousy white tunic—the big red-and-blue stripes centered on the front of it were a clear sign that she was in charge. There was no doubt that she was a skilled warrior, but along with her unmistakable valor she also exuded a distinct poise; Hopper thought she moved like a springtime breeze.

*Firren. Brave and beautiful.*

*And fierce.*

Hopper couldn't take his eyes off her.

Neither could Zucker.

They watched from their lair in the broken rock as she poked at a clump of dirt with the pointy tip of her sword. The scowl on her face was evidence of her frustration, her disappointment with the failed mission. Her soldiers were gone—heading east as fast as their legs could carry them.

In pursuit of a cricket.

Now Firren lifted her chin in a gesture that was at once graceful and intrepid. With a sigh she sheathed her sword and set off on her eastward trek.

And then she halted.

Hopper's blood froze in his veins.

Firren sniffed the air.

She sniffed it again.

Then she turned slowly in the direction of the cracked rock that cradled Zucker and Hopper.

Zucker stiffened and clenched his teeth.

As Firren made to approach, there was a shout from deep within the tunnel:

"Firren, come quick! Firren!"

She hesitated only a moment, to squint toward the split in the rock where her quarry hid, holding his breath. Then she turned on her hind paws and set off running . . . running into the ghostly echo of her own name as it filled the darkness. *Firren . . .*

*Firren . . .*

*Firren . . .*

"Told ya those little bugs were good luck," Zucker whispered.

"What was so lucky about *that*?"

"You're still breathin', aren'tcha? And there's no sword sticking outta your belly, which I'd say also qualifies as a stroke of good luck."

Lucky or not, Zucker and Hopper did not remove themselves from the cleft in the rock until they were sure Firren was long gone.

Hopper was weak-kneed and light-headed when at last they squeezed out from their hiding place.

But Zucker simply raised his arms in a luxuriously casual stretch.

"Well, that was a close one, huh?"

"What?!" Hopper could have bitten him! "Is that all you have to say?"

"C'mon . . ." Zucker gave him an infuriatingly innocent look. "You're safe. I'm safe. So what's the problem?"

"What's the *problem*?" Hopper sputtered, aghast. "Rats with swords are after you! And you sacrificed that poor little cricket to save your own skin!"

"Psshht." The rat waved his paw in dismissal. "They'll never catch that bug. And for the record, kid, I was saving *your* skin too." He leaned so close to Hopper that their noses touched. "Just don't make me regret it, huh?"

Hopper gulped but stood his ground. "Who was she?"

"Her?" An emotion Hopper could not identify flickered across Zucker's rugged face. "Her name's Firren. She's . . ." Zucker furrowed his brow as he searched for the right word. "She's kind of a rebel."

"Against what?" Hopper demanded. "Against whom?"

Zucker's shoulders sagged. He closed his eyes and shook his head. "It's a really long story, kid."

"Well, I've got time."

The reality of that hit Hopper like a punch. The truth was, he had nothing *but* time down here in this hole. He was lost. Stranded. More trapped than he'd ever been in his cage at the pet shop.

Zucker must have noticed the pain in Hopper's eyes because his voice softened to a kinder tone. "Let's just get ourselves to shelter," he said. "We can talk on the way."

This time, by unspoken agreement, they did not run. As they wound their way through the long tunnel at a more manageable pace, Zucker explained.

"Firren and her crew are what you might call anti-Romanus. In other words, they hate us."

Hopper shot Zucker a look. "Go figure."

Zucker chuckled. "Yeah, well, politics are complicated,

kid. Anyway, lately Firren and her gang have been skulking around these parts looking to capture Romanus scouts. She calls her little band the Rangers."

"Are you a scout?" Hopper asked. "Is that why she was after you? Is that why you hid?"

"Uh, not exactly." Zucker cleared his throat. "The thing is, there're a lot of things I'd like to say to Firren. Problem is, that girl's philosophy has always been 'Stab first, ask questions later.' She's unpredictable. So it's hard to say whether she would have given me a chance to speak my piece or . . ."

"Or what?"

"Or captured us and held us for ransom, or maybe just sliced us to ribbons with that dang shiny sword of hers and eaten us for dinner." Zucker sighed and used one scarred paw to smooth the bristling fur on his neck. "To tell you the truth, I'm not sure which of those would be worse."

Hopper had an opinion on that but kept it to himself.

They trudged on in silence.

Now that Hopper's eyes had fully adjusted to the lack of light in the passageway, he was able to make out even more details of his new home—none of which did much to lift his spirits. More stone, more mold, more dirt, more desolation.

Occasionally, though, he would spot something scratched or scraped into the surface of the wall.

Symbols and squiggles, like the ones he remembered from the paper scraps that, in another lifetime, had lined the bottom of his cage. Messages he could not decipher.

*Death to Titus.*
*Romanus Rules.*
*Felina Forever. Long Live the Queen.*
*La Rocha Is the Truth That Shall Set Us Free.*

The phrases meant nothing to Hopper, not even the one scrawled in the largest, boldest hand, although that one seemed somehow more meaningful than the rest . . .

### *THE SQUEAK SHALL INHERIT THE EARTH!*

To Hopper it was just a lot of mysterious gibberish. But there were drawings, too, and these amazed Hopper. Life-size renderings of rats and mice bearing flags and banners of every imaginable color. He couldn't help but marvel at these elaborate illustrations, these epic rodent battles—although whether these wars had been waged in the distant past or were still yet to be fought in some indeterminable future, Hopper could not tell.

"They call these the Runes," Zucker explained. "I haven't been out this far in a while. I'd forgotten how much of this graffiti—" The rat stopped in his tracks so suddenly that Hopper, who was walking behind, crashed right into him.

When Hopper turned to see what had brought Zucker to a standstill, he felt the blood drain to his feet.

There, scraped into the solid surface of the stone wall, was a word Hopper had never seen. It consisted of three squiggles that had been deeply carved into the rock, then painted over and filled in with brilliant color—a rich, royal-looking shade of purple. The squiggles spelled out:

## M Ū S

But there was an image. Beneath the word.

An image of a face. A mouse's face.

And around the right eye someone had carefully, purposefully chalked a perfect white circle.

Hopper's heart pounded in his chest; for a moment, it seemed, the world did not turn. Time toppled over itself, then stood still, upended and off-kilter, waiting for one small mouse to breathe again. One small mouse who could grasp but a single coherent thought in his head: *That's me.*

As Zucker stared at the likeness carved into the stone, Hopper thought he saw a shadow of sadness darken the rat's eyes.

But what baffled him was the fact that Zucker had yet to comment on how much Hopper resembled the face in the rune. The white circle in the drawing was unmistakable. So why hadn't Zucker made the connection? Didn't he see it?

It suddenly occurred to Hopper that perhaps he *didn't*!

After all, Hopper had been rolling around in the muck and mire for hours now. Maybe his white circle was obscured by dirt and no longer visible; maybe it simply blended into the rest of his grungy, grime-encrusted fur.

So if the uncanny resemblance to Hopper wasn't what had caused Zucker to stop dead in his tracks, then what had?

"Who is it?" Hopper ventured, his voice a mere wisp of itself.

Zucker's face was somber. "Just somebody I used to know."

This told Hopper nothing. Was the face in the rune a friend or a foe? Hopper couldn't begin to guess. If Zucker considered this the face of an enemy, how would he react if Hopper were to point out such an undeniable similarity to himself?

He made a split-second decision that for the moment it would be best to keep the information to himself.

Instead Hopper pointed to the three purple letters. "What does that say?"

"It says 'Mūs.'"

Hopper felt a rush of wonder in his belly. "Mews?"

"No, *Mūs*." Zucker quirked a grin at him. "Ya know . . . from the Latin."

Now it was Hopper who was stunned. The last word on his mother's lips had been this one . . . *Mūs* . . . and now here it was written in big purple letters on a wall in the bowels of the earth. Beneath a face that looked unnervingly like his own.

Hopper gulped. "What does it mean . . . Mūs?"

"Depends on who you ask," Zucker grumbled. "And frankly, kid, I just don't have the energy to go into it right now." A strange look came over the rat, and he eyed Hopper more closely. "You know, it occurs to me you never told me where you came from."

"Is that important?"

Zucker lowered one eyebrow. "Could be. Did you travel north or south to get here?"

Hopper looked at him blankly.

"What I mean is, did you come up or down?"

"Down. *Way* down!" Hopper's next words came out in a flurry. "My name is Hopper. I lived in a pet shop and then there was a boy and a snake, so I escaped. My brother got hurt and my sister disappeared after we fell into the rushing river, and then I was carried down by the waterfall and here I am."

"So you *are* an uplander, then." Zucker sighed. "I kind of figured. But jeez, kid, why didn't ya just say so?"

Hopper folded his arms. "Gosh, I don't know. I guess I was just so busy dodging speeding metal monsters, hiding from rat Rangers, and running for my life, that it must have slipped my mind."

Zucker was silent for a good long moment. Then he burst out laughing. "Kid's here less than a day and already he's got an attitude," he said, giving Hopper a sound clap on the back. "Maybe you'll be okay down here after all, little one."

Hopper didn't answer him.

He only hoped the rat was right.

# CHAPTER NINE

EXHAUSTED AND PREOCCUPIED, Hopper could think of nothing but the hauntingly familiar face he'd seen carved into the stone wall: the mouse—nay, the Mūs—with that unique and distinctive white circle surrounding its right eye.

*It looked just like me,* Hopper thought. *But how? Why?* His mother had told him to seek out the Mūs, and now, it seemed, he looked as though he could *be* one. He pictured them, hundreds or maybe even thousands of tiny brown mice, darting around in these dismal tunnels, peppered with pure white markings.

A thriving society of lookalikes, of Hopper doppelgangers.

Of *Hoppelgangers*!

The image was mind-boggling. He desperately wanted to ask Zucker again what a Mūs was, but he didn't think he should chance it. After all, the rat's reaction to the drawing had been unreadable, and Hopper couldn't risk pointing out his uncanny resemblance to a creature whom this tunnel dweller might possibly consider an enemy.

Finally they reached the crest of a small rise in the path, and Zucker had to gently nudge Hopper out of his reverie.

"There it is, kid. Atlantia. Feast your eyes."

At the bottom of the dusty slope lay the vast, walled city of Atlantia. Hopper blinked and rubbed his eyes, certain that what he was seeing could only be an extension of his daydream.

Zucker seemed to read his mind. "You aren't seeing things, kid. It's real."

"My," was all Hopper could think to say. "Oh my."

The sheer scope of Atlantia alone was staggering to a former cage dweller like Hopper, for it seemed to spread a million miles in every direction. From his vantage point atop the small knoll, Hopper could see only glimpses of the sprawling underground metropolis. But if the angled rooftops, stout chimneys, and graceful spires of Atlantia were any indication of what awaited him at ground level, it promised to be extraordinary.

"It's magnificent!" he breathed.

"And that's only the skyline," Zucker reminded him. "Not that there's any actual sky to speak of, since we've got about a billion tons of earth over our heads. But you know what I mean."

Hopper's gaze settled on the wall that surrounded the city; surely it was impenetrable, except where it was interrupted by an imposing metal gateway. Even from this distance he could hear the great din that rose from within the heart of the city—it was the sound of a hundred thousand conversations happening at once. It was the sound of commerce and friendship and *life*; of the myriad everyday dealings that came with residing in such a glorious place. He'd never dreamed there could be that many voices, opinions, ideas.

Suddenly Hopper couldn't get there fast enough.

As Zucker led him down the hill toward the towering gate, Hopper saw that it was fashioned of sturdy iron spikes.

This didn't strike Hopper as particularly welcoming.

And even less welcoming was the burly, uniformed guard who stood on the opposite side of the iron bars with his back to them; his long, hairy tail swishing in an ominous rhythm.

Maybe Hopper wasn't so eager to visit this Atlantia after all.

"Don't worry, little guy," Zucker said. "I can handle that big oaf."

The closer they got, though, the bigger the oaf seemed to get. Hopper estimated that the guard was roughly twice as tall as Zucker, three times as broad, and heavier by many, many pounds.

"He's awfully large," Hopper whispered.

"I think the word you're looking for is 'gigantic,'" Zucker replied, speaking in hushed tones out of the side of his mouth. "Keep it to yourself, though. Clops is a little sensitive about his weight."

"Clops?"

"Nickname. Short for Cyclops. Which, as you'll see, is kind of self-explanatory."

"Is he some special breed of rat?"

"Nope. He's not a rat at all. He's a—"

Just then the enormous guard whirled, swatting at the air with a fat, filthy paw from which sprang claws that looked fatally sharp.

"—cat," Zucker finished.

*Cat!*

The word incited the same instinct in Hopper that the snake had. His blood reacted before his brain did, bubbling with an undeniable impulse. Fear whistled through him, tingling from the tips of his ears to the end of his tail. His senses understood what his intellect didn't:

Cat.

*Run!*

But before Hopper could even flinch, Zucker kicked out his leg and planted his paw firmly on his tail, effectively pinning him in place where he stood.

"Where ya gonna go, kid?" Zucker whispered. "Back into the tunnels to fend for yourself? That's something I'd strongly advise against."

"But it's a cat!" The syllable all but scathed his tongue.

"Don't worry. I've got it all under control."

With his tail pinned to the ground, Hopper realized he had no choice but to believe the rat; still, he trembled as he took in the hair-raising sight that was Cyclops, the cat guard.

He was a hulking creature with angular features and long teeth that flashed like daggers. Several tufts of his orange fur appeared to have been yanked out by the roots, revealing mottled flesh beneath. He was scarred and gnarled in more places than he wasn't, and worst of all, Hopper realized with revulsion, he was missing an eye. The one he did have was bad enough—a sickly yellow-green color that seemed to glow from within, with a pupil that was nothing more than a bottomless black slit.

Whatever had become of his other eye, Hopper was sure he did not want to know; the empty socket had healed into a ghastly purple protuberance that was crusted over in some spots, while from others there oozed a foul-looking slime. One of his teeth—or fangs, in Hopper's estimation—was cracked in half and formed a jagged stalactite that jutted down from the cat's upper jaw. Most of his whiskers were bent or broken.

Zucker threw Hopper a grin. "Good-lookin' guy, huh?"

Cyclops pressed his disfigured face against the bars and hissed.

"Aw, c'mon!" Zucker wiped a paw across his eyes. "Enough with the spitting! I didn't come here to get a face fulla cat saliva. Open the gate!"

"Who's the prisoner?" Cyclops demanded, glowering at Hopper.

"He's not a prisoner, he's a guest."

"Since when do you entertain company?"

"Ha. Funny. You're a regular laugh riot, Clops."

The cat let out a blood-curdling *"Meeeooowww"* as his one good eye bore into Hopper in a way that was almost hypnotic. The compulsion to run was greater than ever, but Zucker's paw remained unyieldingly upon his tail.

"Yer guest . . ." Clops licked his lips. "He looks like a Mūs to me."

Hopper went cold. Something about the way the big cat snarled the word "Mūs" made it clear that whatever a Mūs was, it wouldn't be welcome beyond these walls.

"Wrong again, you brainless waste of whiskers," Zucker snarled. "He's not a Mūs, he's an uplander. And quit lickin' your ugly chops, because he's not your lunch, either."

For a moment the rat and the cat stared at each other.

Hopper felt dizzy. He remembered that Keep had housed smaller, fluffier versions of this monster—kittens—in the shop. They made sweet, mewling sounds and pounced around playfully in their cages, and the patrons loved them. Surely those ill-advised humans could not possibly have known that *this* is what those precious little puff-balls would grow up to be.

"Maybe I should leave . . . ," Hopper whispered.

Zucker shook his head, not taking his eyes off the cat. "You heard me, kid. You're my guest. Now, as soon as Clops here moves his big, mangy self outta my way, you and me are gonna go inside so I can introduce you to my father."

Clops got the message. There was a clattering of keys and then a mighty screech as the iron gate swung open.

*Atlantia!* It was breathtaking.

Hopper's head swiveled right to left, then left to right, then back again, his black eyes drinking in the sights of the bustling city.

Zucker pointed out the marketplace with its stalls containing all manner of delectable edibles. Rats in smocks and aprons hawked their wares while shoppers hurried from place to place, sampling merchandise and haggling for bargains.

"Best grub in the city," barked one plump rat merchant. "Straight from the upland, folks. Get it while it's fresh."

Hopper gaped at the array of foods—sunflower seeds and crusts of bread and dried legumes and juicy chunks of overripe fruit of every sort. He tasted something Zucker called "soda"—a syrupy liquid that seemed to sparkle on his tongue; he marveled over

things like nuts and cheese crumbles and bits of cakes and pastries.

There were booths for clothing and textiles—one snaggle-toothed rat clerk seemed especially proud of a large triangle of faded blue fabric, inscribed with a sweep of bold white squiggles: *DODGERS 1955*.

"It's a commemorative pennant," the clerk boasted to Hopper. "Legend has it that was the year dem bums won the series!"

But when Hopper looked thoroughly puzzled, the merchant snorted. He waved Hopper away in disgust, then carefully folded the precious strip of material and moved on to other business.

"Pennant?" Hopper asked Zucker.

"Forget it, kid. It's a human thing."

As they walked on, Zucker pointed out important places like the school, the infirmary, and the armory.

"And over there's the fire station," he said, motioning to a tall red canister with a chrome nozzle attached to a black tube. Hopper recalled that Keep had one just like it mounted on the wall behind the counter.

Zucker gave an exaggerated sniff in the direction of his armpit. "I suppose I should swing by there later and have them hose me down," he teased. "Ya know, as kind of a 'Welcome to Atlantia' gesture just fer you."

Hopper's cheeks burned with embarrassment. "I'm sorry if I insulted you," he mumbled.

"Ah, no need to apologize, kid. I don't have anything

against bein' clean. A nice long bubble bath every now and then never killed anybody." He gave Hopper a meaningful look. "Remember that."

"Huh?"

"You'll see." Zucker let out a booming laugh, which caught the attention of a female rat selling coffee beans and sugar cubes from a window cut into an overturned cardboard cup. She smiled invitingly at Zucker, but if he noticed her interest, he didn't mention it to Hopper.

"Atlantia has it all, kid," Zucker announced.

Surprisingly this statement was not made with any great expression of pride; in fact, to Hopper, it sounded forced, as though perhaps Zucker wasn't completely thrilled to be a part of life inside the walled city.

"And there . . . ," Zucker continued, pointing ahead a little ways, ". . . is the palace."

Hopper stopped dead in his tracks.

This "palace," as Zucker called it, was truly the most incredible structure in all of Atlantia. Tall and narrow in some places, lower to the ground and broad in others; shimmering and transparent in one section, splashed with opaque color in another. There were rounded sections and octagonal ones; scrollwork balconies; wide stone terraces; pillars and alcoves and staircases that curved around corners and disappeared. It was an architectural masterpiece that was somehow both whimsical and functional at once.

But to Hopper's great distress, the soaring entryway through which they would soon be passing was guarded by not one but *two* of those abominable cats. They were not nearly as gruesome as Cyclops, but they were no less intimidating. They, too, had teeth like razors and glowing yellow eyes that tilted upward wickedly. Their impeccable posture made them seem miles taller than Zucker, and they wore fussy dress uniforms fashioned from shiny cloth and satin ribbon, which were in stark contrast to the heavy weaponry they wore belted around their midsections.

As Hopper and Zucker drew nearer to the two feline soldiers, Hopper again sensed the power of instinct stirring within him; intuitively he shuffled ever so slightly closer to Zucker's side, and without even realizing, reached up to slip his paw into Zucker's— which, as if by magic, was already open and waiting, ready to accept the trembling paw that grasped for it. Suddenly the glimmer of a memory flashed in Hopper's mind.

*He was newly born, snuggled beside his mother's warmth, reveling in the soothing flutter of her heart. But there was something else . . . another heartbeat, just as steady, just as close. In the memory Baby Hopper lifted his tiny head and saw, through the haze of his infant vision, a face— handsome and proud; a loving smile.*

The image vanished as quickly as it had come,

and Hopper was once again aware of the immense structure looming before him.

"Who lives here?" he asked in an awed whisper.

In reply Zucker gave a heavy sigh. His expression clouded briefly with an expression that may have been guilt. Or shame.

"I do, kid," he muttered. "I do."

# CHAPTER TEN

THE PALACE ENTRY OPENED into a grand foyer that was nearly as busy as the city.

Zucker immediately nodded to a pretty young rat in a maid's uniform; she seemed flustered but pleased that he had chosen her as she scurried over and dipped a dainty curtsy.

"Yes, my lord Zucker, sir?"

Hopper's eyes widened. *Lord* Zucker? *Sir?* Was she kidding?

Zucker cleared his throat, uncomfortable with such a formal greeting. "I'd appreciate it if you'd escort my little friend here to the—" He eyed Hopper, then leaned close to the maid to finish his request in a whisper.

Hopper could not hear the destination. But it caused the maid to smile. "Yes, of course, sir."

Then she snapped her fingers, and two burly rats wearing palace livery materialized at Hopper's side. The maid nodded and before Hopper knew what was happening, he was caught in their viselike clutches.

Panic surged in him. He was captured! And at Zucker's command. The sting of betrayal was nearly too much to bear.

Strangely, though, Zucker was grinning. "Remember what I told ya, kid. It won't kill ya."

With that cryptic promise ringing in his ears, Hopper was dragged behind the maid across the grand foyer and up a sweeping staircase, kicking, shouting, and squirming the entire way.

The first staircase led to a second, then a third. The fourth was little more than a ladder fashioned of fraying twine.

Hopper relaxed slightly when he realized they were heading upstairs rather than down, because in his imaginings the worst kind of torture would be found hidden away in a deep, dark, dank place. But as they climbed higher and higher, he began to wonder if perhaps their plan was to hurl him from the rooftop.

"Tell me, how did someone so tiny get covered in so much filth?" the maid asked, her voice rippling with gentle laughter.

The sweetness of her tone surprised Hopper. "Well, um . . . I fell into a dirty river, and then down a waterfall, and I landed in muck. And then I ran for a long time and hid inside a broken rock, where it was pretty dusty." He glanced down at his fur, which had been so soft and pristine just that morning. Now it was stiff and caked with grime. A hot flash of embarrassment burned in his cheeks over his appearance, which was actually kind of silly, considering he was either about to be tortured to death or flung from the roof.

"I'm sorry that you had such a terrible day." The maid gave him a smile so kind and sincere that it made his heart ache a little. His mother had often smiled at him like that. "I'm Marcy, by the way."

"Hopper," he squeaked.

And then he saw the water.

All things considered, he would have preferred to be flung from the roof.

The rope ladder had deposited them on the rim of a large white basin that was mounted to a wall that rose even higher than the great outer wall of Atlantia. The basin was filled with water, and had two silver spigots from which spilled a seemingly infinite stream of water, clear and clean.

And cold.

Very cold.

When the rat guards dropped Hopper into the icy pool, his entire little body erupted in goose bumps.

"Hey!" he sputtered through chattering teeth. "Are you trying to f-f-freeze me to death?"

"Just making you presentable for the emperor," the maid explained. She nodded to the guards, who lugged over a large white block of some fresh-scented substance. A word Hopper couldn't read was carved into the surface: IVORY. When they slid the block into the pool, it floated.

As the stream of water splashed into the chilly water around the IVORY cake, a froth of bubbles filled the pool. Hopper was delighted to find that they felt lovely and smelled even better. As his body adjusted to the water temperature, he found he was actually enjoying himself. He closed his eyes and splashed the sudsy water on his face, feeling the thick layer of dirt rinsing away. After a while one of the guards waded into the pool to scrub his back with a stiff brush and lather the fur on top of his head.

"What happened to your ear?" the guard asked.

"Well . . . um . . ." Hopper eyed the soldier and knew that admitting the truth ("My sister bit me!") would make him a laughingstock. "Sword fight," he lied.

"Best have Marcy patch it up for you." Then the guard ducked Hopper under the surface to rinse.

Marcy brought him a soft, clean towel, patted him dry, and led him back down the twine ladder to a room furnished with plush chairs. She used a long strip of filmy white cloth to bandage his injured ear. Unfortunately, in order to sufficiently cover the wound, she had to arrange the cloth so that it was wrapped around the whole right side of his face, including his eye. Hopper wasn't thrilled about only having the use of his left one, but then it would only be temporary, and the bandage did go a long way toward stopping the throbbing in his torn ear.

When Marcy finished tending the wound, she waited quietly in the corner while another rat appeared to trim Hopper's claws; still another arrived to comb out his whiskers.

"What's with the bandage, kid?"

Hopper looked up to see Zucker leaning in the doorway with his arms crossed over his chest. He, too, was freshly bathed, and had changed out of his ragged leather tunic into an indigo-colored suede jerkin with a high ruffled neck and copper buttons. A loose-fitting chain-link belt encircled his waist. While Hopper admired Zucker's new outfit, Zucker was looking at Hopper's bandage with interest.

"Let me guess—that's your impersonation of Clops the one-eyed imbecile cat?"

Hopper shook his head, careful not to loosen the gauzy dressing. "I hurt my ear upland. But it's okay now. Marcy wrapped it for me."

Zucker sent an appreciative grin in Marcy's direction.

"I told ya a bubble bath wouldn't kill ya, didn't I?"

"Yes, you did," Hopper said, and smiled. "It was wonderful! Thank you for arranging it."

Zucker shrugged. "I didn't have a choice. I'm going to petition to have you take up residence here at the palace, but I can't do that without getting permission from old Titus. And he never would have agreed to meet you if you were stinking like a cesspool."

"Well, I guess you can't blame old Titus for that," reasoned Hopper. Then he frowned. "Uh, exactly who *is* old Titus?"

"Why, he's our fearless leader," gushed Zucker in a voice filled with false reverence. "He's the exalted one. Emperor of all the Romanus." The rat paused, then sighed. "He's also my old man."

Hopper didn't understand. "Your what?"

Zucker rolled his eyes. "He's my father, kid."

"Oh. Your father." Hopper cocked his head. "What's a . . . father?"

Zucker's ears shot upward, curious. "You don't know what a father is?"

"I grew up in a cage," Hopper reminded him. "I don't know much."

Zucker furrowed his brow and scratched his chin, struggling to think of a way to explain. "I guess a father is like . . . well, he's like a mother. You *do* know what a mother is, don'tcha?"

Hopper felt a lump form in his throat. "Yes."

"All right . . . well . . . then I guess you could say that a father is kind of like a mother, only instead of a *she*, he's a *he*. Ya know . . . the male of the species. A father is where you came from."

*Where I came from.* Hopper closed his eyes, and again the hazy memory flashed in his mind—*that second warmth, that second soothing heartbeat.* Deep inside him his instincts were running amok—he just couldn't make sense of what they were telling him.

"I don't think I have a father," he said, shaking his head.

Zucker laughed. "Everybody has a father, kid. Trust me on this one."

"Are you sure?"

"I'm *positive*."

"Why do you want me to live here?" he asked.

Zucker scratched his ear thoughtfully. "Well, I feel kind of responsible for you, having saved your life and all. And since I don't think you'd last five minutes out there alone in the tunnels, I was going to request that you be allowed to stay here." He patted Hopper on the back. "Plus, I always wanted a sidekick."

Hopper wasn't sure what a sidekick was, but he liked the sound of it. He adjusted his oversize bandage, then popped off the chair and began to cross the room. It took a moment for the connection to sink in, but when it did, his mouth dropped open in shock.

"So if the Emperor of Romanus is your father . . . what does that make *you*?"

Zucker let out a long rush of breath. "Very unhappy," he muttered. "That's what."

The throne room was located on the opposite end of the palace. Along the way Hopper and Zucker passed kitchens and dining rooms and drawing rooms and libraries. They passed rooms filled with wall-size maps, flags, and other military trappings where stern-faced rats in soldier's uniforms sauntered about, their weapons ever at the ready.

Maids and valets rushed about the palace, ushering ordinary citizens who'd come to plead with the emperor for favors or forgiveness. There were merchants from the marketplace delivering necessities and provisions of all sorts.

But Hopper noticed that all these visitors had one tendency in common: everyone who passed Zucker either curtsied or bowed deeply in a gesture of respect for the illustrious son of their royal sovereign.

"Are you the emperor in training or something like that?" he asked as they strode through the opulent halls and gilt corridors.

"The term is 'prince,' kid. But I prefer to think of myself as more of a 'knight errant.'" Zucker flashed his crooked grin. "Emphasis on the 'errant,' of course."

Hopper didn't get it. They walked a little farther, and a guard offered a very formal greeting to Zucker. Hopper cleared his throat and whispered to the rat, "Should I be calling you *'Prince'*?"

"What's the matter with 'Zucker'?"

"I'm being serious."

Zucker stopped walking and gave Hopper an impatient frown. "Listen, kid, my list of titles is bigger than you are, but if you insist on going the formal route, here are your choices. You can call me 'Prince Zucker of Romanus' or 'Imperial Highness, Royal Monarch of Atlantia.' I'll also answer to 'Your Grace,' 'Your Majesty,' and occasionally 'Your Excellency,' but my personal favorite title is the one that was given to me by an old friend—he used to call me 'The

Zuck-meister!' So go ahead, kid. Pick a title, any title."

Hopper bristled at Zucker's aggression—after all, it was only a simple question. "I'm sorry," he muttered. "I didn't mean to make you mad."

"I'm *not* mad!" Zucker snapped, then collected himself and sighed. "Look, I've never been all that good at the whole royalty thing, ya know? For lots of reasons." Zucker crouched down so they were eye to eye. "Whaddya say we just keep things status quo, huh? You can call me 'Zucker,' and I'll call you . . ." The rat prince frowned. "Uh, what's your name again?"

"It's Hopper." Hopper lifted his chin. "I'm Hopper."

"Yeah, right. Hopper. Well, you can call me 'Zucker' and I'll just keep on callin' you 'kid.' That way everybody's happy, and you don't have to concern yourself with things like titles or rankings, or remembering to bow in my presence."

"I'm supposed to *bow* in your presence?"

"Technically, yes," Zucker replied. "But frankly, it drives me crazy. So please don't. Now, let's go meet the emperor."

And they were off.


Zucker smoothed his suede jerkin as they approached the throne room. "You wait out here for a minute," he said. "I'll go in first and get the official stuff out of the way, and then you can come in and have an audience with the big guy."

"All right."

Hopper watched Zucker push open the heavy door and amble across the gleaming floor. From where he stood, peering around the doorframe, Hopper could see the throne and the rat who sat upon it.

Titus, Emperor of the Romanus. Everything about him was formidable.

If Zucker was big, then Titus was gargantuan.

If Zucker was a tad cocky, then Titus was downright arrogant.

And if Zucker was handsome and dashing and roguishly charming, then Titus was . . . well, none of those things, really.

"A good day to you, Prince Zucker of Romanus."

Zucker rolled his eyes. "Would it kill you to call me 'son'?" he grumbled under his breath. "Just once?"

"Speak up, Your Grace," the emperor scolded. "I cannot hear you."

"I said it's an honor to be in your exalted company, Your Highness."

"What news? Does the rebel Firren continue to raid our tunnels?"

"I have seen no proof of that," Zucker reported in a level voice.

Listening from the doorway, Hopper was confused. They *had* seen Firren. They'd hidden from her, in fact. Zucker was lying to his father.

The emperor, too, seemed surprised by Zucker's

reply. "Three of our scouts have gone missing in less than a fortnight," he countered.

"Well, that is distressing to be sure, sire, but I'm pretty certain Firren and her Rangers are not to blame. Maybe your scouts got flattened by one of the metal monsters. Or perhaps they just went AWOL." Zucker fixed his father with a contemptuous look. "My money's on desertion."

The emperor ignored Zucker's baiting and mulled over the issue. "I suppose I shall have to put a bounty on Firren's head," he concluded.

Zucker gritted his teeth but said nothing.

"What more?"

"That's about it."

"Is it?" Titus leaned forward. "I believe Firren's ongoing presence is cause for great concern. What if she gets it into her head to approach the Mūs about forming an alliance?" His eyes glittered with intensity. "Such a thing nearly occurred once before, as you well know."

At this, Zucker laughed. "Oh, I seriously doubt she has any intention of doing that," he said, dismissing the emperor's worries with a derisive snort.

"I suppose not, now that she doesn't have that wily Roger to band with."

"His name was Dodger," Zucker corrected. "And besides, even if Firren could talk the Mūs into laying siege, they'd be no threat to us. I mean, c'mon. An army of *mice* fighting the soldiers of Romanus? It'd be a joke."

"I wouldn't be so sure about that," drawled Titus. "They may be small in stature, but they are great in number. With a sufficient arsenal and adequate leadership they could do significant damage. Perhaps I would be wise to mobilize our forces."

"Okay," Zucker agreed with a casual shrug. "Go ahead and mobilize 'em. I mean, if you're *scared* of a bunch of little, itty-bitty *mice*, well, then who am I to—"

"*Scared?!*" Titus's face contorted in fury. "I am not scared, I am merely being cautious . . ."

"Right." Zucker gave the emperor an easy smile. "Tomato, to-mahto . . ."

The emperor glared at his son and fumed for a long moment; then he took a steadying breath.

"On second thought, Prince Zucker, I am inclined to agree with you. An army of mice holding their own against the mighty rats of Romanus is preposterous. The Mūs do *not* present a viable threat. Do you hear me? *No threat!*" His voice thundered across the throne room.

"If you say so, sire." Zucker nodded. "Father knows best."

"Now . . ." The emperor settled back in his jeweled throne. "It has come to my attention that you have brought into our midst a diminutive visitor."

"Yes, I have. A foundling, I guess you'd call him. Little guy. Out of his element."

Titus rolled his beady eyes. "You say that like it's something new."

"Yeah, well . . ." Zucker took a deep breath. "What's new about it is that I feel kind of protective toward this one."

"Why?"

The question seemed to catch the prince off guard.

"Because I saved him from being splattered all over the tunnels by one of those screaming metal serpents."

"Is that all? Surely you have more motivation than that for bringing home a stray mouse." Titus eyed Hopper with disdain. "Mice are not welcome here. So why bring this one?"

Zucker shrugged. "There's just something about him, I guess. Something that makes me want to see to his welfare personally. Which is why I was hoping you'd let him stay here. I'd make sure he didn't get underfoot, and it's not like one little mouse is going to make much of a difference to your . . . cause."

Titus lowered one brow. "I suppose not." He drummed his claws on the arm of his throne. "Bring him forth. Let me have a look at him."

Zucker turned to where Hopper was peeking in from the antechamber. With an encouraging nod he waved the little mouse inside.

The next thing Hopper knew, he was standing alone in the middle of the floor and looking up into the grim face of Zucker's father.

The Emperor of Atlantia.

# CHAPTER ELEVEN

HOPPER COULDN'T STOP STARING.

He was frightened, no question—trembling, in fact. But despite his terror he simply could not pull his eyes from the remarkable rodent who occupied the opulent throne that stood on an elevated platform in the center of the sumptuous audience chamber.

Perhaps the emperor rat had been debonair in his youth, but Hopper could see that in this regard Titus's best days were far behind him. His eyes lacked the mischievous sparkle of Zucker's, and he did not seem to be acquainted with the concept of laughter. He, like Zucker, had battle scars, but whereas Zucker's scars were proof that he was resilient, hardy, and heroic, Titus's scars had the very opposite effect: they made him look ruined—defective, even—giving him an unapproachable, sinister quality.

In a word, Titus was frightening.

And never so much as when he smiled.

This was due to a long, weltlike scar that stretched jaggedly from below his left eye, down his snout, and across his mouth. It was this pinkish-white slash that eerily transformed what once may have been a dashing smile into a truly fiendish sneer. It was that sickening grin that was unnerving Hopper right this very minute.

"Where do you hail from, mouse?" the emperor asked in a voice like hot oil.

Hopper opened his mouth to answer; unfortunately no sound came out.

The emperor Titus was not used to being ignored. He strummed his claws on the arm of his throne and glared at Hopper. "Answer your emperor!"

"P-p-pet shop," Hopper stammered. "Upland."

"And you have come here alone?"

"Alone," Hopper squeaked. "All alone."

Titus considered this for a long moment. "Very well. Ordinarily you would be *housed* with others of your ilk in a special locale that this court has established for the purpose of sheltering the underserved and disenfranchised."

Hopper had no idea what that meant, but he wasn't about to ask. Titus went on coolly.

"However, the prince has requested that I make an exception and allow you to remain in Atlantia under his personal guardianship. Getting in touch with his inner 'big brother,' I suppose." At this comment Titus's eyes clouded a bit, but he quickly cleared his throat and continued. "As I am a father who is fond of indulging my only child, I will allow it, but understand that this is a probationary period. Should you do anything to abuse this privilege, you will be relocated to the refugee camp. Do you understand?"

Hopper didn't, but he nodded anyway. "Y-yes, sir."

"Good. Now then . . . bow to your liege!"

Hopper genuflected, but in his zeal to obey the emperor he whipped his head downward too quickly, and the bandage over his ear unraveled, revealing his torn ear and his right eye.

Zucker, who'd been sitting, tense and frowning, upon an upholstered bench at the base of Titus's throne, leaped to his feet. His eyes were wide and filled with shock. But before Zucker could speak, Titus, who was also gaping at Hopper, shot out a paw to silence him.

Hopper shrank in embarrassment. His wound must have looked vile and disgusting amid the lushness of the palace. Feeling their wondering gazes upon him, he quickly scooped up the length of gauze from the marble tile and turned toward the door.

Without warning, Titus raised his voice to a harsh, bellowing command. "You!" the emperor bellowed. "Do not move so much as a muscle, do you hear?"

Zucker stepped forward fast, placing himself between the emperor and the mouse. "Easy, Highness," he said in a solicitous tone. "Just calm down."

"Calm down?" Titus screeched. "How can I calm down? Do you not see what I see?"

Zucker slid a glance at Hopper, then nodded at the emperor. "Oh, I see it all right."

"And do you know what it means?"

"Sure do." Zucker leaned forward conspiratorially,

lowered his voice, and whispered something into Titus's ear.

Titus considered his son's words with a scowl. "That is certainly in our favor."

Zucker reached down to give Hopper a reassuring pat between the ears. "Our little friend here has a lot of potential."

Titus gave a definitive nod. "It is decided," he said loftily. "Until further notice this diminutive visitor shall be your ward. Of course, he must never be out of your sight. I will also assign a guard."

Zucker stiffened. "Don't trust me, eh?"

Titus's laughter was an unnatural sound that crackled through the audience chamber like breaking glass. "Well, one can never be too careful," he drawled. He again turned his ruined smile to Hopper. "Henceforth, you may consider yourself an honored guest of the royal court. And as such, I shall see to your every comfort."

"Th-th-thank you," Hopper stammered. "But . . . why?"

Titus lifted one gnarled paw to his pockmarked snout and stroked it thoughtfully. "Let's just say that I see something in you. Something unique, something special, someone full of *promise*."

Hopper could not for the life of him imagine what it was the emperor thought he saw, but he was nonetheless flattered to hear it. He quit cowering and stepped out from behind Zucker to return the emperor's smile. Then he hazarded a glance at the prince, whose expression was unreadable.

"Peace and prosperity will be guaranteed in my domain," Titus said quietly, "for as long as you are here . . . Promised One."

"Promised One?" Hopper repeated with reverence. "Me?" He's never had a title before; it was quite a heady feeling.

Zucker frowned but held his tongue.

"Now then . . ." The emperor crossed his legs and tapped his chin with one jagged claw. "Tell me, little mouse stranger . . . what is your name?"

"It's Hopper."

Titus arched one scraggly eyebrow and wrinkled his nose. "That is a ridiculous name."

"Sorry." Hopper lowered his eyes. "But it's the only one I've got."

"Very well." Again the emperor's face contorted into that hideous grin. "So it shall be." He flicked a paw in Zucker's direction. "You may go now, and report your findings to General Cassius."

On cue a hulking rat in military attire stepped into the throne room. Zucker gave him a stony look, to which the brutish general replied with an icy smile.

"I hate this guy," Zucker ground out between his teeth so only Hopper could hear. "I mean, I *really hate* this guy."

Hopper couldn't blame him. General Cassius was even more wicked-looking than Titus. His fur had a greasy sheen, and in places tufts of it were missing, showing mottled flesh beneath. It seemed to Hopper that Cassius was none too fond of Zucker either. And when Cassius at last bothered to glance at Hopper, he did a double take.

"Sire, this mouse has the same—"

Titus quickly held up a paw and silenced his general with a few clicks of his tongue. "*We* are well aware of this development. It appears that *he* is not. Rest assured that we have already found a means by which to use this to our advantage." He turned to Zucker and continued with a wave of his paw. "Go now. Cassius will take you to the Conflict Room, where you can brief him on these recent developments."

Zucker flung a glance at Hopper, as though trying to decide if he should commend the mouse into the hands of the big rat. But it was quite clear to Hopper that Emperor Titus did not make suggestions—he gave orders. No matter how much he might want to stay, Zucker would have to go.

Turning away from the emperor, Hopper offered Zucker a brave smile.

After a moment's wavering Zucker inclined his head to the emperor and took his leave behind the haughty General Cassius.

Titus waited until the echo of his son's footsteps

had faded from the audience chamber before he rose from his gilded throne. To Hopper he looked like a moving mountain as he made his way slowly down the four wide steps of the throne platform and lumbered across the floor. His shadow fell across Hopper like a dark cloud.

"Tonight there shall be a grand celebration in your honor," the emperor declared. "We shall welcome you to our wondrous city and claim you as one of our brethren."

The giant rat reached down to trace the white circle around Hopper's eye.

"Come, let us observe the city," the emperor intoned. "I shall introduce you to our precious way of life, the one we fight for every day."

Hopper wasn't sure what Titus meant by that. On his walk through the market square with Zucker he hadn't seen any fighting at all.

The emperor pointed to Hopper as though he were choosing him for some magnificent mission. When the tip of his claw came to rest on the fur of Hopper's chest, Hopper flinched. The knifelike point did not pierce the skin over Hopper's fluttering heart, but it could have.

"Whether you know it or not," the emperor whispered, "your presence here shall help decide the future. Yours and ours."

Then Titus rested his heavy paw on Hopper's

shoulder and said, "Come with me, dear Hopper."

For the first time in his life, Hopper wasn't sure he liked the sound of his own name.

They stood on a ledge far above the city, with Atlantia sparkling below. Hopper could see all of the metropolis spread out, safe and secure inside its wall. He could also see that the city was enclosed within larger, higher walls that stretched in all directions, disappearing into the darkness of the tunnels. These towering walls were surely of human making, for they were far too broad and high for even a million rodents to construct.

On one of these walls was a sign.

As always, the mystery of the symbols, colors, and squiggles gnawed at Hopper.

Below the sign loomed nothing but vast space.

"What do you call that place?" Hopper asked Titus.

"Forbidden," Titus said curtly. "There is nothing out there except for some odd objects and artifacts left from before the human exodus, from before the Abandonment."

"Oh," said Hopper.

"All that rests outside the wall is dangerous," Titus explained in his slick voice. "We call it the Great Beyond, and only my bravest soldiers are permitted to roam there. I do not allow my subjects to journey out where they might encounter harm. The power of the

Romanus is unparalleled, make no mistake about it, but once a reckless citizen ventures into the Great Beyond, I can no longer guarantee his or her protection."

Hopper nodded, understanding. He remembered vividly that feeling of protectiveness for Pinkie and Pup.

In the excitement of seeing Atlantia and meeting the emperor, he'd been so distracted that he hadn't had time to think of his siblings. Now the guilt kicked him in the chest; the thought of them took the wind right out of Hopper's lungs. And the fact that he'd almost *forgotten* his failure to protect them made it all the worse. The emotion was unnamable, soul-crushing.

But in the midst of it, there was suddenly an overwhelming sense of hope. The fact of the matter was that he really didn't know for sure what had happened to his siblings. He'd assumed the worst, but Pinkie was so tough, so tenacious. Perhaps when they'd lost each other in the raging river, she'd been able to swim to safety and was now searching for him on the sidewalks of Brooklyn. And Pup—it was possible that his fall had not been fatal. For all Hopper knew, his tiny brother was still alive and well, back in the pet shop. Maybe Zucker could assemble a party of scouts to undertake an upland expedition, a mission to rescue Pup. Surely Keep would be no match for an entire troop of Atlantian soldiers.

Buoyant with this new outlook, Hopper looked down on the vibrant city and pictured himself, Pinkie, and Pup living happily among its populace. If they were alive, all he had to do was find them, and with the emperor on his side that shouldn't be too difficult. He was just about to ask Titus for his assistance in locating his siblings when the giant rat patted him on the head.

"Promised One, there is something you must know," Titus said gravely.

Hopper looked up into the gray face of the emperor. "What is it?"

Titus let out a long sigh, his sour breath swirling up a small tornado of dust from the ledge on which they stood. "I believe you bring the promise of safety and peace, but there are those who would see this all destroyed."

Hopper blinked in disbelief. Destroy Atlantia? It was unthinkable!

"Who would want to do that?" he asked. "Why?"

Titus curled his lip and shrugged. "Why, I cannot really say. We assume it is because our enemies are a backward, savage tribe who envy our lifestyle and wish to usurp us, taking our wealth and luxuries for themselves." He shook his head. "They believe they have mystical guidance and justification because they follow the teachings of the one called La Rocha, but their faith is misplaced. La Rocha is evil. La Rocha is the end!"

He paused, allowing this dark truth to sink in. Then he swept his arm over the city as though to bless it.

"And as for 'who' . . . well, there is only one answer. They are the ones who loathe us and seek to bring our world to ruin. They are the hatemongers, the rabble-rousers, the most wicked of all rodents. Once they were led by a diminutive monster called Dodger, the most malevolent of them all. He is gone now, but they honor his memory. They are uncivilized and violent, they thirst for Romanus blood, and they shall not surrender until they have seen every last drop of it spilled from our veins."

"Who are they?" Hopper asked again.

Titus made an odious face, then spat the word into the dust of the ledge: "The Mūs."

# CHAPTER TWELVE

HOPPER FELT THE BILE rise in his throat.

Vicious, bloodletting hatemongers? It couldn't be.

His mother had urged him to *find* the Mūs. Why would she encourage her son to seek out monsters such as the one Titus described?

And what of the rune, the face on the wall—so like *his* face, with its white circle of fur? Zucker had said that it was the face of someone he knew. The face of a Mūs.

Titus had to be confused.

Or misinformed.

Or lying.

Lip trembling, Hopper looked up into the proud face of the emperor and felt his knees buckle. "I'm afraid," he confessed.

Titus lifted one eyebrow as though perhaps he didn't believe it. But when he laid his large paw on Hopper's shoulder and felt him shaking, something in the old rat's demeanor shifted.

"You *are* frightened," he said, a lilt of surprise in his gruff voice. "You truly are."

Hopper nodded hard, dragging an arm across his face to wipe the tear that trickled through the white fur around his eye.

"There, there," Titus hushed. "There, Hopper. It's all right."

The emperor knelt down so that they were eye to eye. "It has been quite a grueling journey for you, has it not?"

"Very grueling," Hopper agreed as he attempted to suppress a sniffle. He was ashamed of himself for crying before someone as powerful as the emperor, but it was suddenly all just too much for him. He was hungry and exhausted and now more confused than ever. The Mūs, according to his mother, were his destiny. But according to Titus, they were to be avoided at all costs. How could he know what to do?

"All will be well, my child," Titus assured him. There was a warmth in his tone that made Hopper wonder if perhaps these were words the great emperor had yearned to say to someone for a long, long time.

"Do you think so, sir?"

"Yes. For you have the friendship of the prince, and such amity is not to be doubted. His affection, when he chooses to bestow it, is as true and as genuine as can be." The emperor gave a sad little laugh. "Not that I personally enjoy such a relationship with the lad. But I have witnessed from afar the depth of his devotion, and you should count yourself lucky to have it."

Titus was quiet for a moment. Then he smiled broadly at Hopper, who inadvertently shuddered in repulsion. The smile disappeared instantly; the emperor actually looked a bit sheepish.

*Now I've insulted him,* Hopper thought miserably. *Wonderful.*

But when the emperor spoke again, there was a softness to his voice that Hopper sensed others rarely heard.

"I apologize for my smile," Titus whispered. "Of course, it is the scar that makes it so unseemly." He used the tip of one arced claw to trace the raised marking that snaked across his mouth. "The result of a brutal slashing I took in my youth, from a feisty feral cat who sought to put me in my place. She succeeded, I will tell you that. Oh, how she succeeded. I carry this scar on the outside, but there are many more I carry within." He waved his paw and shrugged. "The point, Promised One, is that I am well aware of the chilling aspect I give off when I grin, which is why I endeavor not to do it very often."

"So that's why," said Hopper. "I thought it was just because you're the cranky sort."

The honesty and innocence of the mouse's comment inspired a loud, hearty chuckle from the emperor. "I am that indeed," the emperor admitted, rising from his knees to look out once again over his glittering domain. "It may be, Hopper, that you shall find you have quite a long road ahead of you. Decisions. Choices. Challenges the likes of which you cannot yet imagine."

"Great," Hopper muttered. "I don't know how I'll bear it."

"But you will," said Titus, his voice confident. "You see, I understand what it means to be faced with difficult, even impossible choices." His eyes focused briefly on something far off, and his barrel chest heaved with a heavy breath. "Believe me, I understand. We never know what we might be capable of when we are up against enormous odds. In the end we may lose as much as we gain, but even so, we must do what we must do. I have endured it, young Hopper. And so shall you."

Hopper didn't have the slightest notion of what the emperor was trying to express, but he did like the warmth of the words and the gentle weight of the emperor's paw on his shoulder. Could it be that Titus was not so filled with brashness and bluster after all?

Hopper's tangle of thoughts was broken by the sound of a bell tolling below.

"Ah, our feast is ready," said Titus. "Come, friend, let us enjoy the evening. I promise you, the Mūs will not march forth tonight, with their torches and arrows and . . ." He broke off, shaking his head. "I forget myself. I should not fill your head with such insidious images. This night will be a night of joyousness and revelry. Let us go, then, Hopper. Your celebration awaits."

There was more food than Hopper could have ever dreamed of laid out on magnificent tables before him: baked goods, fragrant greens and other produce, and crumbs of too many different kinds of sweets to name. Members of Titus's court—rats, chipmunks, and even a squirrel or two who enjoyed the distinction of nobility—filled the banquet hall to celebrate the arrival of this new mouse. The steady flow of dignitaries and notables who presented themselves to request the privilege of shaking Hopper's paw caused his chest to swell with pride. He would have liked to tell Zucker how giddy he was feeling, but it seemed they were never alone long enough to share a private word.

Marcy was one of the serving rats. For the night's festivities she and the other servants wore more formal uniforms with puffed shoulders and ruffles at the neck and cuffs. Hopper thought she looked lovely, and was touched that she made sure to bring the biggest and best selections of every dish to him first before offering them to the other high-ranking guests. He also noticed that every time she passed their place at the head of the long table, she would pause for just a moment as she passed Zucker.

"I think she likes you," Hopper whispered.

Zucker grinned and bit into a chunk of buttery biscuit. "Marcy's a doll. But, see, I'm really not the sort of rat who settles down."

"Oh." Hopper leaned back in his chair and rubbed his full belly. "I think I like being the Promised One," he said. Then he belched.

"Just don't let it go to your head, kid."

Hopper reached for a grape that was almost as big as he was and began to nibble at the smooth, tart skin.

Zucker laughed. "Careful, little guy, that thing's fermented."

Hopper didn't know what that meant, but he did know that the juice of the grape was sweet and fragrant, and it made him feel warm and tingly the minute it touched his lips. The more he nibbled, the more he tingled.

As the servants cleared the empty plates and goblets from the tables, there was a round of speeches, toasts and testimonials, many of which sang the praises of their beloved emperor, Titus, and cheered the achievements of the Romanus people.

But the most ringing tributes were those in which all present raised their glasses and drank to the great fortune of having Hopper among their number.

By now Hopper's eyelids had grown heavy; the tips of his paws were numb, and his brain felt ticklish.

Zucker grinned and gently removed the sticky, pulpy remains of the grape from Hopper's grasp. "I think you've had enough, kid. C'mon, let's get you to bed."

Hopper felt himself being hoisted up and gently laid over Zucker's broad shoulder. His eyelids fluttered closed, and he sighed dreamily as a memory of crisp, cozy aspen curls drifted through his mind.

He pictured his brother and sister snuggled in the corner, the sound of their breathing lulling him off to sleep.

As Zucker climbed the stairs, Hopper drifted in and out of awareness.

"Prince Zucker," he said in a thick voice, "Imperial Highness . . . Zuck-meister?"

"Yeah?"

"Will you help me find my family?"

"I'll see what I can do, kid."

Then Hopper heard a door opening, closing, footsteps muffled across a thick carpet. His friend was lowering him onto a soft pallet and tucking a fluffy blanket around him. Again his eyelids drooped and he smiled a groggy smile at Zucker, who stood above him. The rat looked amused but also concerned.

"Sleep tight, Promised One," he said softly.

"Thanks." Hopper rolled over and let out an enormous yawn. "G'night . . . Marcy."

The last thing he heard before his eyes closed completely was the sound of Zucker's laughter floating out of the room. He did not hear Zucker send for a guard, nor did he hear the prince instruct the sentry to stand watch outside the door until dawn.

Hopper sighed and snuggled deeper into the softness of the royal bedding to dream dreams he would not recall come morning. It was the end of a night of merry revels; at long last, the palace and all of its secrets fell silent.

And the Promised One slept.

Zucker was true to his word. He wasted no time organizing a band of soldiers to search for Hopper's family. They were his own most trusted officers; their uniforms featured a silver Z-shaped squiggle embroidered directly over their hearts, and they answered to Zucker and Zucker alone.

"We'll begin at the outskirts, of course," one of the officers informed the prince. "As it takes time before the newly lost are discovered and collected. Typically they wander for weeks in the distant regions."

"Yes," Zucker agreed. "If they are still a—" He cut himself off with a glance at Hopper. "Let's just say I doubt they've been found and brought to the camps just yet. So cast our nets wide and start looking in the outermost regions." He turned a placid expression to Hopper. "Tell them who they're looking for, kid."

"Okay." Seated on a richly upholstered chair in Zucker's private chamber, Hopper told the captain—a lean and wiry rat called Polhemus—and his second in command—a stout black squirrel named Garfield— exactly what Pinkie and Pup looked like. When Hopper mentioned the white circle around Pinkie's left eye, Zucker seemed surprised, even a little curious. But he said nothing and urged Hopper to tell the soldiers everything he could remember about the last known upland location of his siblings.

When the soldiers had all this information, they turned to leave the room. Hopper slid off his chair and scampered along after them.

"Where do you think you're going?" Zucker asked, his expression amused.

"With the captain," Hopper replied. "To find—"

"Oh no." Zucker shook his head. "You're not going anywhere. You're staying right here where it's safe. Besides, if Titus got word that you'd left the city, he'd have my head."

Polhemus and Garfield exchanged bemused glances when Hopper lifted his chin and marched to the chamber door to join them. "I'm going."

"Sit down, kid."

A stab of desperation pierced Hopper's heart. "But they're my family."

"Yeah, a family who'll likely be minus one brother if you go out there and try to keep up with my men." He folded his arms and nodded at his officers. "These rodents are pros, kid. And those tunnels, as you might recall, can be awfully dangerous."

Hopper knew Zucker was right, but it just felt all wrong. He'd let his family down once before, and this might be his only chance to make up for that.

"But they're my responsibility," he squeaked. "I don't just want to go—I have to."

"Listen to me, Hopper," Zucker said sternly. "In case you hadn't noticed, every minute counts out there. My soldiers will have to be swift and unencumbered while searching those tunnels."

Hopper's whiskers twitched. "What's that supposed to mean?"

Zucker seemed to be fighting back a grin. "It means they don't need to be worried about having you underfoot while they're trying to save your kin."

Hopper gave Zucker a challenging look. "I won't get in the way," he insisted.

Zucker rolled his eyes. "Pretty sure you will, kid."

Garfield cleared his throat. "Young sir," he began, with a look that might have been warm had the soldier not been such a steely sort. "We applaud your courage, but I agree with the prince. It's best for all concerned if you remain behind. And if we are fortunate enough to find your siblings—"

"*When* you find them," Hopper corrected firmly.

"Yes," said Polhemus. "That is what he meant. *When.*"

"When we find your brother and sister," Garfield continued, "we will bring them directly to you."

Hopper looked from the captain to Zucker, then back to the captain. He sighed and nodded.

"Leave no stone unturned," Zucker commanded, and Hopper realized he meant that literally.

Then the prince nodded to his troops, who clicked their heels and marched out of the chamber.

Hopper watched them until they disappeared down the long palace corridor. He looked up at Zucker with gratitude shining in his eyes.

"Sorry for being so pushy," he said softly. "And thank you—I know your soldiers will find them."

Zucker's face turned serious, his smile fading, his eyes growing dark. "Let's hope for the best, kid, but I have to be honest. The chances of them finding your brother and sister are pretty slim."

What Hopper didn't tell Zucker was that he had a strong feeling deep in his heart that perhaps their chances were better than that.

He also didn't tell him that he had a pounding headache. But Zucker figured that out for himself.

"That'll teach ya to partake of fermented grapes." He chuckled, then rang for Marcy to bring something called "coffee." Marcy brought a wrinkled bean on a silver tray and placed it before Hopper.

"Upland they grind these up and add water," Zucker explained. "Here, we just go right to the source."

When Marcy was gone, Hopper picked up the bean and began to nibble. Zucker pulled up a chair and sat so that he was face-to-face with Hopper. His eyes darted from one corner of the room to another, almost as though he feared someone might be hiding there.

"Okay, kid," he said at last, "there's something I've got to tell you, and it's kind of a big deal."

Hopper's eyes lit as he looked up from the bean clutched in his paws. "Are they planning another party?"

Zucker shook his head. "No, big shot, it's nothing like that. It's—"

Before Zucker could get another word in, the door to the chamber flung wide and a guard entered. But this was not one of Zucker's men with the elegant *Z* emblazoned on his chest. This guard was bedecked in glittering palace livery. This guard belonged to Titus.

"Who gave you permission to enter here?" Zucker demanded.

"His Royal Highness," the guard answered, his eyes vacant, his expression blank.

"For what purpose?"

"To guard the Promised One."

Zucker's eyes narrowed. "I'll bet," he muttered under his breath.

"I am commanded to remain in your and the Promised One's company at all times."

Zucker grumbled, rising from his chair and stomping across the room to his desk.

With no further discussion the guard positioned himself in the corner of the room.

Hopper was mildly curious about the "big deal" Zucker had mentioned, but he was enjoying his coffee bean too much to be bothered by it.

While Zucker busied himself at his desk, Hopper

sat in his comfortable chair and nibbled on the treats Marcy had brought with the coffee. Halfway through the bean, as if by magic, his headache disappeared and his fatigue lifted. He felt energized, even a bit jumpy.

Zucker was just finishing up his work when Hopper leaped off the chair, bouncing on his hind paws excitedly.

"What are we going to do today?" he asked.

Zucker pulled a sheaf of papers off a shelf and spread them across the desk.

Then he smiled.

If the greatest thing Zucker did for Hopper was to save him from the jaws of the speeding metal monster, the *second* greatest thing he did for him was teach him to read.

And in Hopper's opinion it was a very *close* second.

Under Zucker's tutelage the ambiguous squiggles, lines, dots, and slashes Hopper saw everywhere came alive. They began to make sense, revealing mysteries, telling stories, teaching lessons.

It was like a secret code, and now Hopper had been given the key.

Over the next several days Zucker showed Hopper how the once-elusive markings worked, lining up to create words, the words lining up to create meaning.

Together they spent the mornings hunched over

a table in the royal library, where Zucker would patiently explain the sounds made by various combinations of lines and curlicues and squiggles. Hopper was delighted to learn that collectively these were called "letters."

In the afternoons, always under the careful scrutiny of the ubiquitous palace guard, they wandered Atlantia and Zucker would quiz Hopper on what he'd learned. Soon enough he was able to read all the signs in the marketplace.

Then one day Hopper made a fascinating connection: the letters he was learning to recognize were the same symbols that appeared on the sign hanging on the wall of the Great Beyond. Using the skills Zucker had taught him, Hopper tried to sound out the words printed there.

He was able to decipher SUBWAY. Whatever that meant.

And BROOKLYN—Hopper recognized the name of the upland borough where, even at that very moment, Zucker's soldiers were on the march, seeking, searching, and peering into dark corners on their hunt for his lost family.

ATLANTIC AVENUE/BARCLAYS CENTER. That phrase was slightly more complicated, but he assumed it had something to do with Atlantia.

Then came the letters that, for some reason, were printed inside a series of multicolored circles:

B – D – N– R – Q – 2 – 3 – 4 – 5

Either this was a word Zucker hadn't gotten to yet, or it wasn't a word at all. Hopper tried to read it aloud, but the sound that came out of his mouth was meaningless:

"Buh-duh-enn-are-cue."

"Don't waste your time, kid," Zucker advised. "I've been trying to make sense out of that one for years."

Hopper was disappointed. But then Zucker presented him with a tiny, pointy chip of smooth gray substance.

"It's graphite," the rat explained. "From a pencil point. You use it to write with."

Hopper was dumbstruck. Now not only would he be able to read, but he'd be able to record his own squiggles and slashes and symbols and turn them into words. He could set down his own thoughts and ideas on paper.

He would be able to *write*!

As the days went by, Hopper stayed busy, visiting the city and working on his reading and writing lessons. Every few days either Captain Polhemus or First Lieutenant Garfield would materialize in Zucker's office with their report on the search for Pinkie and Pup.

Then Zucker would raise an eyebrow in silent inquiry, to which the solemn-faced soldier would always reply with a curt shake of his head.

And Hopper's heart would break just a little bit more.

But still, he did not give up hope.

On one visit to Atlantia, Zucker was called upon by two merchants to settle an argument, as was his royal duty. While the prince heard the shopkeepers' grievances, Hopper took advantage of the body-guard's interest in the heated debate to slip away unseen. He wandered about, taking in the sights with his usual wonder and awe.

He came across a small park, where several young rats were playing happily, laughing and swinging back and forth, teetering up and down. The sight tugged at Hopper's heart. How Pup would have loved such a place! For a moment Hopper found himself scanning the area just in case his tiny brother, by some miracle, was among the young ones enjoying the delightful play space.

"What are *you* doing here?"

The frightened voice startled Hopper from his daydream of Pup on the swinging contraption. "Me?" he asked.

The boy rat who'd asked the question nodded, eyeing Hopper cautiously. "Yeah. *You!*"

Hopper smiled his friendliest smile. "I'm a guest of Prince Zucker. Just seeing the sights is all."

A little girl rat who'd been jumping rope joined the

boy rat. "I don't think our prince would ever welcome the likes of you!" she snapped.

Hopper frowned. "What's that supposed to mean?"

In reply the girl flung her arm out and pointed; Hopper turned to see a faded paper poster tacked to a pole behind him. The poster featured a headline—boldly printed with words he'd never seen before, but thanks to Zucker's tutoring, he could read it easily:

## BEWARE THE ENEMY MŪS

Hopper's eyes widened. There was a sketch of a face beneath the warning.

And it looked an awful lot like his own! Just like the crudely drawn image he'd seen back in the tunnels, but without a white circle of fur.

"Y-y-you get out of here, Mūs," said the boy, drawing himself up. He was attempting to be brave, but Hopper could see him trembling. "We've heard the stories of your kind! You're vicious and coldhearted. You're the reason why no Atlantian citizen is allowed outside the walls of the city! Emperor Titus makes sure we all hear of it every time your tribe makes a threat to our peace."

"But I'm not a—"

"Now!" the girl echoed, her voice quivering. "Or else I'll scream for the guards!"

Hopper gulped and nodded. He wasn't in the habit of frightening children, and the injustice of this accusation stung him. "I'll go, I'll go," he said, holding up his paws and backing away. "But, truly, there's nothing to be afraid of."

The young rats simply glared at him.

When Hopper had backed up as far as the pole, he paused to take a closer look at the sketch. A roiling sickness filled him. If there had been a toothy chunk missing from the ear and a white tuft around the eye, it could easily have been a drawing of Pinkie.

Or of him!

But the poster was faded, clearly having been hanging on the pole for some time. The color was hard to define, and the edges of the sketch were blurred. It was torn in places; the nose was practically missing, and half the mouth was obscured with grime.

It could be him. Then again, maybe it couldn't.

"I'm not one of them," he told himself. But a tiny kernel of doubt, a sickening little seed of terror had begun to take root in his gut.

At the edge of the park Hopper stopped to catch his breath; his heart was skipping in his chest like the girl with the jump rope. Maybe he *was* a Mūs. Maybe his mother had mentioned them because they were distant relations.

The thought of being descended from the blood-thirsty tribe Titus so loathed, made Hopper dizzy.

But then perhaps the Mūs had been good once. Perhaps his mother had been remembering ancestors who were kind and morally upright. And she had simply not lived long enough to learn of their evil transformation.

That was possible. Sickening but possible.

*Fine,* Hopper decided. *So perhaps there is a chance I may have the slightest trickle of Mūs blood in my veins. That doesn't mean I am anything like the horrific creatures. And it certainly doesn't mean I have to reveal the truth to anyone!*

"There you are, kid," came Zucker's voice from down the block. "Sorry about that. Politics. You know how it is."

Hopper swallowed hard and forced a smile, avoiding the glare he got from the guard. "Yeah, Zucker," he squeaked. "I know how it is."

But he was silent all the way back to the palace, trying to force the poster and the disgusting thoughts that went with it out of his mind. For the first time in his young life, Hopper had a secret. A dark, despicable secret.

He was going to keep it at all costs.

In the evenings Hopper would dine at the royal table with Titus and Zucker, and Titus would ask him about his former life up on the earth's surface.

One night when Zucker was detained by a consultation with his blacksmith over the forging of a new sword, Hopper found himself seated at the table with just the emperor. As always, Titus was gorging himself on sugared morsels of fruit and baked goods.

"Now then, Hopper, what has the prince told you of our philanthropic activities?" the emperor asked. "Has he informed you of the extent of our charity?"

Hopper shrugged. "I don't think so." Then he smiled. "But he did show me the life-size chess board in Atlantia Park. The pawn piece is bigger than I am!"

"So he has yet to tell you about our refugee camps? I'm not surprised." Titus shot Zucker, who was just hurrying in from his meeting, a furious glance. "Our young prince fancies himself quite the warrior, but he has little interest in my benevolent works."

Zucker lowered himself into his chair stiffly. "Benevolent?" the prince challenged through tight lips.

"What are you implying?" his father snarled. "Those unfortunate souls are fed and cared for in our camps. They enjoy the hospitality and guardianship of the Romanus."

"Yeah, sure they do." Zucker narrowed his eyes. "Right up until the moment they—"

A heavily armed footman appeared at Zucker's side so suddenly, it was as if he'd been conjured by black magic. The prince stopped speaking in midsentence, took a deep breath, then changed tactics. "If you're so proud of these camps, why just tell Hopper about them? Why don't you let me take our guest on a tour?"

Titus's eyes widened. "Tour?" he spat. "You know I have expressly forbidden you from setting one paw inside those camps. And with good reason."

"But surely you'll make an exception for the Promised One," Zucker pressed. "Surely you want him to see these delightful communities you've so *benevolently* established." He gave the emperor an exaggerated wink. "After all, sire, what better way to gain his loyalty than to let him bear witness to the very manifestation of your kindness?"

"But I am already loyal to—" Hopper squeaked with enthusiasm.

Zucker's paw came down firmly on his shoulder, silencing him.

"C'mon, Highness. Let me take the kid on a field trip. I'll behave myself."

"You do make a sound point," Titus murmured. "Hopper should see the camps. . . ." The emperor stroked his chin as he mulled over the idea.

"I'd be honored to show the Promised One the refugee communities of which you—indeed, of which all Atlantian subjects—are so justifiably proud."

Titus glared, considering the request.

Zucker shrugged. "But then if you'd rather I *didn't* instill a greater love of our domain in Hopper by showing him your camps—"

The emperor's gnarled paw came down with a slap on the arm of his chair. "You will take the Promised

One to visit the camps tomorrow!" Titus instructed with a glower. "Do you understand?"

The young royal grinned and bobbed his chin in a satisfied nod.

Titus leaned back in his chair, curling his long, spiky whiskers around one long claw. His eyes locked on the circle of white fur around Hopper's eye.

Hopper squirmed. "Is something wrong, sir?"

"I'm just intrigued," Titus said in a raspy voice, "by that peculiar marking of yours."

"Oh." Hopper gulped. He'd never been appraised so intently before, and Titus's gaze was unnerving. What about that mark did the emperor find so interesting? Was it really that unusual? Could it be that only he and Pinkie, in all the world, possessed such a marking?

Then, as swiftly and unbidden as it had the first time, the hazy memory of that second heartbeat leaped into Hopper's head. In his mind's eye he saw a regal face; he pictured two black eyes glinting with love and intelligence.

And one of them was encircled in a ring of pure white.

Hopper felt a jolt of . . . *something*—a sensation that was part recognition, part intuition, but was also mingled with a tremor of fear. It was on the tip of his tongue to tell Titus that the marking was not so special—it was not even unique to him. His sister and perhaps even another member of his family both had borne the same white sphere.

But before Hopper could say anything, Titus wrinkled his scarred nose and made a brushing gesture with one gnarled paw. "Off with you now."

Hopper popped out of his seat, made a quick bow, and went scampering out of the dining room with Zucker hot on his heels. Hopper's stomach was churning; his breath was coming in sharp gasps.

Something in Titus's eyes had made him very nervous.

Hopper did not know why. But he did know he was glad he hadn't revealed what he'd just remembered. It was becoming clear to him that there was a very important mystery behind that white marking of his.

A mystery he wasn't yet ready to solve.

# Chapter Thirteen

Per the emperor's orders, the very next morning Zucker took Hopper to the refugee camps. As usual, Titus's hulking soldier attended them. By now Hopper was becoming used to the burly presence that followed them around like a militant shadow.

As always, Zucker was not pleased about having the guard tag along as they wound their way through the charming residential neighborhoods and onward into the tidy commercial district. Then they took an unfamiliar turn and ventured into an area Hopper hadn't been to before—this was the industrial section.

"What happens here?" Hopper asked.

"That's where the scavenged goods get repurposed for better use," Zucker explained absently.

"Scavenged?" Hopper asked.

"Uh, well, that's when merchants or scouts get special permission to go outside the city walls and travel upland to where the humans are. They seek out all sorts of items—objects and articles the humans leave lying around—and they transport them back here, where the factory workers resize or reimagine them to make them suitable to our needs."

"Scavenging sounds a lot like stealing," Hopper said.

Zucker frowned at him. "We're rats, kid. It's what we do. And if you're going to judge, then judge the humans for being so sloppy and wasteful and cavalier. That's not our fault, and besides, our survival depends on their carelessness!" He shook his head. "Well, on that and some other significant factors. But the point is, if the humans can't be bothered to protect their belongings, why should we feel bad about appropriating them?"

"Okay, okay," muttered Hopper, dropping the subject. Zucker was particularly edgy this morning. Hopper wondered if the prince was just nervous since this would be his first time visiting the camps in a while.

They made their way through the block of smoking factories without another word.

It was a long walk, and Hopper's legs were beginning to ache from the effort of keeping up with Zucker. In an alley he had to pause to catch his breath.

"Tired, kid?"

"A little."

Zucker poked two claws into his mouth and let out a long, shrill whistle. The next thing Hopper knew, the opening of the alleyway was filled by the face of a gigantic gray cat.

Hopper looked up into the shining yellow eyes of the feline, then squealed and ducked behind a trash can.

"Easy, Mr. Promised One," said Zucker. "She's our ride."

"Excuse me?"

Zucker swept Hopper up from behind the garbage can and boosted him onto the cat's silky back before gracefully leaping up himself. The guard climbed on as well, but even the presence of his heavy sword failed to calm Hopper's fears.

"She's going to eat me!" Hopper cried.

"No, she won't." Zucker made a clicking sound with his tongue, and the cat began to walk in a graceful, slinking stride.

"Back in the day the cats down here pretty much ruled the place. It wasn't safe for a rodent to roam the tunnels for fear of being flattened by one of their gigantic paws, or torn to bloody shreds—"

Hopper cut him off with a shudder. "I get the picture."

"Right, sorry." Zucker reached out and tugged gently on the nearly transparent tip of the gray cat's ear; obediently she veered left. "Anyway, Titus was just a flea-bitten commoner at the time, but he had big goals for himself. So with nothing but his wits and his political wiles, he boldly presented himself to the Queen of the Ferals, a steely white angora named Felina, and made a revolutionary proposition."

"What was it?"

Zucker grimaced and cleared his throat. Before he began speaking again, he flicked a cautious glance at the guard. "Well, it was before I was born, and the details are kind of difficult to explain. Suffice it to say, Felina was intrigued. For weeks she and Titus met in secret, negotiating and debating, until finally Titus—raggedy little nobody that he was— emerged from the queen's lair with a newly forged peace accord. And from that day to this, the felines have been sworn to refrain from preying upon any rodent who resides in the city of Atlantia or who is in any way associated with the Romanus. They do this in exchange for certain"—again Zucker eyed the guard before making a rasping sound deep in his throat—"*arr-hmm* . . . for certain mutually profitable trade considerations."

Hopper couldn't imagine what mutually whatever-able trade whatchamacallits might be, but there was something inspirational about a lowly tunnel rat having the guts to strike a bargain with the Queen of the Ferals.

"Needless to say," Zucker continued in a pinched tone, "Titus's truce placed the entire rodent population in his debt. So he proclaimed himself emperor, commissioned the construction of the palace, and the rest, as they say, is history."

"How do you know all this?" Hopper asked. "If it happened before you were born, I mean?"

"It's the story of our proud beginnings," Zucker said dully. "All Atlantian children learn it as soon as they're old enough to understand. Me, I had a royal tutor when I was a kid. When he wasn't nodding off and snoring, he imparted the historic details to me." The prince gave Hopper a mirthless grin. "The ones deemed suitable for public knowledge, anyway. But I knew there was more to the story, so I did what you might call an independent study, furrowing out and piecing together the bigger picture for myself." He leaned closer to Hopper so the guard couldn't hear. "I'll tell you all about it, kid. Very soon."

By now they had arrived at the mouth of a rusted pipe, and the gray cat lowered her head to allow them to disembark.

Feeling brave, Hopper reached up to gently pat the soft fur of the cat's lean leg.

"Thanks for the ride, girl," he said.

The cat smiled and rubbed the side of her silky face against him.

Zucker told the feline to wait for them, as they'd only be a few minutes.

Then Hopper followed Zucker into the pipe, and with the guard close behind, they began their descent.

Halfway down, the trio had to press themselves against the pipe's curved wall to make room for two burly sentinels who were making their way up the narrow passage. They were dragging a filthy, wriggling rucksack. Hopper could hear faint but frantic shouts coming from within the burlap sack.

"I call upon the mystical power of La Rocha to strike you down! La Rocha's spirit will see to my safety!"

One of the guards jerked his paw toward the sack, landing a good hard kick in the center of the slight bulge within it. Instantly the squirming ceased.

Hopper's bodyguard grinned. It was the first expression of emotion Hopper had ever seen him display.

Hopper, on the other hand, felt queasy.

When the guards had gone on their way, Zucker sighed and continued down the scooped pathway of the pipe.

"What was that all about?" Hopper asked with a shiver.

"Mūs captive." Zucker's voice dripped with revulsion. "Every now and then some rogue Mūs scout pretends to be a lost uplander and infiltrates the camps."

"Why?" asked Hopper.

"To cause trouble, maybe incite an uprising." The prince rolled his eyes. "I guess the Mūs don't understand what a great and generous service these camps provide to the poor, lost, wandering ones."

Hopper thought Zucker sounded like he might choke on his words.

He remembered the face on the poster in the park, and his stomach flipped over. "Are the Mūs truly as bad as Titus says?"

Zucker looked at him closely. The ever-watchful palace guard lifted his chin in anticipation.

A coldness flickered in Zucker's eyes as he began to speak:

"The Mūs are a primitive and violent tribe of mice who reside deep in the tunnels below the outlying areas of Atlantia."

He spoke as though he were reciting something he'd memorized, in a tone that was devoid of any conviction.

"Not much is known about them," Zucker continued dryly, "except that they worship a mystical being they call La Rocha. This in itself is a violation of royal decree; belief in omnipotent beings such as this so-called La Rocha is vehemently forbidden by the throne. Still, according to the Mūs, La Rocha has prophesized that their humble clan will one day rise up to conquer Atlantia, oust the Romanus, and restore life here in the tunnels to the way it was before Titus's reign." Zucker paused to chuckle. "Of course, we enlightened, intelligent Romanus citizens look upon such a prophecy as pure fantasy."

Hopper darted a glance at the guard, who was nodding as though Zucker's speech consisted of undisputed truths. Indeed, everything the rat had just said confirmed what Titus had told Hopper that evening on the ledge.

"So . . ." Hopper's mouth felt sticky, and his voice seemed to cling in his throat. "You're saying that the Mūs are . . . *bad*?"

"Yeah, kid," Zucker answered tightly. "The worst."

Hopper couldn't stand it any longer. "But, Zucker," he breathed, "I think *I'm*—"

"Afraid?" Zucker cut him off quickly and pointedly. "Well, sure you are, kid. But there's nothing to be afraid of. That whole prophecy thing is ridiculous. And nobody with a brain in their head believes there even *is* a La Rocha." He laughed, but it sounded forced to Hopper. "It's a fairy tale. And as for the Mūs—they're nothing. Just a rabid little bunch of underdwellers. Mice! Everybody knows mice are not only weak and puny but ignorant, too. Uh, no offense . . ."

"None taken."

"The thing is, the Mūs aren't even worth thinking

about. Because no matter what that cockroach deity of theirs has predicted, they won't attack Atlantia. Even they know they'd get crushed."

Again the guard nodded his agreement.

Hopper took a moment to digest this. Except for that crack about mice being rabid and puny, the rest seemed logical. Still, the fact that his mother had invoked the Mūs and had urged him to find them continued to baffle him. Before he could question Zucker about that, however, the prince clapped his paws together decisively and resumed walking.

"Okay, so now that we've cleared that up . . ." Zucker let out another burst of phony-sounding laugher. "Let's get this show on the road, huh? I'd like to finish touring these camps in time for lunch."

The pipe deposited them at a gate cut into a wire fence. Two cat guards—friends of the surly Cyclops, no doubt—patrolled the perimeter.

"New blood?" one of the cats asked, eyeing Hopper.

"The Promised One," Zucker corrected coolly.

When the cat opened the gate, Zucker motioned for Hopper to enter first, then followed him inside. The bodyguard, as always, remained within earshot.

Aside from Atlantia, Hopper had never seen so many rats, mice, chipmunks, and squirrels in one place. There were elderly ones and young, virile-looking ones. Hopper even saw a few families scampering about. Everyone looked healthy, cared for, and well fed. And undeniably *happy*!

Hopper wasn't sure what he'd been expecting exactly, but this thriving city-beneath-the-city was a very pleasant surprise.

"Welcome to the refugee camps," Zucker said flatly.

"It's nice," Hopper observed.

"Sure. That is, if you aren't overly concerned with little things like rights and freedom."

The guard cleared his throat loudly. Hopper thought it sounded almost like a warning.

"What I mean is," Zucker amended stiffly, "if ya want comfortable lodging and three squares a day, this place is paradise. Titus likes to call it a 'gated community for the marginalized.'"

"Where are they from?" Hopper asked.

"Well, let's put it this way: some rodents willingly relocate, and others have relocation thrust upon them. These refugees have all come from the upland. Some of them just kinda 'dropped in,' like you did. Others found their way into the tunnels after they were forced out of their nests by the most vile form of human being there is—the Exterminator."

"So they're strangers here too? They came from above like me?" An instant sense of kinship bloomed in Hopper. "Well, this is wonderful. These rodents are lucky to be here."

"Yeah, kid," Zucker said. "They're downright blessed."

"I know it's not as grand as the palace," Hopper admitted. "But at least they don't have to worry about those speeding metal serpents or that Firren and the Rangers."

At the mention of the rebel's name the guard's ears pricked up; he scowled at Zucker, who muttered a curse beneath his breath, then raised his voice so that the guard could hear him.

"Titus thinks Firren and her band of mercenaries present a danger to Atlantia, but I say she's more of a nuisance than anything else. I guess you could say she believes her own hype. She thinks she's fighting on the side of justice, but she's really just a little girl with a big sword and an even bigger ego." Zucker patted Hopper's shoulder. "The point is, kid, you're right. These poor lost refugees are *much* safer here in the camps, living as wards of the state, than they would be out in the tunnels."

The guard nodded, satisfied, but Hopper thought he detected some sarcasm in Zucker's tone.

"In fact," Zucker continued, "let's see if there are any lucky new additions to the camp."

He gave Hopper a quick wink as he waved over one of the cat guards.

"I'd like to have a look at some of your more recent arrivals," he said with all the authority of his royal station. "Where would we find such newcomers?"

"Hmm." The cat frowned in thought. "Well, just

this morning we got a litter of baby chipmunks. And I'm expecting a wave of full-grown field mice later today."

"No." Zucker shook his head. "Not that recent. I'm interested in any refugees who might've arrived in, say, the last few weeks or so?"

Hopper tugged on Zucker's tunic. "What are you doing?"

"I'm doing exactly what I came here to do," Zucker whispered. "You didn't think I baited Titus into sending me down to this god-awful place for nothing, did you?"

"Baiting?" Hopper repeated. "God-awful? Zucker, I don't understand!"

"I've sent my men here every day to search for your family, but the guards would only allow them very limited access. I thought of sending some in undercover, but it was just too risky." Zucker grinned at Hopper, his eyes twinkling. "So I figured the only way to get it done right was to do it myself."

Now the cat guard was pointing to a far corner of the fenced-in space.

"Try the southwest quadrant," he suggested. "That's where you'll find the Orientation Building. New arrivals spend their first few weeks there being debriefed and reeducated."

"I think the term is 'brainwashed,'" Zucker grumbled. Hopper's gaze followed the cat's pointing paw across the vast yard to the southwest corner of the camp. And what he saw there filled him with a joy he could scarcely contain.

"What is it?" the bodyguard asked.

But Hopper was already running across the yard.

"Halt!" the cat commanded.

Zucker ignored the feline's reprimand and hurried to catch up to Hopper. "Both of them, kid?" he whispered knowingly.

Hopper shook his head, tears welling in his eyes. "Just one. But it's a start."

"That's the spirit. Okay, show me—which one is it?"

Hopper's mouse heart nearly burst as he pointed across the distance with a trembling paw. "That one right there. The tiny one. He's my brother! He's Pup!"

# CHAPTER FOURTEEN

"PUP!" HOPPER CRIED OUT. "Pup, over here! It's me! Hopper!"

But Pup could not hear him; in fact, no one could. Because Hopper's joyful shout was drowned out by the sudden earsplitting sound of a horn blowing somewhere just outside the fence.

Hopper turned to Zucker. "What's going on?"

A tiny grin spread across Zucker's face. "I'm guessing it's a rebel raid."

As the enemy's horn continued to blare, the guards reacted, blowing their whistles and shouting orders for the refugees to return to their barracks immediately. The rodents obeyed, running as fast as their legs could carry them. Hopper watched helplessly as his baby brother disappeared into a rolling sea of fur and whiskers and tails.

Hopper darted toward Pup, but Zucker quickly grabbed his arm. "We gotta get outta here, kid!" He was shouting to be heard above the commotion. "It's about to get ugly!"

"No!" Hopper cried. "Not without Pup."

"He'll be okay!"

"But—"

The first wave of panicking rodents reached them, and Hopper clung tightly to Zucker as the mob jostled him. Again Zucker raised his voice to be heard above the din.

"Listen to me, kid! This is important. Everything I said back there, about the Mūs being bad and the camps being good and Firren . . . it was all a big, fat—"

*Fwump!*

Hopper shrieked as the heavy hilt of a sword came down hard on the back of Zucker's head; horrified, he watched the prince crumble to the ground. His stomach flipped over when he saw who'd wielded the weapon.

Standing above Zucker's lifeless form was the bodyguard.

"What have you done?" Hopper breathed.

The guard was returning his sword to its sheath. "Accidents happen."

Did they?

Hopper wasn't so sure. It was *possible* that in the chaos the guard had misjudged and unintentionally brought his sword down on Zucker's skull. It was *possible*, but if it had been a mistake, Hopper couldn't help but notice that the bodyguard did not look especially troubled by it.

Now the guard was slinging the unconscious prince over his shoulder. Hopper was glad for that, at least; the hysteria was escalating, and in another moment Zucker would have been trampled in the stampede of refugees.

"It is my duty to see you to safety," the bodyguard barked at Hopper. "Follow me."

With no intention of following the guard, Hopper turned his attention back to where he last saw Pup and started to claw his way in that direction. But in the next instant the camp began to fill with the smell of burning wood and choking clouds of thick black smoke.

Panic became pandemonium. Hopper glanced over his shoulder and saw flames flickering just outside the gates. He heard screaming; he heard crying. There were pleas for help and commands for order. The rodents still ran, although now they could not see nor even breathe.

Determined, Hopper squinted into the swirling cloud and called for Pup. He thought he caught sight of him leaving the southwest quadrant, but when he tried to change course to reach his brother, a fleeing refugee stepped on his tail and Hopper fell to the ground. Above him the terrified camp rodents were pushing and shoving in their mad quest to find shelter—if Hopper didn't get out of their path, he would be crushed.

Hopper hugged his arms close to his chest, squeezed his eyes shut, and began to roll sideways out of the way of the running paws, out of the path of destruction.

He kept rolling until he collided with the fence, safely out of the fray. Dizzy, he stood up and struggled to find his bearings. The bodyguard was long gone, but if Hopper could find the pipe by which they'd arrived, he could make his way back up to Atlantia. Then he would return to the palace to see if Zucker was all right.

Unsure of his direction, he did his best to stumble along as the smoke continued to swirl. Bodies rushed past in a charcoal-colored blur, but no one seemed to notice him as he crept along the fence, searching in vain for the gate through which he had entered the camp with the Romanus prince.

When Hopper's paw caught on a plank of splintered wood, he pushed the plank aside and saw a hole beneath it. It seemed bottomless.

Then he heard the heavy clank of metal on metal.

A duel? An execution? He could not say for sure.

Another clash of swords and then:

"*Meeeoooowwww!*" A keening howl filled with pain.

Hopper turned to see where the wail had come from. He saw nothing, but in the next heartbeat he heard a deep thud.

Then through the haze of smoke and flame Hopper spied a petite figure, running toward him with sword drawn.

"*Aye, aye, aye!*"

Firren's battle cry!

As she drew nearer, he could see that the sword was bloody.

*"Aya, aye, aye!"*

Hopper had no choice. Holding his breath, he flung himself into the dark chasm of the bottomless hole.

Unfortunately Firren had the same idea.

Hopper found himself facedown in the muck. Again.

Again the world was dampness and shadow.

Again he was lost and alone.

But not for long.

*Thump!*

Something—make that someone—had dropped out of the darkness and landed on him, hard. Luckily it wasn't a particularly heavy someone.

Firren.

Sword and all.

She quickly scrambled off him and raised her weapon.

But Hopper was too overwhelmed with despair to even flinch. Fighting was definitely out of the question, and running would have been pointless.

Besides, he didn't care.

He had lost Pup. Again. So maybe a sword across his throat wouldn't be such a bad thing after all.

Firren's sword poked Hopper in the shoulder.

"Are you all right?"

The voice startled Hopper. He had been expecting her blade to cut; he hadn't been expecting conversation.

"Hey . . . I asked if you were all right."

For a ruthless killer rebel, she certainly had a sweet-sounding voice.

"Just get it over with, please," Hopper said into the mud, sighing. "I won't put up a fuss."

"Well, a fuss wouldn't do you much good against my blade," Firren pointed out on a ripple of soft laughter.

So now she was laughing at him? Hopper's humiliation was complete. He summoned his last ounce of energy to spring up and meet her gaze.

When Firren saw his face, a little gasp escaped her lips. Her eyes widened in surprise, and perhaps something else—disbelief? Excitement? Hope? Hopper wasn't sure, and right now he didn't care.

"Go ahead," he snapped, throwing his arms wide to make a better target of himself. "Plunge that bloody thing right into my heart. I'm done. I can't do this anymore."

For a long moment the warrior just stared at him. Her eyes threw glints of light into the darkness. Hopper could see that her silvery cape was rumpled, and her white tunic with its red-and-blue stripes was smeared with dirt and splattered with red splotches—*cat blood*. He stood there, waiting for the tip of her sword to slice into his belly. Or better yet, his heart. "C'mon!" he prodded. "What are you waiting for?"

Firren opened her mouth to speak. Then she closed it. And then she laughed. Again.

"You've got spirit, uplander. I'll give you that! You're standing here on the business end of my sword, and you don't even have the good sense to plead for your life."

"Maybe because it's not worth pleading for," Hopper said with a sigh.

"Still, I applaud your bravery. I mean, it's foolhearted bravery, but it's bravery nonetheless."

Hopper blinked. Had she just called him brave? Yes. She had. He chose to ignore the "foolhearted" part.

"I am Firren," she said in that lilting voice. She reached out a paw to shake. The gesture reminded Hopper of his first meeting with Zucker.

"Hopper," he said, accepting her paw. "Um, how did you know I was an uplander?"

Her eyes flickered to the white circle around his eye. "I just knew."

"But how?"

Firren sighed. "Well, for one thing, the locals know better than to go jumping into mysterious dark holes of unknown origin."

"You did," Hopper reminded her.

"That's because *I* knew where it ended." Then she smiled at him, and it was one of the loveliest things he'd ever seen. "You look like you could use a friend. Come with us. We'll give you true sanctuary." She raised her eyes to the arched ceiling of the tunnel and shook her head. "Not like that evil sham up there."

"Titus cares for those refugees, Firren."

She frowned. "Already brainwashed, I see."

"Those refugees live a good life. They're fed, given shelter." Hopper stopped as he saw the cynicism grow on Firren's face. "Why is that bad? I don't understand."

"You will. Unfortunately today's raid was unsuccessful. But next time we'll get it right. We'll strike again, and we'll annihilate that camp."

But Pup was in that camp! If Firren annihilated *it*, then she would be annihilating *him*! This was a reminder that Titus was right about her. She was a dangerous monster.

Something ignited in Hopper, just as it had the day Pinkie had bitten him. With a growl he sprung forward, prepared to fight this rebel rat with every last breath in his body.

But she sidestepped his attack, and in one strikingly graceful maneuver she had both his arms pinned behind him and the tip of her sword pressed to his throat.

"Like I said. Foolhearted."

"My baby brother is a refugee in that camp," Hopper blurted. "And all those other poor, lost rodents! They've suffered enough already, and now you want to burn down the only home they have! Titus was right about you! You're evil. And Zucker—he said you were just a little girl with—"

Firren did not release her grip, but Hopper was

aware of an immediate change in her bearing. "You know Zucker?"

Hopper nodded.

The rat was silent for several seconds. "Zucker is a faithless, self-serving traitor," she said finally. Her tone was calm, but there was a note of sadness in it.

"That's not true!"

"Well, I say it is, and I'm pretty sure I've known him longer than you have."

Firren released her grip, and Hopper adjusted his posture.

"I'm going back, Firren. I need to find my brother."

"Believe me, going back to that place will be your doom." She smiled. "Your brother is safe for now. I won't be mounting another invasion for days." She reached into a pocket sewn into the underside of her tunic and removed a length of rope.

Then Firren cupped a paw around her mouth to call out in a shorter, quieter version of her battle call. "Aye!"

Two of her Rangers appeared from out of the shadows. She handed them the rope, and they immediately set about binding Hopper's paws behind his back.

"Sorry about the rope," Firren said, "but I can't be sure you won't try to escape. You're with me now, and I swear upon the honor of my very soul that I will keep you safe." She reached out reverently and traced the white circle as Titus had, only much more gently. "Actually, I swore to protect you long ago."

"Huh?"

But she would say no more.

They waited only long enough for her to wipe the feline blood from her sword. Then they set out.

"Where are we going?" Hopper asked.

"To commune with the Mūs," Firren answered.

"Will they welcome us?" he asked nervously.

A little grin tugged at the corner of Firren's mouth as she once again eyed the tuft of white fur on Hopper's face. "Something tells me they might."

Paws bound and heart aching, Hopper fell into step with his captors.

Away from Atlantia, away from his brother, and into the dusky unknown.

# CHAPTER FIFTEEN

THE JOURNEY TO THE homeland of the Mūs was long and grueling.

Back in the pet shop Hopper had been able to note the movement of the sun beyond the big glass. It had been reliable and constant, and he realized now that he'd never really appreciated what a simple comfort it was to see a new day dawn, then burn itself out and fade into the next.

Here in the belly of the earth there was no way at all to gauge the passage of time.

For all Hopper knew, they had been walking for days in search of the Mūs. Maybe even weeks.

The little party rarely stopped to eat, because they had almost no food to speak of. On those occasions when they did break for a meal, Firren made sure that the Rangers shared their meager rations with Hopper. And fairly. Once or twice Hopper thought she took less for herself, giving up most of her own share so that he could be fed.

And when they camped for the night, Firren never forgot to gently loosen Hopper's bindings so that he could rest more comfortably; then she'd sit up all night to make sure he did not run off into the darkness.

He would have too. And he told her so.

"That's why I stay awake," she replied.

"Because you want to keep me as a hostage!"

"No, because I want to keep you from fleeing into the tunnels, where you would be certain to endure a slow and painful death."

She sounded so sincere that Hopper almost believed her. But he'd heard what Zucker had said—Firren was malevolent and misguided. She could not be trusted.

And yet she shared her food and loosened his ropes for comfort.

Still, he was a prisoner.

It was all too confusing, and he would fall asleep attempting to reconcile the heartless creature Zucker had described with this kind and gentle rat who watched over him while he slept. Try as he might, though, he just couldn't make sense of it, and eventually he would doze off to the lulling, far-off sounds of the crickets chirping.

Once they saw one of the musical bugs go hopping past. The Rangers seemed disquieted by its peculiar appearance—those strange antennae and the bent, craggy legs.

"They're crickets," Hopper explained.

"We know what they are," one of the Rangers snapped. "We just don't see them around much, and they're awfully odd-looking."

"Well, there's nothing to be afraid of," Hopper informed them. "Zucker says crickets are harmless. Except when they swarm."

Firren chuckled. "That Zucker is just a wealth of knowledge, isn't he?"

"He taught me to read," Hopper said defensively.

Firren's ears perked up, and she nodded her head. "He did, did he? Well, I'll admit, I'm impressed." Then she called to her Rangers, and the group decided to make camp for the night.

As the Rangers began setting up their gear, Hopper gathered his courage to ask Firren the question that had been nagging at him: "Why do you want to destroy the Atlantian refugee camps?"

Firren took a moment to think before answering. She helped herself to a piece of crusty bread from her knapsack and brushed off a few mold spores before tasting it. Then she turned to Hopper and replied carefully, "Because I believe those rodents would be better off liberated."

"Liberated?" Hopper scoffed. "They'd starve to death. They'd be at the mercy of those screaming metal serpents."

"What is he talking about?" one of the Rangers asked, biting into the stem of a wild mushroom. "What serpents?"

"I think he means the trains," Firren said. "Otherwise known as the subway." She broke off a piece from the scrap of moldy bread and handed it to Hopper.

"Thanks," he said. "So if they aren't serpents, what are they? What is a train for?"

"It's how the humans move around," Firren explained. "They stole the idea from the earthworms, actually. Long ago the humans burrowed into the earth and created a whole labyrinth of tunnels. These tunnels go from the places where the humans are to the places they need to reach. Those monsters you speak of are the carriers—they ingest the humans, transport them at a truly mind-boggling velocity through their man-made warren of tunnels, and then spit them out at their destinations."

"That's amazing," said Hopper. "But why do the trains need to go so fast?"

"Because." Firren tossed off a delicate shrug. "Humans are by far the most impatient species there is."

"And how do they know where one or another train will take them?"

"That's the mystery," the Ranger with the mushroom said. "We suspect they have some sort of homing instinct that tells them which train arrives at which place, but that is merely speculation."

"Right," said the other. "And besides, as long as they leave us alone, we don't care where they go or how they get there."

Hopper couldn't argue with that logic. Still, he couldn't help wondering about those speeding trains and their comings and goings.

As he polished off the paltry shred of crust Firren had shared, he closed his eyes and tried to pull into focus that sign from the Great Beyond, with its cryptic circles and colors and letters. There was some connection there, if only he could puzzle it out.

But at the moment he was too tired and hungry and cold to do it.

When the Rangers packed up their sacks and turned in for some much-needed rest, Hopper put his head down in the dirt to shiver himself to sleep. Sometime during the night his slumber was interrupted when he felt something brush over him; in his dreams it was the silvery wing of a giant butterfly gently encircling him to keep him safe, keep him warm.

Hopper's eyelids fluttered, and in his half-wakeful state he saw Firren, sitting vigil beside him.

As he snuggled into the warmth of the butterfly's wings and drifted back to sleep, he wondered what had become of her cape.

They had arrived at the end of the world.

Or so it seemed to Hopper. An enormous gray wall stood before them, putting an end to their travel.

"Now what?" he asked.

"We go through," Firren replied simply.

"Through?" Hopper repeated in disbelief. "How?"

Firren smiled and rolled her eyes. "Didn't you know we have a battering ram in one of our packs?"

It was a moment before he realized she was teasing him.

One of the Rangers stepped forward and was about to knock on the gray expanse of concrete.

"Wait!" cried Hopper. "Are you sure you want to do this?"

Firren's mouth twitched into a tiny grin. "Pretty sure."

"But you're wrong about Titus. Look at all he's done for the lost rodents. He's given them a safe haven, a civilized place where they can live out their lives in peace and comfort. He's the most unselfish monarch to ever sit upon a throne."

The rebel shook her head. Her voice was filled with sadness. "You're wrong on all counts. There is no one more selfish than the emperor Titus. He has turned your head with his propaganda and his lies."

"B-but . . . ," Hopper stammered.

"Take my advice." Firren's voice was tender and wise. "You'd do well to pay better attention to your instincts. If you have a feeling in your gut, trust it."

Her hand went to the hilt of her sword as she nodded for the Ranger with the red armband to go ahead and knock. "Stay back," she told Hopper.

He was perfectly fine with that.

"And keep your head down."

"Why?"

"Just do it," she said firmly. "And keep it lowered until I say otherwise. Much depends on it." She gave his arm a gentle pat. "And please, do not let anything we say trouble you. You will understand in time, I promise."

Then she nodded to the Ranger to rap on the wall. A scant second later a small wooden door slid open. Hopper couldn't get over it. The door had been virtually invisible, completely camouflaged in the gray expanse.

"Who goes there?" came a voice from the other side.

"Allies," Firren said stoutly. "That is, if you will allow us to be."

A sentry mouse poked his head out of the door and studied the small traveling party. At the same time, from where he waited in the gloom, Hopper was able to study the sentry with his downcast eyes; a strange sense of familiarity washed over him.

The mouse did not share Hopper's white marking but he was brownish in hue, with the same oval ears as Hopper and the same chubby little form. His tail was exactly like Hopper's, as were his paws.

In fact, the only discernible differences between Hopper and this Mūs sentry were the glint of fierceness in the sentry's eyes and the powerful aura of strength and purpose that emanated from him.

Hopper had to admit, those were pretty big differences.

"You are the one they call Firren?"

"I am. And I am here to humbly request a meeting with your Tribunal Council."

The Mūs sentinel looked taken aback. "That would be highly unusual."

"True. But these times in which we live might also be considered unusual."

The guard hesitated, then nodded.

"So you will send word that we have come in peace for the purpose of forming an alliance."

The sentry turned over his shoulder and shouted for one of his fellow soldiers to relay Firren's request to the council leader.

"May we wait inside?" Firren asked. "We have traveled far and would be grateful for clean water, perhaps a meal?"

The sentry looked dubious. "I am not sure that would be wise. Even here in the depths of Mūs territory, wc have heard stories of your hostile nature."

"I am only hostile toward those who are deserving of my hostility," Firren countered. "We have ventured here with only the best intentions. To urge you once again to form an alliance of good, as Dodger once advised. Remember, many Mūs have suffered at Titus's hands."

The sentry did not deny it. "I will need a promise that your motives are genuine, that once inside this wall, you will not attack us. I will need proof."

"All right." Firren reached into her sheath and, with a *whoosh*, removed her sword. Her Rangers did the same. They all placed their swords gently at the feet of the sentry.

"How's that for proof?" she asked.

The sentry opened the gate.

Hopper had thought the tunnel was mystifying. He had believed the city of Atlantia the most spectacular place in the whole wide world, and he'd been certain Titus's royal palace was the most dazzling thing he would ever lay eyes upon, an incomparable feat of imagination and luxury.

But nothing—*nothing*—could have prepared him for what he found on the opposite side of that big gray wall.

Even Firren seemed a bit waylaid by the sight of the black behemoth that lay before them. The Rangers came up short, halting their single-file march so abruptly that they crashed into one another and toppled comically to the ground, dumbfounded by the appearance of the massive and alien *thing* that lay before them.

"The humans used to call it a locomotive," the sentry explained. "It's been abandoned and buried here for decades."

"Is it alive?" Hopper asked. He sincerely hoped the answer would be "no."

On further inspection it was clear that it was not. This gargantuan object was made of steel, polished to a brilliant sheen. Its body was angular in places, rounded in others. It had wheels and a smokestack and glass windows, and made Titus's palace look not only stunted but shabby—inferior in every conceivable way.

"It's incredible," breathed Hopper.

"It's home," said the sentry.

Around the enormous object on the floor of the tunnel was a sturdy village of brick, mud, and stone. The party made their way through the little town as they headed for the black structure.

Hopper kept his head down as instructed, but he was able to watch the Mūs going about their daily tasks—filling pails from their pipelike water source; mending walls made of snugly piled pebbles; children playing in the streets, happily wielding swords fashioned from twigs. Even in these most simple and menial of chores, the Mūs gave off an air of power and purpose. And something else: unity.

These were the ones his mother had begged him to seek. And now he was here, among them. It was as thrilling as it was frightening.

*Savages,* Titus had called them.

Here they were acting anything but.

As Hopper, Firren, and the Rangers wound their way through the tidy lanes and courtyards, Hopper began to notice the delicious smells that wafted from the windows of the cozy cottages.

The sentry pointed to a quaint nest on the corner. "You can stop here for food."

Hopper's stomach growled appreciatively.

Inside, an elderly Mūs couple led the travelers to a small space where the group circled around a platter full of bread.

The meal was different from the fancy fare Hopper had grown used to as a guest in the palace, but it was no less tasty and just as filling. He obediently kept his head down the whole time he was eating.

When they were finished, Firren offered their hostess a warm smile. "Our deepest gratitude for a delicious meal. Thank you for your kindness. We shall not forget it."

The old mouse smiled back and gave the Rangers a loaf of bread to take with them.

Certainly nothing savage about that.

"Head down," Firren reminded him softly.

Then the cottage door swung open, and they were once again following the sentry through the village toward the gleaming locomotive.

# CHAPTER SIXTEEN

THINGS WERE DECIDEDLY LESS cozy inside the locomotive.

They climbed a metal ladder and found themselves in a cavernous space, a steel fortress. On one end of it was a veritable mountain of mechanicals, a tall tangle of metal cords, dials, springs, meters, and cranks.

"What is this place?" Hopper asked.

"Another human leftover," Firren observed. "Bigger than most."

"Very true," came a voice from the shadows.

Hopper turned away from the guts of the locomotive to see another Mūs. At the same moment two of Firren's Rangers very purposefully stepped in front of Hopper, effectively shielding him from the Mūs's view. Hopper had to peer through the tiny gap between their bodies to see what was happening.

This Mūs was not dressed in military attire like the sentry, nor did he wear the plain serviceable clothing worn by the elderly couple with whom Hopper and the Rangers had just dined.

This Mūs was draped in a long, hooded robe—gold, with colorful needlework around the wide cuffs and hemline. The hood, which hid most of his face, was also embellished with bright embroidered trim.

He continued, "We believe this engine, as our

research tells us it was called, is the ancestor of the sleeker modern ones that zip through the tunnels above us."

"I think you're probably correct," said Firren. "In any case, it is a suitable place for such an exalted tribunal as yours to convene. And for La Rocha to dwell."

"I agree," he said. "Although we never see La Rocha. Being mortal, we are not fit to lay eyes on such greatness. He comes and goes under the cover of darkness, and we speak to him from a distance only, and then only rarely. Most of his prophecies and commands are communicated to us in the written word."

"I thought La Rocha was a mystical being," Hopper whispered to the Rangers.

"That's one theory," one whispered back. "Others believe that La Rocha is just an earthly creature blessed with plain, old-fashioned wisdom and good sense. Still others think that he—or perhaps she—is some fantastical combination of both. His lengthy lifespan lead most to believe he is at least part cockroach. Mixed with dragon, perhaps."

Now the Mūs pushed his hood back, and again Hopper felt that same sense of recognition wash over him. Same brown fur, same gently pointed snout.

The robed Mūs introduced himself. "I am Elder Sage, of the Tribunal Council. We have heard of your recent escapades and know that you are—how shall I say it?—*rattus non grata* within the walls of Atlantia.

I am no fan of the Atlantian emperor, but I fear it is not in our best interests to form an alliance with you at this time."

"At *this* time?" Firren repeated, struggling to remain calm. "With all due respect, sir, this may be the *only* time!" She took a deep breath. "Dodger and I began a quest to end Titus's reign." Firren's pretty face tightened with anger and sadness. "We had a third associate, who was equally committed to our cause. Or so we thought. But when we lost Dodger and it became clear that we could not win the fight alone, this traitor shifted his allegiance. He is now staunchly aligned with the Romanus." She lowered her eyes to murmur, "Perhaps he always was."

Sage let out a long sigh. "Dodger had set out from us so bravely. But then he was gone for so long. We told ourselves it was because he was accomplishing his goals, but eventually word reached us that he'd met a tragic end. Then not long after we learned of Dodger's demise, La Rocha's greatest prediction was revealed. A prophecy of a Chosen One who would come to follow in Dodger's footsteps, and most importantly that this Chosen One would be Dodger's progeny. But Dodger left no mate behind when he set out on his mission. For this reason the prophecy has perplexed us. Until—" Sage seemed to catch himself, as though he'd said too much.

"Until when?" Firren prompted.

"Never mind. Continue. Please."

"There is so much we do not know," said Firren. "But I have always had a feeling. A hunch, you could say. That perhaps things then were not as they seemed."

"Is that so?" Sage cocked his head, his whiskers twitching. "Enlighten me."

"Early on in our crusade against Titus, Dodger had entertained the notion of going upland to recruit more forces."

Sage gave her a curious look. "So you believe a Mūs would willingly subject himself to the horrors of the Lighted World?"

"Not ordinarily," Firren clarified. "But he might, if the time came that the horrors of his own world left him no choice."

Sage blinked, allowing this to sink in. "Are you saying you believe he retreated upward, to live among the surface dwellers?"

"It's only a theory," Firren admitted. "Or perhaps just a strong wish. But I propose that Dodger was not mortally wounded by that vile Atlantian officer. I propose that he feigned death as a means of escape. The only place he could go and be truly safe would have been upland to, as you call it, the Lighted World. There he could avoid Titus's bounty hunters and also take opportunity to gather reinforcements." A tiny smile flickered on her lips. "And maybe some other opportunities as well."

Sage considered her words carefully. "If that were the case, then where is this upland army and why has Dodger not returned to us?"

"I honestly don't know the answer to that," said Firren with a sigh. "As I say, it is only a theory and a new one at that. I've only just come upon certain, shall we say, 'evidence' that leads me to believe Dodger may have lived long enough to sire a litter, thus making the prophecy of a Chosen One possible."

Elder Sage mulled this over, his expression unreadable. Finally he spoke, but it seemed as though he were talking only to himself. "So the stranger was speaking the truth . . ."

"What stranger?" Again Firren's curiosity was piqued. "Who spoke the truth?"

Sage shook his head. "La Rocha's prophecy gave us hope for an offspring of Dodger's—a Chosen One— to come in glory and lead us as he did. But nowhere in the prophecy did La Rocha suggest that the child would hail from the upland."

"Well." Firren allowed a small smile. "Maybe La Rocha was saving that as a surprise."

Sage clapped twice, and two more robed figures entered from behind the mechanical mountain.

Sage introduced his brethren—Temperance and Christoph. They were, like Sage, advanced in age with an aura of quiet strength about them.

Now the trio of council members put their hooded

heads together and whispered for a long moment. From his place behind the Rangers, Hopper struggled to hear but couldn't make out a word of it. Finally Sage stepped forward.

"What exactly do you wish of us?" he asked Firren.

"To continue the work that Dodger so bravely began. You know of the refugee camps beneath Atlantia. You know that in addition to innocent upland migrants, Titus would think nothing of capturing and sacrificing a Mūs."

*Sacrifice?* Hopper felt the word like a punch in the gut.

"Yes, we know that," Sage replied. "Which is why we instruct our citizens to remain here, behind the gray wall. Now only our scouts are allowed to venture out, to patrol or to scavenge for provisions." His eyes clouded with regret. "And yes, a number of them have been lost to Titus."

"Well, if you are aware of the atrocities he is committing," said Firren, her voice taking on a fiery tone, "then you are morally obligated to join with us in our efforts to put an end to it. To all of it! His reign of terror, his barbaric rituals . . ." Her body was quivering now with adrenaline and fervor. "My Rangers and I can't defeat him on our own! With you as our allies we can raise a sizable and well-trained army. That is what Dodger wanted. You know this is true because he appealed to you, and I know you had, however reluctantly, begun the process of recruitment and training. But when he disappeared, you abandoned your efforts. Now the evil that Dodger so detested is worse than ever. Elder Sage, join forces with us. We must liberate the camps and destroy Titus. We must rise up against him, and we must do it now!"

"No!"

The Tribunal elders whirled at the sound of Hopper's voice coming from behind the Rangers.

"Titus is not a villain—" Hopper began, but one of Firren's soldiers quickly clapped a paw over his mouth.

"You have to join us!" Firren cried, her voice filled with passion. "That was Dodger's wish."

"How do you know that?" Christoph demanded.

"Because I fought side by side with him. Dodger was your trusted leader. And he understood that Titus was a monster who must be stopped. His greatest goal was to put an end to the tyranny!"

Hopper was trembling now. Rise up against Titus and Atlantia? It was unthinkable.

The elders again retreated to their circle and whispered among themselves. From what Hopper could see, it appeared that Temperance was nodding emphatically, but Christoph shook his head in opposition. Finally Sage turned back to the visitors.

"I am sorry, Firren. We must think of our Mūs citizens. A rebellion against Titus and Felina would endanger us all. Especially without one so worthy as Dodger to lead us."

"And what if there *were* one as worthy as Dodger to lead? Would you agree to help us then?"

The council members exchanged veiled glances. It seemed to Hopper that they knew something they weren't sharing with Firren, as though they were keeping a secret.

With a deep breath Firren motioned to the two Rangers who had been concealing Hopper. Without hesitation they stepped aside, revealing Hopper to the Tribunal.

Sage reacted with a visible jolt. His eyes locked on Hopper's with an expression that was a charged blend of excitement, amazement, and reverence.

Hopper felt a jolt of his own. This was *something.* The sense of connection, of belonging, of purpose. But he had to fight it. His loyalty was to Zucker; according to Titus, he was the promise of Atlantia's future. He didn't want to feel connected to the emperor's enemies. The other council members looked as moved by the sight of Hopper as Sage did.

"Another one!" Temperance breathed.

"He, too, bears the mark," said Christoph.

"*Another* one?" Firren frowned. "He, *too* . . . ? What do you mean?"

But Elder Sage was walking slowly toward Hopper with his arms outstretched. When he reached

Hopper, he bowed, then cupped Hopper's face in one trembling paw.

"You," he whispered. *"You."*

Hopper swallowed hard.

"It seems we have received an even greater gift than has been foretold to us," Christoph observed.

"It is a miracle that blesses us twice over," agreed Temperance.

A very baffled Hopper glanced at Firren, whose brow was knit. She seemed as confused as he was, on the verge of asking a question, when from behind the locomotive's pile of cranks and dials there emerged a fourth robed figure.

All eyes turned to watch this stranger approach Hopper. The hood cast a deep shadow, so no face was visible. But there was something in the stranger's carriage that seemed eerily familiar to Hopper.

"Well, well, well," came a voice from inside the hood. "Look what the *rat* dragged in."

Then the hood was flung back, and Hopper felt his heart flip over in his chest.

"Pinkie!"

There she was. White circle, wounded ear. A near mirror image of Hopper.

Except, of course, for the fact that she was dressed in a golden robe.

Hopper felt a rush of brotherly joy. "Pinkie!" he

cried again. "You're alive! You're all right! And . . . you're a Tribunal Council member?"

"I'm the Chosen One, you idiot," she said in her icy way. "Although now it seems I'm half of the Chosen Two."

"Again with the 'Chosen' nonsense?" Hopper was exasperated. He turned imploringly to the members of the Tribunal. "I'm not the Chosen *anything*. We were five minutes away from being some snake's breakfast when we escaped. I don't understand what it is you think you see in us."

Before the Tribunal could respond, Firren grabbed Hopper's arm and jerked him forward. "Honored members of the Mūs Tribunal Council, she's not the Chosen One. I respectfully present to you the true Chosen One. Dodger's son."

# CHAPTER SEVENTEEN

HOPPER WAS VAGUELY AWARE of Sage explaining to Firren how Pinkie had wandered up to the gray wall weeks ago, exhausted and nearly starved to death. The presence of the white marking had so shocked the sentry on duty that he'd immediately summoned the council. They had then covertly transported Pinkie to the engine, where they nursed her back to health and argued among themselves whether or not she was the Chosen One of La Rocha's prophecy.

When Pinkie was well enough to speak, she told them she was from a far-off land called Petshop, which was utterly unheard of to the Tribunal. Ultimately they determined from her description of this foreign place that she had come to them from the upland. As far as they were concerned, this fact put a significant crimp in the likelihood of her being Dodger's offspring, the one they had so long awaited. But as there was no denying the marking of white fur, they had decided to keep her hidden here in the train engine until they could determine the truth.

Now they were beside themselves with joy over the fact that they had received a matched pair of Chosen Ones. Joy and confusion.

As thrilled and relieved as Hopper was to have found his sister, he was finding it hard to stay focused.

When Christoph called him forth to receive a golden robe of his own, Hopper didn't even realize he'd been addressed.

Firren gave Hopper a firm nudge in the elder's direction, but he could barely get his paws to work.

"Wait," he said. "Please. I need a minute to think about this."

Firren gave him a curt nod, and Hopper closed his eyes, allowing his thoughts to swirl.

Dodger's son. He was Dodger's son.

Dodger. Hero of the Mūs. His father.

And Pinkie's father too, of course, and Pup's.

So what did that make Hopper? He had moments of anger, but he believed himself to be good and fair and peace-loving. And who could be sweeter and more innocent than Pup? How could he and his brother be any of those things with Dodger's Mūs blood coursing through their veins?

Although it certainly explained a lot about Pinkie.

Now Christoph was slipping the elegant robe over Hopper's head; he placed his arms into the wide sleeves and felt the sweep of the embellished fabric swish around his legs.

Hopper's head swam. Zucker had known his father. Known him, fought with him, and, according to Firren, betrayed him. But Hopper refused to believe that. Zucker was loyal, even if he did give his father misinformation about Firren. That was probably nothing more than a simple mistake. Firren was a liar! She was thirsty for power and would do anything to get it.

Hopper knew the sanctity of Atlantia must be defended at all costs, and he would do everything he could to see it done.

As Temperance stepped forward to adjust the hood around Hopper's shoulders, Hopper made a silent vow.

He would escape Firren. He would get back to Atlantia and warn Zucker of her infernal plot. He would tell Captain Polhemus and First Lieutenant Garfield that the Mūs were now aligned with the Rangers and that the Romanus army should mobilize at once.

If need be, he would go directly to Titus himself and reveal Firren's plan.

For the first time in his life, Hopper was ready to fight.

Pinkie had changed out of her golden robe. She was dressed like a warrior now, in britches of rough cloth, and a thickly padded leather jerkin.

In addition, someone had given Hopper's sister a dagger.

To Hopper, who knew her best, that was unsettling indeed.

It was while Firren and the Tribunal Council

worked out the details of their agreement and Hopper found himself waiting alone in the shadow of the metal mountain that Pinkie turned to face him.

A wave of brotherly affection rolled over Hopper, a connection that seemed to sing in his blood. Despite their tendency to argue, and Pinkie's constant bullying, she was family. Now more than ever he understood the importance of that, and he couldn't wait to tell her that Pup was not only alive but safe in the refugee camp.

At least he had been the last time Hopper had seen him. But Firren's raid may have changed that. A stab of fear shot through Hopper's chest. *Pup.* Where was he now? Was he safe? Had the fire . . . ?

He shook his head to dispel the thought.

But what he couldn't ignore was that Pinkie, with the help of this powerful and determined band of mice, was preparing to attack the camp again. Who knew what would become of poor little Pup if Firren's next raid succeeded?

As his sister stared at him, Hopper felt a surge of hope—maybe if he explained about Pup, he could get Pinkie to help him sabotage the rebel plan to destroy the camp.

She was crossing the floor of the engine room now.

His heart thudded. He would ask for her assistance, beg if he had to. They would work together as they had in that cardboard box. Oh, how long ago that seemed now! But they were still family. For better or for worse, they were the children of a mighty leader. Surely they had victory in them.

Hopper closed his eyes and returned to the memory—the heartbeat, the proud posture, those kind and gentle eyes—it didn't seem possible that his father would willingly endanger those helpless rodents who were the wards of Atlantia.

But it was so.

Again Hopper shook off the image and set his mind on the moment at hand. He would explain all about Firren's lies and Titus's good works to Pinkie, and she would understand. Together they would defeat the rebels and the Mūs. Or perhaps as the Chosen Ones they could make the Mūs see that there was no reason to wage war with Titus. Maybe they could persuade them to change their ways.

Pinkie now stood directly in front of him.

He was about to open his mouth and tell her his plan, but she narrowed her eyes and spat at his feet.

"You've ruined everything," she growled. "Again."

"What? No! I—"

"Mother is gone because of you. Pup is gone because of you," she said. "And I was the Chosen One. I was the one who would lead them. But now . . . I'll be forced to share my leadership with a sniveling weakling! This mission is doomed already, Hopper. And it's all your fault."

"You don't understand!" His voice was desperate. "Firren is a liar. What she said about Zucker is wrong. He found Pup! The prince led me right to him, and guess what! Pup is safe and unharmed, being cared for in one of those camps!"

Pinkie's paw went to the handle of her dagger, and Hopper gasped.

"Listen to me, brother. You will say nothing. The Mūs have agreed to follow Firren and attack this Atlantia you love so much. So it shall be. . . ."

Her claws curled around the dagger's hilt.

Hopper gulped. She was threatening him! His own sister! What had happened to her down here? She'd always been tough. Mean, even. But deadly?

She turned and stomped away to where Firren and her Rangers, along with the council members and several Mūs military officers, were huddled around a long, rough-hewn table; a large metal chest sat upon it.

Grimly Hopper joined the others at the table.

"We have agreed to join with the Rangers," said Sage, "but before we embark on this quest, we must consult the Sacred Book. It may shed light on this quandary of having two Chosen Ones in our midst and remove any doubt as to who will lead us." He looked from Pinkie to Hopper, then nodded to Christoph, who unlocked the metal chest. Temperance reverently lifted a sheaf of yellowed pages out of it and spread them carefully across the surface of the table.

"These pages have been in the possession of the Mūs for ages," Temperance explained. "They contain not only the writings of our forefathers but also antiquated texts of unknown origins. We believe these have been delivered to us over the decades by many an anonymous hand, none of which even La Rocha can name. We have endeavored to interpret these scrolls and books and leaflets, but many remain a mystery to us."

Firren looked interested and impressed. She reached out and cautiously lifted a brittle page from the collection.

Christoph took the page from Firren and turned it over.

"Here are the prophetic words of La Rocha, transcribed soon after we lost Dodger." He cleared his throat and read aloud:

*". . . There shall appear One who will lead them*
*Small of stature but brave of heart*
*Only He can destroy what evil did start*
*Innocence tempered with wisdom shall guide Him*
*    in His quest*
*His bearing may be gentle, but it is courage He*
*    wears best*
*A marking of white shall bear the proof*
*That He alone brings purity of vision*
*Exalt and hail Him!*

For He, the child of brave Dodger, shall lead our
noble mission . . ."

The engine room went perfectly silent as all eyes
turned to Pinkie. But in the next moment Sage's voice
broke the silence.

"'*He* alone brings purity of vision,'" he repeated. He
turned his wise face to Hopper and nodded. "This
prophecy states clearly that the Chosen One shall be
of the male persuasion."

Pinkie let out a furious snort. "That is ridiculous.
Sexist and chauvinistic and just plain wrong. I have
more guts and zeal in the tip of my tail than Hopper
has in his whole chubby little body!"

But Temperance shook her head. "Sage is correct.
The Sacred Book proclaims it thus. 'Exalt and hail
*Him*.'"

Hopper took the page and read it to himself. Indeed,
the prophecy described the Chosen One as gentle.
Pinkie was the complete opposite of gentle. But it
also predicted this leader would be brave of heart.

Hopper had never been brave before. But Firren
herself had said he was.

So perhaps it was true. Pinkie may bear the mark
and the heritage, but Hopper fit every criteria from
the Mūs text.

"It is decided, then," Sage proclaimed in a solemn
tone. "Hopper shall lead us."

The look Pinkie hurled at Hopper was heated enough to singe his whiskers. But Hopper barely noticed. He was too astounded by the announcement that they were appointing him to lead a mission.

The thought nearly paralyzed him.

First of all, he was utterly untested and inexperienced in the ways of war. And second of all, he wasn't even on their side!

Of course, they did not know that.

Firren must have seen the panic in his face. Quickly she removed herself from the crowd and drew Hopper aside.

"Chin up, little one," Firren said softly. "I'll be with you every step of the way. I know you're afraid. I know this is a daunting proposition for one so small and untried. But the prophecy says that the Chosen One will be innocent. And I've never met anyone more innocent than you!"

Did she think he was worried about failing her and the Mūs? That was ridiculous.

And yet there was such sincerity in her words and such kindness in her voice.

*Liar!*

"Courage," she continued, "is a complicated thing. Most think that having courage means never being frightened. But that is untrue. Real bravery is doing what needs to be done, even if what needs to be done terrifies you to the depths of your soul. Being immune to fear isn't courage—it's idiocy! Life holds many dangers. It is the mouse who feels fear but takes action in spite of it who is the most heroic of them all!"

Hopper remembered how frightened he'd been in the camp when the rebel horns had blown and the smoke had swirled in like a dark spirit. He remembered the fear that overtook him. And he also remembered that in spite of it, he could focus on only one thing: finding Pup. He would have walked through those flames to get to his brother, if only he'd known where Pup was.

Maybe Firren, vicious, dishonest usurper that she was, for once was speaking the truth.

They returned to the table, where the Mūs General DeKalb was showing them maps that were included in the Sacred Book. They were old and also faded, and the pathways they marked seemed to be a pointless tangle.

Hopper immediately recognized the word "Brooklyn" on the big map, and the familiar colored circles with the letters inside. This was a map, a map of the rails and tracks that carried the speeding monsters—the subway trains! Their destinations were clearly noted, and there were numbers that indicated which trains arrived at which stops.

So that was how the humans did it. They had a map! And a schedule.

A quick glance around the table told Hopper that none of the other mice or rats had made the connection.

Good. He would keep this to himself. He had no idea how the information might be useful to him, but on the chance that it would, he was not about to share it with Firren and these dreadful Mūs soldiers.

# CHAPTER EIGHTEEN

**ALL THAT WAS LEFT** was to receive La Rocha's blessing.

Sage excused himself and disappeared into the sanctuary where the deity lived in seclusion from all except the Tribunal. This sacred chamber was built into the long, narrow smokestack of the engine and was heavily guarded by armed sentinels.

The assemblage waited.

It seemed to Hopper that in the entire time Sage was gone, no one moved. No one even breathed.

When at last he returned, he opened his arms and said, "The wise and benevolent La Rocha deems it right and necessary that we join with Firren and her Rangers in this worthy endeavor to defeat Titus."

A cheer went up from the gathering, echoing off the gleaming steel of the engine's walls.

"A small contingent shall go forth with the Rangers now. The remainder of our forces will prepare and follow soon after. Pinkie, sister of the Chosen One, shall go along at this time, and assist her valiant brother in leading this mission."

Pinkie's whiskers twitched as she scowled, not happy about "assisting" anyone, let alone her brother. But there was nothing Hopper could do about that.

Well, fine, then. If they were going to follow him,

he would take his cue from Firren and become a boldfaced liar. She'd twisted the true purpose of the camps in order to enlist the Mūs. So why shouldn't he be equally conniving?

And Zucker—he'd already played this game, making Firren believe he was on her side when all along he'd ... well, Hopper wasn't exactly sure what Zucker had been doing back then, but he'd fooled Firren—that much was clear.

So if Firren could lie, and Zucker could make believe, then Hopper could too.

He would pretend. He would fool Firren, letting her think he welcomed this role of the Chosen One. Then the very first chance he got, he would dash for freedom. Somehow he would find his way back to Atlantia and warn Zucker that the Mūs had united with the rebels.

Titus deserved at least that much. He had treated Hopper with kindness and respect. Sure, he was gruff, and sometimes Hopper felt nervous around him. But Titus was powerful, and under great pressure to protect his city and his subjects. That kind of responsibility would make anyone short-tempered.

Summoning his most dignified voice, Hopper lifted his chin and declared, "I gladly accept this honor." *For Titus,* he added silently.

His announcement was met with more shouts of celebration, followed by a flurry of activity. The

Rangers marched off to the bladesmith with General DeKalb to collect more weapons. Firren conferred with Temperance and Christoph while Sage and a handful of attendants went off to the village square to inform the populace of this new alliance and the importance of their support.

Pinkie stood in the corner, toying with her blade. And brooding.

Hopper, still dressed in his flowing golden robe, watched it all with a worried but resolute heart. Then he went back to the antique table to again examine the mysterious map unfolded upon it.

The lines, the circles, the letters. He would pretend about this, too. He would pretend he hadn't solved the elusive mystery of the train routes.

He was sure that knowing this was the answer to something.

If only he knew what.

There were a dozen Mūs soldiers led by General DeKalb, Firren and her Rangers, Pinkie, and Hopper. This was the company that set out through the door in the great gray wall.

They made their way through the tunnels, the Rangers leading since they were most familiar with the labyrinth of passageways. At times they heard the rumble of the trains speeding above their heads.

Firren went over her plan with the general, and

Hopper made it a point to listen carefully.

She explained that the rebels had managed to breach the perimeter of the refugee camp in several spots. They had dug holes and tunnels, creating entry points and escape routes, and then with the help of some brave Rangers posing as refugees on the inside, they had camouflaged these egresses so that the camp guards would not detect them. One of these was the hole near the fence down which Hopper had gone on the day of the fire.

Firren would lead the Mūs to these various entry points, and at the sound of the rebel horn, which Hopper now knew was a hollowed-out piece of bone that hung from a rope around one of the Ranger's necks, the company would storm the camp.

Without warning, Hopper was filled with a strange sensation. His whiskers began to twitch and his fur stood on end. Something was about to happen. . . .

Firren knew it too. She lifted her nose into the air and sniffed.

Hopper remembered what she had said the first time he'd seen her: *I can smell him.*

It was as if merely thinking of him had magically conjured him. Hopper looked up just as Zucker appeared on a high mound of dirt and rubble.

Hopper had never been so glad to see anyone. Polhemus and Garfield and a handful of foot soldiers joined him, and the sight of the silver *Z* on their vests filled Hopper with joy and relief. In addition, there was a battalion of palace soldiers who wore the emperor's livery.

And there were cats! Felina's warriors had come along to aid Zucker and his troops.

Rapier drawn, Zucker leaped down from the dirt pile. Firren, too, sprung into action, her sword slicing through the air as she rallied her Rangers with a blood-chilling cry:

"*Aye, aye, aye!*"

These rebel shouts were answered with the screeching cats' meowing. Their green-gold eyes seemed to light up the darkness as they surrounded the Mūs army.

Without thinking, Hopper grabbed Pinkie.

She fought him, of course, but he held fast, dragging her out of the melee.

"What do you think you're doing?" she hissed.

"Keeping you safe!" Hopper answered, pushing her behind the pile of gravelly dirt.

"I want to fight!"

"Against an army of cats? Not even *you're* tough enough to defeat a feline. Dagger or no dagger. Now stay here and be still!"

As Hopper scampered away from the dirt mound, one of Zucker's soldiers, a powerful rat named Ketchum, caught him and pressed him against a wall, creating a shield with his body.

Hopper did not resist. He knew what this was. A rescue!

Now the sound of a multitude of swords clanking and warriors shouting out in fury and pain filled the tunnel.

The Mūs were no match for Zucker's band. And the feral cats! They swatted at the tiny mice, batting them around as though they were playthings. Still, one of the burlier Mūs soldiers managed to plunge his sword into one of the cats' paws, and the resulting howl seemed to shake the stone walls of the tunnel.

Undaunted, the Rangers attacked, advancing again and again. But they were outnumbered by the Atlantian soldiers. Zucker's troops were skillful and agile. Titus's soldiers were ruthless and well armed.

"Retreat!" DeKalb commanded.

Obediently the Mūs and the Rangers withdrew from the scuffle. Hopper saw Pinkie dart out from her hiding spot and hesitate as though she would ignore the general's order and stay to fight. But she must have thought better of it, because in the next moment she turned and took flight with the others. This was not cowardice; it was good judgment. Hopper was just glad that Pinkie had escaped with her life.

Ketchum grabbed Hopper's arm and began tugging him away.

But Hopper stopped short when he saw Zucker and Firren, toe-to-toe in the center of the tunnel. The

Mūs and the Rangers had already disappeared into the darkness, and most of Zucker's men and their feline counterparts had begun a sprint back toward Atlantia.

Firren raised her sword, twirling it in tiny circles above her shoulder.

Zucker swung his rapier in broad, graceful swishes.

Their eyes were trained on each other's. Neither wavered; neither glanced away.

Firren stepped left; Zucker leaned right.

She snarled.

He growled.

They pounced! Each at the same time, colliding in midair with a bone-knocking thud.

Metal crashed on metal; Hopper swore he saw sparks.

Zucker dodged and parried; Firren thrust and swung.

Then he kicked out with his hind paw and tripped her! She stumbled and fell to the ground as Zucker lunged forward, his sword high above his head.

In one fell swoop he could have put an end to her.

Hopper held his breath. He watched Firren watch Zucker, who in turn watched his would-be victim with fire in his eyes.

Again he growled, low in his throat.

And then silence. The stillness was utter and complete. Even the dust motes swirling in the dank air seemed to halt in their orbits as the rat prince hovered like a statue above his prey. Three seconds, four . . . five . . .

Hopper could not believe what happened next: Zucker stood down. Sword still aloft, teeth still clenched, eyes still flashing like flame, he *stood down*.

One step back, then another . . .

At last he tore his eyes from Firren's.

"We ride!"

Ketchum swept Hopper into his arms as a tremendous tabby appeared. Zucker leaped onto the cat's back. The soldier handed Hopper up to him, then clambered up himself.

"Yah, yah!" cried Zucker, spurring the cat forward. "To Atlantia! Yah!"

As the cat bounded forward, Hopper took one wild glance back over his shoulder.

Firren was rising from the ground, brushing the dirt from her tunic, shaking her head and scowling.

She did not give chase. Instead she merely stared after them until the tabby took a corner.

And then she was gone.

They found the rest of the rescue party waiting for them at a bend in the tunnel. There were tracks running down the center of it, so the rats and ferals were careful to keep to the edges.

Zucker swung down from the striped back of the

tabby, then helped Hopper to the ground.

"Nice to see ya again, kid. How've ya been?"

Hopper looked up into Zucker's grinning face in amazement.

"I've been better," he grumbled.

Zucker casually examined the tip of his rapier, then returned it smoothly to its sheath. "Well, all things considered, you look okay to me." He lowered one eyebrow. "Nice robe."

Hopper couldn't believe Zucker's aplomb. He reached up and clutched the front of Zucker's vest, shaking him with all his might. "They're planning another raid. We need to get to Atlantia as fast as possible!"

"Easy, kid." Zucker shot a quick glance at the tabby cat and the palace soldiers, who were listening intently. Then he lowered his voice so only Hopper could hear. "This ain't the time or the place. Trust me."

"But, Zucker, I can help you—"

*"Trust me,"* Zucker repeated in a tone that brooked no argument. Perplexed, Hopper let go of Zucker's vest. His hands felt strangely wet, and as he examined them, he saw why; his hands were covered in blood.

"Zucker! You're hurt."

The prince smiled. "Just a scratch, kid." But there was a waver in his voice, and his eyes were beginning to glaze over. With great effort he waved to the palace soldiers. "You and the cats go on ahead. Bring word to my father that the Promised One, or should I say, the Chosen One, is safe."

The breath caught in Hopper's throat. Zucker knew! He knew that Hopper was part of the Mūs legend! But how? And why had the prince been so kind to the chosen leader of Atlantia's archrivals? For a fleeting moment he feared that Zucker's friendship had all been a sham, that the rat had been using Hopper somehow, as a pawn in this baffling game of war. But the fear vanished as quickly as it had come. He knew in his heart and soul that Zucker cared for him. So there had to be another reason. Right now he was simply too overwhelmed to imagine what, but he would give Zucker the benefit of the doubt.

"I think we should hear what the mouse has to say," said one of the soldiers.

"Well, sure," said Zucker in his most amiable voice. "Of course. In fact, as soon as we get back to Atlantia, we'll have a nice, cozy little summit meeting in the conflict room, and the kid can spill his guts over tea and crumpets."

A high-ranking officer of Titus's army stepped forward. "But Atlantia is days from here, even with the ferals to carry us."

Zucker lowered himself to a sitting position on the ground; Hopper was sure this was to conceal the fact that he was beginning to sway. "C'mon, Colonel, have a heart, huh? The kid's been through a pretty major ordeal here. I'd like to give him time to calm down before we start interrogating him."

"But—"

"I promise I'll bring him straight to the conflict room the minute we get back. Now, you and your troops go on ahead."

The officer looked as though he might protest again, but Zucker lifted one eyebrow in a challenging expression. "You've just been given a direct command from the royal prince, in case ya didn't get that."

The colonel frowned, but he obeyed. Titus's men climbed onto the cats and took their leave, the ferals galloping off at a good clip.

Zucker's guards remained behind with their prince; he motioned to Ketchum, who was at his side in a split second.

"How long before they reach Atlantia, Ketch?"

"Three days at the most," Ketchum replied, then called over one of the soldiers to assist him. Together they carefully removed Zucker's vest to reveal a deep stab wound, bleeding steadily.

Hopper reached a paw toward his friend. His limb shook with fear and fury. "Did Firren do that?"

"Nah. It was one of the Mūs soldiers. Hurts like crazy. Apparently those little guys have good aim." He laughed, then winced. "We've got to get back there before Titus's men do," he continued between clenched teeth. "We've got to divert the palace army and prepare for the siege."

Divert? Hopper still didn't understand. Why would Zucker want to *divert* the Romanus troops? Perhaps the pain and the loss of blood were affecting the prince's mind. Hopper was about to suggest this to Ketchum, but he was interrupted by a rumbling sensation under his feet.

"Look out!" cried one of the other soldiers.

Ketchum hoisted Zucker onto his shoulder and ran for the edge of the tunnel; the rest of the group dove from the tracks and pressed themselves to the cold stones of the wall.

As always, the light came first, then the train, filling the tunnel with explosive noise and rocking the whole world.

When it was gone, Hopper turned to Zucker, who seemed to be hovering close to unconsciousness.

"Forget those mangy ferals," the prince grumbled, even as his eyes rolled back in his head. "*That's* what we need. Speed."

"You're losing a lot of blood, sir," Ketchum said grimly.

An idea hit Hopper like a lightning bolt.

"I can get you back to Atlantia in a matter of minutes," he said. "Way before the palace guards, and in plenty of time to prepare for the Mūs invasion."

Zucker's face contorted in pain. "Really, kid, this isn't the time for jokes."

"I'm not joking. And I'm not crazy." Hopper smiled. "We can ride a train back to Atlantia!"

The soldiers looked at him as though he'd gone soft in the head. Even Zucker, in his semiconscious state, looked stunned.

"Those silver things that speed around are called subway trains," Hopper explained.

"We know what they are," snapped one of the soldiers. "We aren't the ones who are new around here."

"Oh." Hopper felt his cheeks tingle with embarrassment. "Right."

"But we don't know much else about them," another admitted.

Hopper brightened. "Well, then you probably don't know that they follow these tracks, with a purpose and not just willy-nilly."

"Did he say 'willy-nilly'?" whispered the first guard.

"They follow a pattern," Hopper clarified. "I know because I saw a map. Certain trains stop at certain places. That's what the circles and letters are all about. They tell the humans which trains go to which places."

"You're suggesting we actually ride one of those devils?" said Ketchum. "It's madness!"

"Madness," the second guard agreed.

Hopper felt his desperation rising. "I know it's risky. But it will get us to Atlantia in minutes instead of days." Hopper closed his eyes and pictured the map on the table in the engine room. He saw it, with all its lines and swerves and circles imprinted with letters and numbers. "Red circle with a two or a three in it. That's the one we need."

Zucker grimaced as another jolt of pain slammed through him. "C'mon, kid. This isn't a game."

The soldiers exchanged glances. Hopper thought that for all their muscles and silver *Z*s and swords, they looked a little bit nervous. Maybe even scared.

Hopper wasn't scared.

He was petrified.

He knew in his heart that jumping on that moving monster was the only way they could get to Atlantia in time to prepare for the raid. But the thought of riding that train as it barreled through the tunnels was nearly too frightening to bear.

*It is the mouse who feels fear but takes action in spite of it who is the most heroic of them all!*

A wise thought and inspiring words.

Zucker's cloudy eyes met Hopper's as he summoned his most powerful, royal voice. "I forbid you from riding the train!" he wheezed.

It was the last thing Zucker would say for quite some time. In the next second his eyes fluttered, and the prince slipped into oblivion.

# CHAPTER NINETEEN

THE SOLDIERS BEGAN THEIR march toward
Atlantia.

Ketchum and the others took turns carrying Zucker,
who, even from the depths of his unconscious state,
would occasionally groan out in pain.

Hopper scampered along behind, his mind reeling.

Zucker wanted to arrive at Atlantia before the
palace guards did. Probably because he didn't trust
that stuffy old colonel of Titus's to fortify the camps
against Firren's attack. This was a job for Zucker's
soldiers. They were younger and stronger.

And besides, the Mūs wouldn't be far behind.
Hopper didn't know much about the military, but he
did know that Atlantia would be at a much greater
advantage if they had more time to organize, prepare.
They needed to know that Firren was on the warpath,
and they needed to know now.

It wasn't long before the small band of soldiers had
to again slam themselves into the wall to dodge a
speeding subway train. As it screamed past, Hopper
squinted into the light in search of the colored circle
branded on the monster's forehead.

*F.*

No.

He sighed.

As the train disappeared, Hopper caught a glimpse of its hindquarters. Jutting out from the bottom was a metal nub, like a stubby tail.

Sturdy. And just big enough for a determined little mouse to hitch a ride on.

Hopper felt his pulse quicken.

Could he . . . ?

*Should* he? The prince had forbidden it. But Zucker was worsening with every step, every jostle, every movement of this long, difficult hike. Hopper could see from the deep crimson stains seeping into the fur and vests of the prince's loyal guards who carried Zucker that he had lost a great deal of blood. Zucker needed to get back to Atlantia fast, back to the infirmary. If they couldn't get him there in time . . . well, Hopper didn't even want to think about what could happen. Every time Zucker cringed or winced, Hopper felt as if he himself were being stabbed . . . right in the heart.

*Real bravery is doing what needs to be done, even if what needs to be done terrifies you to the depths of your soul.*

Minutes later, when the far-off rumble began, Hopper came to a decision.

Zucker had saved him once. Now it was up to Hopper to save Zucker.

And Pup.

And all the helpless rodents back in the camps who,

in days, would be senselessly slaughtered if someone did not get to Titus in time to warn him of Firren's approach.

The light bloomed in the distance, and the roar grew. He heard the sound of metal rattling metal and the growl from the subway's belly.

But this time, when the soldiers flattened themselves safely against the wall, Hopper did not cower; instead he took a deep breath and prepared to leap.

"Hey, get away from there!" shouted Ketchum.

Hopper didn't budge from the edge of the track. He stared into the light, searching and hoping that the symbol emblazoned on the front would be the one Hopper needed, the one that identified this as *the* train.

And there it was.

A circle, plainly visible on the face of the train.

Like a birthmark.

Like a white circle naming the Chosen One. And just as Hopper's unique marking had told Titus and Zucker and Firren and the Tribunal who *he* was, this red circle with a bold, white number 2 in the heart of it told Hopper what he needed to know: *I will take you to Atlantia, and I will take you there fast!*

The train sailed past in a silver blur.

Behind him Hopper was aware of motion—one of the soldiers was coming to snatch him away from the rails.

The train cars clattered past. And then the last car.

Timing would count; timing and strength and grace.

And courage. With a little madness mixed in.

Now Hopper saw the rusted metal shelf extending outward at the bottom of the car.

Behind him the soldier's paws were reaching to pull him back....

But Hopper leaped.

Leaped into the wind and the speed and the danger.

"Nooo!" screamed the guard, but his voice vanished as the train swept past.

*Thud.*

Hopper landed on the chunk of metal, scampering frantically to get his footing. But the train swerved and he was thrown! He slid toward the edge, scratching and flailing, sure he would be hurled to the rusty rails to meet his own tragic end.

There was a sharp tug around his shoulders, and he stopped slipping.

The hood of his golden robe had caught on some metal outcropping attached to the stub!

The train sped on with Hopper swinging madly as he dangled by his hood.

Again the train took a turn, and this time the momentum swung him closer to the shelf. He reached, grasping, and managed to grab hold of a large bolt; he wrapped his paws around it and hung on tight, panting, sweating.

Twice he tried to sweep his body upward onto the shelf, but the wind sucked at him and kept him from getting enough momentum. Finally he resigned himself to traveling the rest of the way suspended by his hood and clutching the jagged bolt.

It was a miserable way to take a ride.

But it was a ride. And it would get him back to Atlantia in time.

That, as far as Hopper was concerned, was all that mattered.

The ride was mere minutes, but they were filled with thrill and terror, whipping and winding through the labyrinth of tunnels. When at last the train pulled into the station Hopper needed—ATLANTIC AVENUE/ BARCLAYS CENTER, the sign read—the noise was a deafening shriek of metal grinding against metal. Speed to stillness, and then a windy *huff* as the doors opened and the humans were expelled.

Hopper was able to disengage his hood and jump to the platform, where he scampered along among the foot traffic, which reminded him of the upland sidewalk, but this path was paved in smooth squares. He forced all thoughts of being stomped or crushed or kicked out of his mind and ran. For once, his stature worked to his benefit. No one noticed the brown mouse dressed in gold hurrying across the sticky, grimy tile floor.

Hopper, on the other hand, noticed plenty. The light from overhead was pale but fierce enough to illuminate a veritable minefield of garbage and lost articles. It was just as Zucker had described—the humans were careless with their belongings and sloppy about their castoffs. Hopper hurdled over plastic forks, broken glass, and half-used packs of matches. On many occasions he was forced to scuttle around or over hefty pieces of baggage the humans had rested unguarded on the floor beside their feet. Many of these cases had been left to gape open, threatening to spill their contents everywhere. Hopper only just avoided one catastrophe—he'd scaled the slippery leather outer wall of a ladies' handbag, but his tiny claw had caught on the zipper and he'd toppled inside.

Once he'd managed to free himself, he made a frenzied dash to the far wall of the tunnel and kept close until he found what he needed.

A gap! It was the tiniest fissure, where the floor failed to meet the base of the wall; it was all Hopper needed. With a deep breath and a quick prayer, he squeezed through.

And again he was falling.

He landed with a thud in the silence of the Great Beyond, the walls of Atlantia just mere yards away.

He got to his feet and brushed the grime of the human upland from his fur.

And he ran.

He barely paused to acknowledge Clops, who regarded him with a cold look as he opened the gate.

"You," the cat sneered. "Thought you were a goner for sure."

Hopper scuttled past the guard station, then flew through the marketplace, ignoring the hawkers and the shoppers who paused in their tasks to stare at the little mouse in the elegant golden robe.

He went directly to the palace and entered the great hall. As it happened, Titus was passing through the grand space at that moment; the sight of Hopper made the emperor stop in his tracks.

His eyes glittered. "Promised One! You have come back to us."

"Titus. You have to listen to me."

Titus looked over Hopper's head to the broad door behind him. "Where are the others? The colonel, my troops, Zucker and his battalion?"

"Delayed, Majesty. They should be back in three days. Zucker was badly injured and—"

"Three days?"

Hopper nodded. A small crowd of servants and palace officials had gathered, even a few Atlantian townsfolk, curious at this excited exchange between their emperor and the royal guest in his elegant golden attire.

"I don't understand." Titus scowled down at

Hopper. "How is it possible that you have arrived so far in advance?"

Hopper shrugged. "I took the two train."

"You took a *train*?" Titus blanched. "That is very reckless, Promised One."

"Uh, well ..." Hopper gulped. "I was in kind of a hurry."

Titus studied him. "You appear unharmed," he said, sounding relieved as he reached out to stroke the embroidered cuff of Hopper's robe. "What urgency demanded you travel so quickly?"

"Firren has formed an alliance with the Mūs, and I suspect they are marching forth even as we speak. It will take them the whole of three days to get here, according to Officer Ketchum, but I think if we start organizing the Romanus army immediately, we will be ready for them."

"Excellent advice." Titus patted Hopper's head with a gnarled paw. "It would appear that you are the Chosen One for good reason."

This brought Hopper up short. "You knew?" His voice was a gasp of disbelief. "Even when you called me Atlantia's Promise, you knew the Mūs awaited me as their Chosen?"

"I am the emperor," Titus said simply. "It is my job to know."

Hopper had no idea why Titus would keep such crucial information from him, but now was not the time to ask.

"There's more," Hopper piped up. "I listened to the rebels talking, so I know much of their plan." He caught himself, embarrassed. "I'm sorry, I'm sure there's something else you'd rather know first."

Titus frowned. "What could possibly be more important than hearing what you have to say about defeating the Mūs?"

Zucker's condition, of course. It was wrong, Hopper realized, that Titus was not worried for Zucker, his own son. It was a sign, an indication . . . of *something*. A cold tingle pricked Hopper's spine.

And then there was Firren's voice whispering far back in his mind: *Pay attention to your instincts . . . a feeling in your gut . . . trust it . . .*

Abruptly Hopper bowed to the emperor. "Pardon me, Your Highness, but I feel a bit weak. I think I should lie down for a bit." When he straightened, he saw the emperor's eyes glint with fury.

"I wish to thank you, from the bottom of my heart, and on behalf of all of Atlantia, for your most courageous actions. You put the greater good ahead of your own safety. I can only imagine what it must have taken out of you, and I want you to know how very, very much we appreciate such sacrifice."

Hopper froze; the word shot into his ear like a poison arrow.

*Sacrifice.*

His chest tightened, and the sensation of alarm coursed through him.

Something was wrong. Something was very, very wrong. And Hopper suddenly had the very unsettling feeling that he was to blame.

"Summon Cassius immediately," Titus barked to a young rat soldier standing near. "Tell him we have a hostage."

The word snapped out of the emperor's mouth and hit Hopper like a whip. "Hostage?"

"Of course." Titus's voice was as hot as embers. "You are the Chosen One. The Mūs have been awaiting you with bated breath. You are the answer to all. And that is why I kept you. Didn't you find it odd that, but for you, there was not a single mouse in the entire city of Atlantia?"

*No, I didn't,* thought Hopper. *Because I was too wrapped up in my own importance and the mission to save Pup to even notice.*

"That rule was instated so that no Mūs spy could ever get behind these walls. So you can imagine my surprise when my own son deposited the Chosen One right at my feet. He didn't know it at the time, you'll recall, but the revelation of that white marking was undeniable."

"And he agreed to keep me here," Hopper rasped, "as a hostage."

"He's the prince. It was his duty."

The sense of betrayal caused Hopper's knees to buckle. Zucker had been lying to him all along, playing him for a fool. A chosen fool.

Cassius strode into the entry hall, eyes glittering. His excitement over Hopper's capture caused his oily gray fur to give off a faint but sickening musk. Hopper felt instantly ill. "Your plan to broker an armistice with the Chosen One's life has come to fruition, I see."

"Yes," Titus drawled. "And you know what we must do now."

Cassius nodded. "I will send word to the enemy that the Chosen One is being held prisoner. If they are smart, and I think they are, they will retreat immediately." The general's filmy eyes bore into Hopper's. "After all, it is the only way to ensure that I will not sever the Chosen One's tail from his body and strangle him with it."

At that, Titus frowned. "Now, Cassius, there is no need for such violent talk. The important thing is that the Mūs army will stand down. And then . . ." He paused and shrugged. "Well, we will address that issue when we come to it."

"Yes, Your Majesty," Cassius huffed, then added, so only Hopper could hear, "We will address it with my dagger across this Mūs's throat and my sword through the prince's belly."

Hopper began to quake.

"Oh, don't be overly frightened, Hopper," the emperor said breezily. "I'm certain your tribe will be reasonable. They have great concern for your well being, even if that irksome little rebel, Firren, doesn't give a rat's ... well, you know." He flicked his paw at Cassius. "Now get this mouse out of my sight. You, Cassius, will guard him personally. And send a royal messenger to the Mūs village with word that a highly valuable hostage is currently in our possession."

"Wait."

Titus, Cassius, and Hopper turned to see the maid, Marcy, standing at the bottom of the stairs.

"If I may, Majesty?" she asked, dipping a ladylike curtsy.

"By all means, pretty one." Titus waved her over, flashing his sinister smile. "You have something to say?"

"Yes, I do. I heard what you just said, and I applaud you on your keen military instincts."

Titus beamed. "Thank you. I try."

"However . . ." Marcy batted her eyelashes, then shook her head. "No. Never mind. I'm sorry. I fear I overstep myself."

"Nonsense," said Cassius, his musky stink growing stronger. "Speak your mind."

"All right." Marcy tilted her head and lifted her shoulders in a dainty shrug. "I know I am but a lowly chambermaid, but it seems to me that the general's military prowess might be better employed. Surely his gifts for warcraft and his ease with violence would be wasted guarding such a pathetic little mouse."

Cassius stroked his pointy snout and looked at Titus. "She has a point."

"Which is why I propose you allow the general to direct his undivided attention toward the impending battle and let someone else act as jailer to the captive."

Hopper couldn't believe what he was hearing. Marcy, who had been so kind and gentle, who blushed whenever Zucker smiled at her, was offering to oversee his imprisonment. He could have wept.

"That is a brave and dutiful offer, miss," said Titus, his eyes narrowing. "But how do I know that you are worthy of such a crucial task?"

"Because I am a loyal citizen of Atlantia and I consider any creature who would have a hand in destroying the Romanus way of life to be my greatest enemy."

"But you are a female," Cassius scoffed. "How do we know that you will not be soft on the hostage?"

"I assure you, I will not."

Cassius snickered. "We would need proof."

Without hesitation, Marcy marched across the hall, raised her arm, and slapped Hopper hard across his face, the force of the backhand blow knocking him to the floor.

"And there it is!" Cassius laughed. "All the proof we need."

Marcy reached down and grabbed Hopper by the scruff of his neck. "I will not take my eyes off of him, Highness. I will see to it that Hopper is treated exactly as he deserves to be. And so that you and Cassius can begin planning for the attack posthaste, I will also take it upon myself to find an appropriate messenger to send word to the Mūs."

"Excellent," said Titus. "We thank you for your allegiance, little maid. You are quite the resourceful young lady."

Again, Marcy batted her eyes. "Oh, Your Majesty. You have no idea."

# Chapter Twenty

When the bedchamber door closed behind them, Marcy threw her arms around Hopper and hugged him.

"I'm so sorry I had to hit you," she cried. "But it was the only way I could make them believe me."

"Believe you?" Hopper rubbed the sting from his face.

"That was all just a ploy to get you away from Cassius."

Hopper's heavy heart seemed to rise up. "So you *don't* want to see me strangled with my own tail, then?"

"Never!"

"And you aren't going to send word to the Mūs about this hostage business?"

"Absolutely not. I just wanted to buy you some time to execute your plan." She gave him a hopeful look. "You do have a plan, don't you?"

Hopper began to pace.

"You should lie down," Marcy coaxed. "You've been through a great trauma and you'll need your rest if you're going to put this all to rights."

Hopper shook his head.

"Would you like some food? Or a drink?"

"No, thank you," said Hopper.

Marcy glanced nervously toward the door, then

stepped closer to Hopper. "Is this about the camps?" she whispered.

Hopper stopped pacing and stared at her in shock. He remembered how kind she'd been when she'd bandaged his wounded ear.

"I . . . I've *heard* things," she confided.

"What kinds of things?"

"About the true purpose of the refugee camps."

Hopper's stomach turned to stone. "The true purpose? I thought Titus had created the camps to protect the lost ones. To provide shelter for the wanderers."

"That's what we're supposed to think. But I've often heard Titus talking to his advisors. Servants have a way of being invisible, you see. The emperor is so used to our comings and goings that when we are around, he hardly knows we're there. He speaks freely about things he shouldn't."

"What does he say?"

Marcy frowned in thought. "Well, he often talks of a place called the hunting ground. And of needing more lost rodents to appease Felina and her clan."

Hopper didn't like the sound of that.

"And I've overheard Zucker . . . I mean, His Royal Highness the Prince . . . in conference with his general. They, too, speak of this hunting ground, but it makes them very, very angry."

Hopper let the words settle into his brain. He must

have been pondering this for some time, because Marcy cleared her throat.

When he looked up at her, he saw great worry in her face.

"How badly is the prince wounded?" she asked softly.

Hopper felt tears prickle behind his eyes. "Pretty badly. The wound was deep, and he lost a lot of blood."

Marcy looked away.

When Hopper spoke again, his voice was small and soft. "Marcy, do you believe Zucker has betrayed me? Do you think Titus speaks the truth when he says that all this time, the prince has seen me only as a hostage to use against the Mūs?"

"Not for a minute do I believe it," said Marcy, her face flushing with the strength of her avowal. "Zucker loves you. If he pretended to agree with Titus, then he must have had a very good reason."

Again, Hopper's heart soared with relief. Marcy was right. Zucker was his friend.

"I wish I had told them about the trains," Hopper said.

"Maybe I can help," Marcy offered, her voice eager. "I can send my brothers. They're young and strong. They can go out into the tunnels and find the prince's battalion, and bring them a message."

Hopper's heart lightened. "That's a wonderful idea."

As Marcy went off to find her brothers, Hopper

found some scraps of paper left over from his writing lessons with Zucker. He quickly wrote a note explaining to the prince that he had arrived safely at the palace, and that he had almost revealed everything about the Mūs invasion, but at the last minute something told him to keep the details to himself. Still, he wrote, he feared that the damage had been done and that the only way for Zucker and his soldiers to get back in time would be to ride the train, as Hopper had. He explained how Zucker would know which train to ride and added instructions advising him and his soldiers to hop onto the train's metal stub of a tail.

Then he signed it:

*I remain, as ever, your loyal servant, Hopper.*

After a moment's thought he crossed out "loyal servant" and wrote "devoted friend."

Soon Marcy returned with her brothers. They were twins, Bartel and Pritchard, and were possibly the most robust and athletic-looking rats Hopper had ever seen.

"We are loyal to Prince Zucker," said Bartel. "We plan to enlist in his elite corps when we come of age."

"We are honored to have this opportunity to assist him," said Pritchard. "Just tell us what you need."

Hopper explained that he wanted the boys to go

off into the tunnels and find Zucker and his troops. Their first order of business would be to see to the prince's injury.

Hopper then sketched a map indicating the path Zucker and his soldiers would be traveling. Very carefully and as neatly as he could with his tiny chip of graphite, Hopper drew a circle with a 2 in the center.

"Tell them that they must board this train and this train only," Hopper said. "No other. Do you understand?"

Bartel nodded.

"We understand," said Pritchard.

Hopper gave Bartel the letter, and Marcy handed Pritchard a small sack filled with medical items.

"Be careful," she called as they scampered out the door. "And send the prince my love."

Hopper could see from the way she blushed that she hadn't meant to say that out loud.

"It's okay," he said with a grin. "He's a lovable guy."

Marcy smiled, and then her face grew serious. "When I went to fetch my brothers, I saw Queen Felina arriving. One of the footmen told me she had come for an urgent meeting with Titus."

Hopper cocked his head. "And?"

"Well, I was thinking that perhaps you would want to hear what they were saying."

Hopper's eyes widened. "Is that possible?"

The next thing Hopper knew, he was following Marcy down a long, shadowy corridor that ended in a small, forgotten antechamber at the back of the throne room.

"You can hear everything from in there," Marcy whispered. "Just remember to keep quiet."

"What is Felina like?" asked Hopper.

"Like all cats," Marcy replied. "Sly. And vicious. But the legend goes that she was not always a tunnel dweller. The evidence is the jeweled collar she wears, although after all this time below, it no longer sparkles like it once did. The story says that Felina was once the privileged house pet of a human family who doted on and spoiled her. And then one day they turned her out. She found her way here and rose to power, some say, on beauty and cruelty alone."

"Great," grumbled Hopper. "Another scary monarch."

As he crept into the dark nook and pressed his ear to the long-unused door, he couldn't help but wonder how, in such a short time, he had gone from being a simple pet-store mouse to being the Promised One who would insure the promise of a safe Atlantia, to being the Chosen One foretold of in Mūs legend.

And now from being the Chosen One to being a spy.

Felina was, in a word, gorgeous.

Pure white, with enormous tilted eyes—one gray-green, the other the clearest icy blue. This peculiarity was not off-putting; rather it only added to her mystique. The queen had a perfect little pink nose; her ears were proudly pointed, and her fur looked almost too soft to touch. The gem-studded band that encircled her throat was proof of her pampered background.

It was hard for Hopper to believe that this elegant creature was a member of the same species as that heinous-looking monster Cyclops. The other ferals had a roughness about them, but Felina was lithe and elegant.

And mean.

"You are failing me, rat," she hissed through her glistening white teeth. "My subjects are hungry not only for food but entertainment. We were exceedingly disappointed by the last sacrifice."

There was that word again: *sacrifice*. Hopper shivered.

"I assure you, Felina, I am doing all that I can." Titus smiled his hideous smile at the beautiful queen. "The tunnels have been empty. My soldiers can only do so much."

Felina responded with an ominous purr. "Our peace accord is based on my contentment."

"I serve at your pleasure, Highness," Titus croaked, growing jittery. "And believe me, I know verily well the conditions of our agreement."

"Do you, Titus? Because it seems that you've

forgotten. Do you still understand exactly what is keeping me from ripping your head from your body and sucking out your innards right this very minute?" She looked down her pert nose at the emperor. "Not that I imagine you would be especially tasty."

Hopper was beginning to understand why her humans had turned her out.

Titus trembled as the color drained from his face; Hopper thought he looked ready to faint. "I assure you, you will be presented with a suitable number of refugees as per the conditions of our treaty. The delivery of said refugees will be on schedule—I guarantee it."

"Small price to pay," Felina purred, "for your life."

"You think I worry only for myself?" the emperor replied, his voice quivering. "I carry out these conditions not only to ensure my own safety but for that of all the citizens of Atlantia. I worry for my subjects as well." Titus swallowed hard.

"Of course you do," Felina purred again. She let out a razor-sharp peal of laughter. "And those furry little idiots believe you are actually colonizing the tunnels."

The sound of that laugh made Hopper want to upchuck.

"I must say," Felina went on, "my subjects thoroughly enjoy their monthly sport of stalking these unsuspecting rodents you deliver to the hunting ground. Not that it's much of a contest, of course."

A shriek rose in Hopper's throat; he fought it back, but his stomach lurched as he began to realize the nature of this treaty.

"Naturally it would be far more exciting and rewarding if we just attacked your precious Atlantia," Felina cooed. "But I wouldn't dare violate *my* side of the bargain, now, would I?"

Titus shook—in fear? Anger? Hopper couldn't tell.

But then the emperor's shoulders lost their strength, and the old rat hung his head, his body slumped as though in shame.

"We both win, Titus. Everybody wins," Felina hissed joyfully, then tossed her head and smiled. "Well, everyone but the refugees, that is."

Like a poisonous gas the words seeped into the tiny nook where Hopper hid. His eyes burned with tears, his head pounded, and his heart felt near to splitting in two. This "treaty," this "arrangement," was anything but peaceful—it was an agreement to murder, a regularly scheduled slaughter. And Titus had the audacity to call it peace.

Peace for *some.*

*Death* for others.

No wonder Firren wanted to liberate the camps! A hot wave of disgrace washed over Hopper as he thought of how he'd misjudged her. She was a hero, fighting for freedom, for justice. What had he done? How could he have been so stupid?

"Now," Felina was saying as she whipped her tail so that it snapped dangerously close to the emperor's ear. "What are these rumors I am hearing of a raid on your camp? That would greatly displease me, Titus—the loss of all those delicious little rodents."

*Delicious.* The word almost made Hopper gag.

But Titus gave a dismissive wave. "You have nothing to worry about there, Felina. We have been told of this forthcoming invasion, and as you know, forewarned is forearmed. Which we are. And I believe that this time we shall put an end to their efforts for good."

"Does your handsome son continue to remain true to the Romanus way of life?" Felina asked. "I have always wondered about him. He seems too liberal by half, and it was once believed that he had befriended the Mūs leader, Dodger, and was working with him to bring down our precious camps."

"That is absurd," cried Titus. "Those were rumors, falsehoods. Disparaging scuttlebutt perpetrated by those who would see me defeated. Zucker would never align with a Mūs or a rebel like Firren, not even in his misspent youth. And in this case, as in all others, he will abide by my wishes. He is irreverent and reckless, but he is not stupid." A tone of dread crept into the emperor's voice when he added, "Zucker knows that if he betrays me, the royal advisors will place a bounty on his head."

Hopper went cold. The emperor would put a bounty on his own son? No. But his advisors would. And Titus would be obligated to allow it.

Felina meowed in amusement as she looked the emperor up and down. "Don't tell me this treaty still pains you after all these years, Titus," she said with a smile. "It's a necessity, after all, not to mention the reason we get on so well together." She crossed the throne room, her soft, padded paws as silent as ghosts on the gleaming floor. "Still, your reaction concerns me. Could it be that you're finally discovering you have a conscience? Or worse . . . a soul?"

"A soul?" Titus shook his head. "No. I relinquished that long ago, the moment you and I first shook paws on this agreement and I opened the first camp. You have nothing to concern yourself with, Majesty. The refugees will be delivered. On schedule, as always."

Felina narrowed her eyes. "I sense some hesitation. And I don't like it at all. Which is why I suddenly find myself unwilling to give you a chance to reconsider. I am going to insist that we do not wait out the remainder of the month before enjoying the next sacrifice. On the chance that you are going soft, or that perhaps we have underestimated Firren and the Mūs, I would like to arrange a hunting party for . . ."

She paused, considering. The purr that came from deep in her throat was a threatening sound.

"The day after tomorrow," she decided. "First thing

in the morning. Oh, and I would like double the usual offerings. After all, you owe us from last time, and if those rebel invaders get lucky, there might not *be* a *next* time." She swished her tail again, creating a breeze that caused Titus's whiskers to quiver. "I don't suppose I need to tell you that *that* would be the end of our peace treaty."

Titus opened his mouth to answer her but only succeeded in making a pathetic wheezing noise.

"And it also goes without saying," purred the beautiful white queen, "that you will be the first one to feel my wrath."

With a swish of her luxurious tail she turned and strutted out of the throne room.

When she was gone, Titus crumbled into his throne, then pointed a knobby paw at one of the footmen. "Bring word to the camp guard immediately. There shall be an unscheduled delivery two mornings hence. We are to supply double the amount of quarry for Felina's hunters. Instruct the guards to feed them well. The fatter the hunted, the fuller the hunters. Go now, make haste!"

Hopper remained huddled in the dusty alcove until the soldiers and attendants had all left the throne room and Titus was alone.

Then the enormous rat let out a whimper and dropped his scarred face into his gnarled paws.

Perhaps he laughed. Perhaps he wept. Perhaps he

merely sat and thought about what might lie ahead for his empire.

Frankly, Hopper didn't actually care what the emperor was feeling. His kindness had been a sham. He was as devilish as Firren had said. All Hopper could think of now was Pup, alone in that camp— the camp that Hopper had stupidly believed was a paradise but now knew was merely a holding cell where innocent rodents awaited certain death. His eyes stung with tears. He had to get Pup out of that vile place before something terrible happened. Teeth gritted, Hopper slipped out of the anteroom and ran back to his bedchamber as fast as he could. There was much to do.

And it had fallen to him to do it.

# CHAPTER TWENTY-ONE

"WELL, IT'S ABOUT TIME, kid. Where ya been?"

Hopper nearly tripped over his own paws at the sound of the voice coming from the bed on the far side of his room.

"Zucker! Are you okay?"

The prince grinned. "Well, I been better. But then again, I been worse. And keep yer voice down. Nobody knows I'm here, and I'd like to keep it that way."

Zucker was propped up on the pile of plush pillows that adorned Hopper's bed. His chest was securely bandaged; other than a small bloom of red that seeped through the gauze, he looked well. Bartel and Pritchard stood beside the bed. Ketchum was posted near the door, and Marcy sat on a chair close to the prince, feeding him steaming broth.

"I'm so glad you made it back," said Hopper, scurrying over to sit at the foot of the bed.

"Thanks to you," said Zucker. "I would have never thought that crazy metal monster would take us to Atlantia so fast if you hadn't figured it out. And I'm pretty sure I wouldn't have had the guts to ride it, until you went ahead and did it first."

Hopper flushed with pride. "Thank you for rescuing me, by the way."

Zucker shrugged. "All in a day's work, kid." He took

a sip of broth, then turned a serious expression to Hopper. "Now, I need you to tell us what you know. Firren and the Mūs—she finally has the support of their army?"

"Yes."

Zucker let out a hushed whoop of joy. "Thatta girl, Firren!"

"Zucker, I'm so confused. Nothing makes sense. I thought the Mūs were bad and Titus was good and Firren was just plain trouble."

"Well, I can't blame ya for that. After all, I was the one who told you those things. It was part of my plan." The prince sighed. "I'm bettin' you've got some questions."

Hopper barely knew where to begin. "Why did you lie to me about Firren and the Mūs? You told me they were savages."

"I know what I told you. But think back, Hopper . . . every time I said something negative about the rebels and the Mūs, who was listening?"

Hopper struggled to recall. "Titus's guard?"

"Right!"

"So you wanted him to *think* you hated the Mūs?"

"Right again, kid."

"But why?"

"Because this reign of Titus's has to end. And Firren, with the Mūs as her allies, is our only hope. And I've been feeding my old man false information to make it easier for Firren and her Rangers to infiltrate the camps."

"So that's why you didn't put an end to her, back there in the tunnel?"

"That's one reason."

"Then she really *doesn't* despise you?"

"Oh no . . . she pretty much hates my guts." When Zucker shifted against the pillows, the movement caused him to wince. Or maybe it was the thought of Firren that caused him pain. "She doesn't know I've been sabotaging Titus all this time. She thinks I really did switch sides after Dodger . . ." Zucker looked away, then cleared his throat. "Anyway, it's better like this; Firren needs to attack at full throttle, and if she's worrying about me getting hurt, she might hold back."

Hopper remembered how considerate and protective she'd been when he was her captive. He could see how she might let her concern for Zucker's safety affect her mission; her hating him definitely solved that problem.

"What about the Mūs?"

"The Mūs . . . are complicated. Titus wants us all to believe they are ferocious warriors, which they are. They have a natural gift for battle, but they only engage when provoked. They much prefer to live in peace if possible. It took a lot for Dodger to get them to agree to form an army. After they lost

Dodger, they tried to look the other way and ignore the injustice of Titus's camps. From what you tell me, Firren's finally made them see they can't sit idly by anymore."

Hopper's next question came out in a whisper: "So you did know Dodger? You knew . . . my father?"

A shadow of sadness passed over Zucker's face. "Dodger was my best friend. We met in the tunnels when we were young. He was the one who first told me the truth about Titus's peace accord. I knew he was going to lead his tribe against Atlantia one day, and I vowed to help him."

"Did you know I was his son?"

Zucker nodded. "As soon as that bandage fell off your ear. That white circle said it all."

"So the first day, when you told Titus the Mūs were not a threat and Firren wasn't a danger, you were just throwing him off the scent, to give them a better chance."

"Exactly. I'm what you might call a double agent."

"And now Firren is planning a mighty assault."

"Yep. And as long as Titus doesn't know that, they've got a really good shot at succeeding this time."

A sick feeling filled Hopper's gut. He turned to Marcy. "You didn't tell him?" Marcy shook her head.

"What's the matter, kid? You look a little queasy."

"I told Titus!" Hopper blurted. "When I got off the train, I went straight to the palace and told him that

Firren had united with the Mūs army and an attack was imminent."

Hopper curled up at the foot of the bed and buried his face in the blanket. The guilt and disgrace were nearly overwhelming. "If anything happens to Firren and the others, it'll be my fault. I told the emperor they were coming, and now he'll be ready for them."

Zucker sat up, ignoring the pain that shot through his chest, and placed a gentle paw on Hopper's back. "You didn't know, kid. And besides, we've got a few weeks before the next sacrifice, so—"

"No!" Hopper groaned and sat up. "We don't. Felina ordered Titus to reschedule the hunting game."

"Reschedule it? To when?"

Hopper gulped. "Day after tomorrow. There's no way Firren will be here by then."

"Maybe she will, kid. That little rat has a lot of tricks up her sleeve, believe me."

"Even if she does, it's going to be a catastrophe. The Rangers and the Mūs army will be walking into a deathtrap." Hopper collapsed into the rumpled sheets. "And what about Pup? And Pinkie? They're in danger too, and it's all because of me. Oh, Zucker, what have I done?"

"Easy, kid. Don't do this to yourself." Zucker let out a long rush of breath. "It's not all your fault. I was the one who filled your head with that negative propaganda. It wasn't like you had the inside scoop."

Hopper bolted upright, his teary eyes wide, his heart racing.

Something Zucker had said had struck a chord.

"Inside!" he cried.

"Inside?" Zucker raised his eyebrows. "Inside *where*?"

"The camp."

It took Zucker a second to comprehend, but when he did, he shook his head. "Ohhh nooooo! Not happening, kid. Ya hear me? Way too much of a risk."

But Hopper rambled on. "What bigger risk is there than doing nothing? If Firren and the others don't arrive before the sacrifice, all those innocent creatures will be tortured and eaten. And if she does, and we don't do something, the palace soldiers will be ready for her, and she and her troops won't stand a chance."

Zucker glanced over Hopper's head to where Ketchum was still guarding the door. The officer shrugged and gave his prince a nod. Hopper was right, of course, and both Zucker and Ketchum knew it.

"What exactly are you thinking?" Zucker asked.

Hopper had no idea. All he knew was that he wanted to get inside that camp and find Pup. He'd hide him or break him out, or, if all else failed, he'd give his little brother a weapon and tell him to fight for his life.

"I suppose you could sneak me in. Tell them I'm a new refugee you found in the tunnels. They'll be happy about that. With the sacrifice just a day away they're looking for as many victims as they can get. Felina ordered Titus to double the numbers for this one. Did I mention that?"

Zucker looked grim. "No. You didn't."

"Well, she did! So that means Pup's chances of being sent to the hunting ground are even greater."

Zucker did not deny it, which made Hopper both more frightened and more resolute.

"If I'm inside, I can warn the refugees. I'll tell them the truth about the camps. I'll tell them that the colonist story is a lie and that if they want to get out of there alive, they're going to have to fight. That way, when Firren attacks, the guards might not be surprised to see her, but they sure will be surprised when the refugees start fighting! I can tell Ketch where Firren's entry portals are, and we can have your soldiers sneak a whole bunch of weapons in for the refugees to use."

"Wait a minute," said Zucker. "If you know where those escape portals are, why don't we just sneak the refugees out?"

"I thought of that," said Hopper. "But if all those rodents go missing, the soldiers will notice. They'll send search parties into the tunnels and bring them right back."

When Zucker glanced at Ketchum, the officer was biting back a grin. "He's got a point, Highness."

Zucker rolled his eyes but smiled. "Yeah, I guess he

does. But then he is the Chosen One, right?"

Hopper whirled to face Ketchum. "If I tell you where Firren's secret entrances are, can you arrange to have Zucker's soldiers deposit a cache of weapons there?"

"It's a brilliant plan," said Ketchum, but he looked skeptical. "But I'm afraid if Titus knows about the attack, it's safe to assume he's already begun assembling an arsenal by requisitioning every available weapon in Atlantia, including those that belong to Zucker's corps. That leaves us with only the ones we brought on our mission to save you. Not nearly enough to arm ourselves, let alone the refugees."

Hopper felt the disappointment like a crushing blow. Arming the imprisoned rodents and convincing them to defend themselves was the essence of the plan. But how could they supply the refugees with weapons if Titus had seen to it that there was not a single blade or sword left in all of Atlantia?

They would simply have to go beyond the city.

Beyond and above.

It had taken some doing, but Hopper was finally able to convince Zucker and Ketchum that what he wanted to do was not, in fact, suicidal but sound. Moreover, this quest was necessary and unavoidable.

"You came through the upland station just like I did," Hopper reminded the soldier. "Didn't you see all that *stuff*? It was everywhere. And those humans don't keep their eyes on any of it."

"I hate to admit it," Ketchum said with a sigh, "but I think it's our only hope."

Zucker hesitated but finally nodded his consent. "Who will we send?"

"Ketchum and me and the twins," Hopper decided. "And two others, perhaps—strong ones who can carry the haul. But they must be fast and stealthy as well. We'll instruct them to gather anything jagged or pointy that can be used in lieu of swords, as well as any article that might be turned into ammunition. Fiery things, toxic things, blunt or heavy things."

Ketchum nodded. "I understand. I'll go gather our best soldiers, and you meet us on the south side of the palace in half an hour, and we'll venture upland to carry out this important mission."

Ketchum turned to leave, then turned back. With a grin he offered Hopper a salute.

Hopper squared his shoulders and returned the gesture with a wary smile.

Soon he would be traveling upland, but even with the twins and three soldiers to protect him, he felt a twinge of worry. He did not want to poke his whiskers into the bags and totes and cases of humans and steal their belongings.

He did not want to, but he had to.

As Ketchum had said, this was an important mission

and it was up to the Chosen One, the long-awaited son of the brave Dodger, to lead it.

Zucker motioned to Marcy's brothers, who were still lingering at the prince's bedside, eager to be useful. "Hopper, you tell Bartel and Pritchard everything you know about Firren's plan, especially the whereabouts of the secret exits. They'll bring the information to General Polhemus."

So Hopper spent the next hour telling the twins everything he'd seen and heard. He told them about every secret entrance point, every hidden portal, every concealed exit that Firren had mentioned to General DeKalb. He described the kinds of weapons he'd seen or heard about and estimated the number of soldiers the Mūs would be sending. He talked about strategy and tactics.

Bartel and Pritchard were then swiftly dispatched to seek out Polhemus and Garfield and make a full report. They would join Hopper, Ketchum, and the others at the assigned spot to the south of the palace, and together they'd go off to find weapons with which to arm the refugees.

The minute the twins left the chamber, Zucker threw back the covers and put his paws on the floor. With great effort he rose from the bed.

"What are you doing?" Hopper protested. "You're still hurt. You need to rest. And finish your broth!"

Zucker sighed, picked up the bowl, and swallowed

the remaining soup in one long gulp. "There. Ya happy? I finished the broth. But I'm way too worked up to rest any more than I already have. Oh, and for the record, kid, if you're going into the camp tomorrow, then so am I."

"You are? Why?"

"Because . . ." Zucker reached into the pocket of his breeches and pulled out a scrap of paper. It was the message Hopper had sent him via Bartel and Pritchard. "Because you're my friend, that's why." Zucker smiled and pointed to Hopper's signature at the bottom. "See? Says so right there."

Hopper hesitated only a second; maybe it wasn't the act of a courageous warrior or a brave rebel, but he couldn't help himself. He threw his arms around Zucker and hugged him for all he was worth. It went a long way toward bolstering his courage for the mission, but he knew he needed just one more thing to inspire his bravery.

He released the hug and took a deep breath. "Zucker?"

"Yeah, kid?"

"Would you . . . um . . . would you do me a favor?"

"You mean *besides* taking my life in my hands by heading into enemy territory to fight a bunch of evil cats and palace soldiers?" Grinning, Zucker reached for his sheath and sword. "Sure, kid. Anything you want."

Hopper opened his mouth to ask but was suddenly overcome by his nerves. Zucker noticed, and repeated his question in a much gentler tone.

"What is it, kid? What is it you need me to do for ya?"

Hopper drew in a long breath, then let it out slowly. "Tell me about my father . . ."

Zucker had never been out in the tunnels before. Titus had strict rules that forbade all Atlantians—even the royal ones—from venturing beyond the city walls. But the prince could not be happier about his newfound freedom. He was curious and confident and hopeful all at once.

It never occurred to him to be afraid.

After he and Dodger tripped along for several yards, Zucker cleared his throat and asked hesitantly, "It doesn't bother you that I'm . . . ya know . . . royal, does it?"

Dodger crooked a half smile. "Not as much as it bothers you."

"Do you live near Atlantia?"

"Nope. I'm what you might call an underdweller."

"Aren't we all underdwellers down here?"

"Well," said Dodger with a shrug and a grin, "there's 'under,' and then there's under."

Zucker had no idea what that meant, but he found himself enjoying the company of this outsider. Dodger had an energy that Zucker admired, and even though he looked no older than Zucker, Dodger seemed wise—or at least experienced—beyond his years.

The young prince and his new mouse friend chatted amicably about nothing in particular as they scampered along the dirt floor of the tunnel. Zucker's nose was in a state of perpetual twitching as new scents assaulted him from every angle. There was more darkness than light, but when his sharp eyes adjusted to the shadows, he was amazed at the barrenness of the passageway. No buildings like the ones in Atlantia. No marketplace, no public parks. And almost no rodents to speak of.

Once he had caught sight of a lone and hungry-looking rat creeping quietly along the stone wall in their direction. Dodger had hastened over and whispered something to the stranger. Zucker had not heard the exchange, but the result was that the rat had turned tail and run as fast as he could in the opposite direction.

Zucker had not asked Dodger what he'd said to the wanderer, and Dodger had offered no explanation.

As they went along, Zucker snuck furtive glances at the mouse. He was chubby, with a sandy-brown coat speckled with gray flecks. Most striking was an odd marking on his face—a perfect circle of pure white fur around his right eye.

Zucker was so entranced with the white mark that

he was not watching where he was going and nearly collided with a hideous eight-legged creature that seemed to be floating in midair. The sight of the thing nearly scared the daylights out of him.

"Spider," Dodger explained as the beast quickly scurried upward on an invisible thread. "There're plenty of them crawling around down here, but mostly they keep to their webs." He pointed upward with his tail to a gossamer thing that stretched the width of the enormous tunnel—a feat of engineering and embroidery. The delicate-looking net seemed to glisten in the gloom.

"Not sure how those creepy little bugs do it—those webs may look fragile, but they're stronger than you'd think." Dodger laughed. "Just ask the flies! Oh, and try not to brush up against one of those stringy things or you'll be sticky for days."

Zucker took note and kept walking. After a while he asked Dodger, "Where are the colonies? I thought we'd have reached them by now."

Dodger gave him a dubious look. "What colonies?"

"The Atlantian colonies. My father chooses rodents from his refugee camp and sends them out to colonize and build new cities in the tunnels."

Dodger stopped dead in his tracks. "Is that really what you think the emperor is doing? Even you?"

Zucker nodded, then frowned. "Isn't it?" A knot of dread had begun to form deep in his belly.

Dodger shook his head. "Not even close, Your Majesty. Not even close."

"Well, then what is—"

Zucker's question was cut off by a voice in the distance shouting, "Aye!"

Dodger replied immediately with a clear, high-pitched whistle.

There was a rustling sound of dainty paws in the dirt, and there she was: the prettiest, most charming-looking rat Zucker had ever seen in the whole of his young life.

She blinked her big, dark eyes at him and smiled. "Hello."

Zucker nodded. It was all he could manage.

After a moment she turned to Dodger. "Is he a new recruit?"

Dodger laughed. "We'll see."

The pretty rat slid a grin in Zucker's direction. "What's his name?"

"I think for now we'll just call him"—Dodger's eyes twinkled—"the Zuck-meister."

The girl rat's eyes went round with surprise as Dodger turned to Zucker. "Is that name okay with you?"

Zucker nodded, grinning. "I like it."

"Have the others gathered?" Dodger asked.

"Aye."

"Let's go, then."

"Wait," said Zucker. "You were going to tell me about the colonies."

"Come along with us," said Dodger. "If you really want to learn something."

Zucker did want to learn something. He wanted to learn everything.

Most of all, the pretty rat's name.

They had come to a spot in the tunnel that seemed to be a sort of makeshift meeting place. There were several sturdy stones set in a wide circle around a scorched spot on the ground—the site of repeated campfires, Zucker surmised.

A handful of young and rugged-looking rats perched on these stones, eyes filled with interest and anticipation.

Zucker took a seat, and Dodger thanked the other rats for coming. He introduced himself as the leader of the Mūs tribe, and this sent a shudder through the prince. The Mūs, according to his father, were a band of diabolical little beasts who had but one goal: to overthrow the peaceful reign of Romanus.

Zucker sprung to his feet, not sure whether he wanted to bolt into the tunnel or strike out at Dodger.

"I know what you're thinking, Highness," Dodger said, grinning easily. "You've heard horrible things about my brethren. But I promise you, it is nothing but propaganda designed to vilify us. In truth, we are good souls and would never harm anyone unless duly provoked."

Something in his expression told Zucker to trust him. Slowly he returned to his seat on the rock.

Dodger motioned to the girl rat and told the gathering that she was Firren.

She nodded at the small assemblage, then turned to the wall and began to sketch something with a sharply pointed stone.

Firren; just thinking her name caused a fizzy sensation in Zucker's brain.

Dodger explained to the burly rats that he and Firren had summoned them in the hope to draft an elite unit to patrol the tunnels against the insidious Romanus scouts.

Zucker tried to listen to the mouse's eloquent speech, but he was mesmerized by Firren scratching the drawing into the stones of the wall. Her back was to them, and Zucker could not see what she was working on, but the scraping sound of her stone was steady, determined, and intriguing.

He noticed that there were other drawings stretching out along the wall: intricately detailed renderings of battle scenes featuring bold armies of mice and rats engaged in combat.

"It will be a dangerous undertaking," Dodger was telling the recruits, "but never before has there been a more worthy cause. You have heard the rumors and the gruesome tales of what the Atlantian emperor is doing . . . and I am here to confirm for you that even the grisliest of those reports are true. And so I urge you now to go back to your nests and consider what Firren and I are asking of you. I am in the process of convincing the Mūs to assemble an army, and if they agree, I will bring Firren in to explain to them precisely what needs to be done. If the Mūs will not agree to meet with her, then I will go upland to the Lighted World to seek more assistance."

The scraping sound stopped abruptly. Zucker watched as Firren whirled, gaping at Dodger.

"You aren't serious."

"I'm very serious," he assured her. "We'll need all the help we can get, and if it means leaving the tunnels to recruit more soldiers, then that is what I'll have to do."

Zucker was amazed. He knew little of the world above the tunnels. Mostly he'd heard that it was unforgiving and dangerous. And yet Dodger would go there willingly in service of his cause. Zucker realized this was a testament to either his new friend's great courage or his incredible stupidity.

"We will reconvene here in two days' time," Dodger told the group, "and if at that time you remain inclined to join us, we will be proud and happy to sign you up."

As the rats took their leave, Zucker stood and made

his way to where Firren remained drawing on the stone wall. He motioned to the mural-like scenes that stretched outward from where she stood.

"Did you sketch all of those?" Zucker asked.

Firren nodded. "These are battles I see and long for in my dreams."

"I thought pretty girls dreamed of fancy weddings."

Firren rolled her eyes and let out a snort of disgust.

"Not this pretty girl," laughed Dodger. "She's a warrior, through and through. It was her idea to recruit the others and form an elite corps to go up against your father's scouts. She herself plans to lead them."

"Lead them where?" Zucker asked.

"To your father's camps," Firren informed him, still focused on her drawing. "For now we'll just try to protect the lost ones who wander the tunnels, and we'll stem the flow of rodents into the camps. But once we've enlisted and trained enough soldiers, we're going to attack. We're going to fight! We're going to free all those poor imprisoned refugees."

Zucker turned a puzzled expression to Dodger.

"She's feisty," he replied with an indulgent grin.

"I prefer the word 'rebel,'" Firren corrected, bending to pick up a fresh stone from the rubble.

Now Dodger reached beneath one of the sitting stones and dragged out a parcel of bound papers. "This is kind of her inspiration."

"What is it?" asked Zucker, taking the pages.

"A sacred book. One of many. We find them scattered around down here. I believe they come to us from some greater power, some source of infinite knowledge and wisdom beyond these passageways. This one tells the story of a mighty human army called the Rangers. According to the words printed here, they're the conquering heroes honored with a silver treasure from someone called Stanley."

Zucker looked at the red-and-blue uniforms the soldiers wore. They did look intimidating. "But I still don't understand the problem with the camps. Why would you wanna destroy them?"

Admittedly he'd never taken much interest in his father's philanthropy, but as far as he knew, the refugee camps were exactly what they appeared to be. Temporary housing for unfortunate rodents who'd wound up lost in the tunnels and who would eventually be sent out to build new towns and villages in the name of the Romanus empire.

"You mean other than the fact that they are vicious and evil?" hissed Firren. "And a complete and utter abuse of your father's power?"

"What are you talking about?" Zucker shot back. "The camps aren't evil."

Dodger placed a calming paw on the prince's shoulder. "Clearly you've been kept in the dark about the reality of Titus's peace accord."

"Okay, so gimme the details. I'm listening."

Dodger's voice was gentle and patient. "Firren . . . ?"

It was a long moment before Firren began to speak. When she did, her voice was level, but her tone was a mixture of sadness and fury. She did not turn away from her work but continued to draw as she spoke.

"My mother and father and I were captured by Romanus scouts and held in the camps."

A sour taste filled Zucker's mouth at her use of the word "captured."

Firren kept her eyes firmly on her artwork. "When it was our turn to go off to the so-called colonies, we were so excited. Right up until the minute they let loose the hungry cats into the hunting ground, a place we thought to be our new home, a place we believed was safe and wonderful. But that was not so. The cats were particularly hungry that day, and my mother and father were gone in a matter of seconds." Her voice caught in her throat and she paused. "I hid—a broken cup lined in silver metal. I was so tiny back then, I think the ferals missed me entirely, or else the metal lining of the cup must have masked my scent. Whatever the reason, I stayed crouched until long after the slaughter was over. Then I rolled out of my cup, vomited in the dirt, and cried until I had no tears left to shed. In pitch-darkness I burrowed out of that horrible place. I was tiny and weak, but do you know where I found the strength? By remembering the screams, and the pleas for mercy, and the sound of teeth gnashing and bones snapping in two—"

"Stop it!" cried Zucker, the bile rising in his throat.

Now Firren stepped away from her artwork, turning to face him. Tears had welled up in her eyes, but her jaw was set. "That's exactly what I intend to do," she said in a quiet voice. "Stop it."

Zucker did not know what to believe. The story was so outrageous, but her tears seemed undeniably real. A hunting ground? Sacrificial rodents? It couldn't be true.

At last Firren moved away from her drawing, and the prince could see that she had sketched a face. It was a pleasant, proud face with wise eyes and a gentle aspect. Brown and furry with small oval ears and a bristle of whiskers.

It was a face filled with goodness and purpose. It was Dodger's face.

But something was missing.

Zucker stood and walked toward the portrait. Silently he bent and selected a chalky white rock from the pebbles on the ground.

With a steady hand he drew a perfect white circle around the right eye.

"Still listening," he said softly.

And so for the next hour Dodger and Firren explained everything to Zucker: Dodger was a member of the Mūs tribe—a proud and intelligent clan of mice who valued peace and fairness above all else. Dodger, though young, held a highly respected position in the tribe. He worked closely with their governing body, the Tribunal, and was gifted at interpreting the writings of La Rocha and the mysteries contained in the Sacred Book.

"Who is La Rocha?" Zucker asked.

"That's a story for another time," Dodger told him. "The point is, my kind is a strong breed. If Firren can assemble a company of Rangers to assist her, and I can convince the Mūs military to join with her, we will begin the process of bringing down the camps."

"And bringing down your father," Firren said pointedly. "Are you with us?"

Zucker was paralyzed by indecision. He waited for a sense of anger to overtake him. He waited for some feeling or instinct that would compel him to defend his father to these strangers. But no such feeling came. What this mouse and this pretty rat were telling him was simply unbelievable. He didn't think they were lying, but perhaps they misunderstood the purpose of the camps and the conditions of Titus's treaty. Titus had a responsibility to all who entered the gates of Atlantia. Atlantian citizens were safe. Titus cared about his subjects. Surely he would not—could not—do what these two were accusing him of.

Finally Zucker shook his head. "I'm sorry."

Firren opened her mouth to shout at him, but

Dodger raised his paw, silencing her. He seemed utterly unsurprised.

"This is a sign of character," he said. "I would have been disappointed if the prince had simply taken our word for this. These are serious crimes we are pinning on his father, and we have offered no real proof of them. He is right to be wary."

"But we speak the truth!" Firren insisted, stomping one paw in the dirt. "I know. I was there!"

"He will need to find out for himself," Dodger said, and smiled a genuine smile at Zucker. "I applaud your loyalty, Your Highness. And although I wish it were not the case, I believe that when you have investigated, you will find out that we tell you no falsehoods. It is a well-guarded secret, a matter of royal security, to be certain. But if you look for the signs, you will find the answers. Even if you don't want to accept them."

"Is there any way you could be mistaken?" Zucker prodded. "I mean, sure, my old man can be cold and arrogant and self-involved, but what you're describing is genocide. And my mother, the empress. She's gentle and kind. She would never allow this kind of stuff to go on in Atlantia. She'd have definitely done something about it." The words "if she knew" came unbidden to his mind, but he dared not speak them aloud. Instead he shook his head and reiterated, "You've got to be mistaken."

Firren's eyes flashed with loathing. "We are not mistaken."

"No." Dodger shook his head, confirming her words. "We are not."

A charged silence passed between the three of them.

At last Zucker sighed. "So I guess this is where we go our separate ways, then, huh?"

"For now," said Dodger with a slow nod. "For now."

Zucker turned to Firren, but before he could meet her eyes, she'd snapped her head away. This saddened him more than he cared to admit.

But there was nothing to be done about it.

He was the scion of the royal house, the only heir to Titus's throne. Without more compelling evidence he was duty-bound by blood and custom to remain loyal to his family, to defend his exalted emperor.

No matter how much it hurt him to do it.

"So long, Dodger. Firren."

Dodger sighed. "Farewell, Zuck-meister."

Without another word Prince Zucker turned away from his new friends and made his long, slow way back to Atlantia.

# Chapter Twenty-Two

**With a full heart, Hopper** led his fellow rodents up to platforms in search of viable weapons.

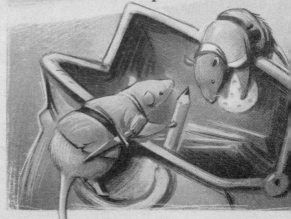

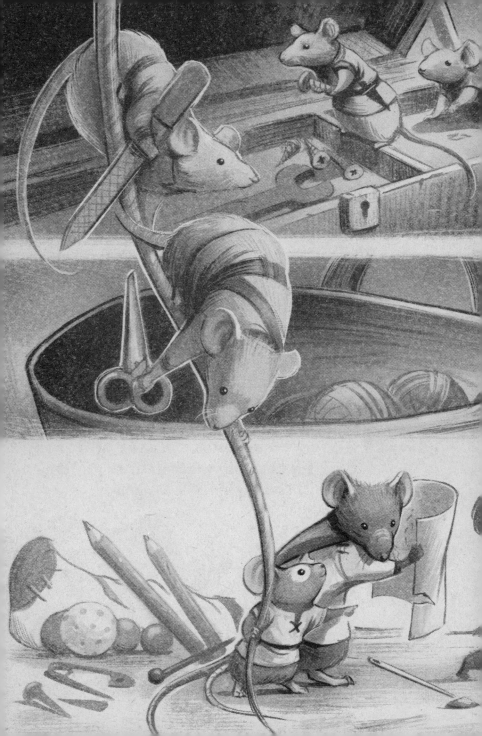

# CHAPTER TWENTY-THREE

IT WAS LATE THE next morning when Hopper and Zucker ventured out of the palace.

Marcy had unbound Zucker's chest and applied a salve to the wound, which, Hopper was happy to note, had stopped bleeding at last. Then she had bandaged him up again, muttering all the while about how he should really stay behind to rest.

Thanks to Marcy's handiwork, they were both disguised as servants, out for a simple stroll through the marketplace.

But there was a nervous energy in the city that made Hopper's fur stand on end. Many of the merchants had closed their stalls, and the few citizens who hurried along the streets seemed eager to get home, or at least indoors.

Word of the impending violence must have trickled out among the masses. It was apparent to Hopper that no one knew where or how this trouble would manifest, but still they were wary.

Afraid.

And worse, no one really knew why. The city was enjoying its usual comfort and prosperity, and below, the emperor's greatest charity project—his camp for homeless rodents—was a thriving entity where lost souls found solace and refuge.

Still, something was *not right*, and the pampered citizens of Atlantia sensed its approach like a storm in the air.

As Hopper and Zucker made their way to the refugee camp, Hopper snuck glances at Zucker to see how he was holding up. The prince's wound was still fresh. He really should have been back in the palace, under the care of a royal physician.

But of course, there was no time for such a luxury.

"So tell me about your little scavenger hunt," Zucker prompted as he and Hopper meandered through the gritty industrial district of the city. "Good haul?"

"Exceptional," said Hopper, pleased and proud. The soldiers had managed to retrieve a sizable arsenal of human items that, while not technically designed to function as weapons, could easily be of use against the camp guards and Titus's army. Zucker's soldiers, Firren's Rangers, and the soon-to-be-recruited refugees would have to use their imagination to turn these unfamiliar upland discards into viable weapons, but if they worked together, there was hope.

Always hope.

Hopper's only fears were that Firren would not realize in time that Zucker was working *with* her and not against her, and that she couldn't possibly be expecting the captive rodents to join in the fight. This could create a great deal of confusion when the rebels stormed the camp.

And there was the issue of the hunt. If Firren and her army didn't arrive before the sacrifice, many of the rodents would be lost to the ferals.

Hopper knew that at that very moment, Ketchum and the twins and several others from Zucker's personal army were stockpiling the found weapons at the portals he'd heard Firren describing to General DeKalb and the Tribunal. His and Zucker's job would be to rally the refugees and enlist their help in hiding the weapons inside the camp to be used against guards when the rebels finally arrived. Hopefully before the "colonists" were removed and transported to the hunting ground.

As they reached the mouth of the pipe that would carry them downward to the camp, Hopper expressed this concern to Zucker. "Firren's not going to be prepared for the refugees to fight. That could present a major complication."

"That's a good point, kid," said Zucker seriously. Then he bent a grin at Hopper. "Thought so myself when it came to me last night."

"Last night?"

Zucker nodded. "Which is why I snuck out of the palace and into the tunnels to warn her."

"You snuck out? Injured and alone?" Hopper was stunned. "When?"

"The minute you took off on your weapons mission."

Hopper sighed. He didn't even want to think about

what could have happened to his wounded pal out there in the passages. "Well, did you find her? Did you tell her our plan?"

"Nope. But I did leave her a message."

Now Zucker chuckled and gave Hopper a nudge into the pipe. "C'mon, kid. One thing at a time. We've got to focus on our part of this grand design before we can worry about Firren's role. For now let's just go find your brother and get this thing rolling."

Together they crept down the rusted pipe.

They avoided the main entry to camp.

Not surprisingly, extra guards had been posted. But the sentries were, at that very moment, being briefed by Titus's most favored general, Cassius, about the potential invasion; they had their backs to the pipe's opening.

"How's that for irony?" Zucker whispered.

The prince and the Chosen One kept to the shadows and made their way to one of the concealed entrances Hopper recalled Firren mentioning.

Zucker was impressed. "The girl's got the touch," he observed as they pushed through an all but undetectable cut section of the wire fence.

Once inside, they immediately went in search of Pup. Hopper's misguided alert had compelled the guards to confine all the refugees to their barracks. Hopper and Zucker made quick work of peeking in windows until Hopper spotted his tiny brother, curled up on a rickety old cot in one of the dormitories.

Zucker boosted Hopper up through the window, then climbed in himself.

The refugees stared in wonder but, thankfully, did not sound an alarm.

"No need to be afraid, folks," said Zucker calmly. "We bring news."

Hopper, his heart full near to bursting at the sight of his brother, had gone immediately to Pup, who blinked up at him.

"Hopper?" the tiny mouse asked in his wispy voice. "Is it really you?"

"It's really me," Hopper promised, wrapping him in a crushing hug.

"Hopper, you'll never believe what happened after I fell! I was—"

"You can tell me later, Pup. I'm here to save you."

"Save me? From what? It's lovely here."

He turned a quizzical look to Zucker, who was under the curious scrutiny of the entire barracks. None of the refugees recognized the Atlantian prince, of course. To them he appeared to be just another disenfranchised rodent, enjoying the kind and generous hospitality of the Romanus, eagerly awaiting the good fortune of possibly being chosen as a colonist.

In a steady voice Zucker explained to the wide-eyed

refugees the truth about Titus, the peace accord, and the true purpose of the camps. As he spoke, one old female mouse cried out in horror, wringing her paws on her apron; a young, powerful-looking squirrel snorted with disgust, as though he had suspected as much all along. But to Hopper's shock, the overall response was one of disbelief.

A male rat, who shared a cot with his mate and their young litter, stood up. "Why are you saying such frightening things?" he demanded. "Isn't it bad enough that we have to worry about those infernal rebels who threaten to attack? Now you tell us that Titus, too, is our enemy?"

"Titus is the *only* enemy," Zucker clarified. "The rebels are fighting to free you."

"Why would we want to be freed?" a female chipmunk asked. "This hunting ground is just an old wives' tale. It's a story told to keep unruly children in line when they misbehave. 'Be good or be hunted,' they say. And it works!"

"If Titus were planning to dispose of us," the father rat reasoned, "why would he feed us so well?"

"To make you more appetizing to the cats," Hopper cried. "Scrawny, starving rodents can be found all over the tunnels. Felina only keeps her end of the bargain with Titus because he provides fat, healthy rodents for her and her ferals to feast upon."

"We're telling you the truth," said Zucker. "If you

want to save yourselves, you have to listen and do what we tell you. Even as we speak, my soldiers are planting weapons all along the outer perimeter of the camp."

"Your soldiers?" asked the powerful-looking squirrel. "Who are you that you have soldiers?"

Zucker sighed. "That's a long story."

Suddenly the sound of a bell tolling shattered the uneasy silence outside the barracks.

"What's that?" Hopper asked Pup.

"It means they're going to be choosing a new batch of colonists!"

*Or an unscheduled hunt . . . with double the prey!* Hopper whipped his head around to meet Zucker's gaze.

Clearly the prince was thinking the same thing.

One of the refugees ran to the window. "They're coming this way!" he cried gleefully. "They're entering the barracks right next door."

A cheer rose up, although the old mouse and young squirrel looked worried.

Hopper had to make them understand. Mind reeling, he turned his desperate eyes to Zucker.

"We have to stop the hunt," the prince said gravely. "We can't wait for Firren and the Rangers and the Mūs army—who knows how far off they are? I have to bring in my soldiers *now*."

Before Hopper could protest, Zucker leaped over a

cot, sprung through the window, and hit the ground running. Hopper flew to the open window and leaned out as far as he dared, watching as Zucker reached the fence and frantically searched for the hidden exit Firren had made. His paw connected with the opening, and Hopper's heart soared—until he noticed a hulking presence looming behind the prince.

General Cassius! Hopper recognized him even at this distance; his booming words echoed across the camp.

"Going somewhere?"

Slowly Zucker turned away from the fence and came face-to-face with his father's most revered officer.

Hopper felt a chill as he saw the expression of hatred that darkened Zucker's face. Of all Titus's advisors, Hopper knew, Zucker despised Cassius the most.

"I've long suspected that you never truly abandoned your youthful ideals," the general hissed. "I will take great pleasure in telling my liege that I have been right about you all along." He eyed Zucker with a sneer. "Much as I once took similar pleasure in doing away with that mangy Mūs friend of yours." The general's paw went to the hilt of his heavy sword as he added in a deep, rasping voice, "You remember, do you not, my young lord?"

"Oh, I remember. I remember it every day."

"Good. Because it would be a shame if I should have to do the same to you."

The panic rose in Hopper's throat as he watched Zucker's eyes harden. He imagined a million different thoughts churning in Zucker's mind.

But Hopper knew the only one that made sense would be the one Zucker hated most.

Eyes flashing, teeth grinding, the royal heir to the Romanus throne let out a long rush of breath. Then he raised both his arms above his head and lowered himself to his knees in the dirt.

"I surrender," he said.

# Chapter Twenty-Four

At that very moment the barracks door burst open.

"No!" cried Hopper, shielding Pup with his body. Two heavily armed rat guards stood smiling in a menacing manner. One had a series of daggers tucked into his belt; the other had a broad sword at his hip and a club propped casually upon his shoulder.

"Congratulations, rodents," said the one with the daggers. "You have all been selected to go forth and establish a new colony in the name of Emperor Titus of the Romanus, and for the greater glory of Atlantia!"

A cheer went up that rattled the barracks windows. Hopper looked from the smiling guards to Pup's joyful face to the celebrating rodents.

The hunt was happening. Now. And they were the ones who were about to be the hunted.

As the guards marched the newly elected "colonists" through the quiet camp, Hopper made sure to lag toward the back of the line. He held fast to Pup and kept his head low so as not to call attention to his unmistakable white marking. Several other lines of rodents trudged ahead of them. More were being led out of their barracks to join the march.

*"Psst."*

Hopper glanced up to see the strong young squirrel marching beside him.

"The name's Driggs," said the squirrel. "And I want you to know I believe what you and your friend were saying back there. So does the old lady, you know, the mouse." He shook his head sadly. "Seemed to me right from the start this whole camp and colony thing was too good to be true."

Hopper felt the relief wash over him. "Do you think you can convince any of the others?"

"Sure," said Driggs. "I've got friends in some of the other barracks. A couple of tough rats and a bunch of wiry mice. They'd be great in a fight. I can spread the word about the rebels and those hidden weapons, but only if I can get out of this line without the guards noticing."

By now the old lady mouse had slowed her pace and was lagging along beside them. "I can help there," she said.

"How?" asked Hopper.

In a sweet but determined voice the old lady whispered her plan.

Hopper nodded.

"Okay," he decided. "Let's try it."

They continued their march toward the main entrance. When they were a few yards from the front gate, Hopper gave the old mouse a silent signal.

On cue she tripped, let out a squeal, and went sprawling into the dirt.

"Ohhhh!" she wailed. "Oh no. My hind paw! I think I've hurt it!"

As her barracks-mates gathered around, fussing and fretting and trying to help, Hopper pointed to Driggs; the squirrel ducked low and scampered out of line just as the guards appeared from the front of the line to see what the commotion was about.

"Someone's been hurt!" cried Pup.

The guards did not look as though they welcomed such a complication. One of them stooped to examine the old mouse's paw while his partner urged the others to stand back and give her breathing room.

"What if I can't march anymore?" the old mouse cried.

The guard touched her ankle, which, of course, was perfectly fine. When she howled out in pain, Hopper bit back a smile.

"Sorry, ma'am," said the guard. "Maybe next time."

"Oh, please," she implored, reaching out and encircling his waist with her arms. "Can't you carry me?"

"Against regulations," the guard sputtered, trying to shake out of her grip. But she held fast, clinging to him with all her might. Finally his fellow guard had to step in and give the old mouse a firm tug. She came away from the first guard and collapsed into a sobbing heap.

"Leave her here," said the second guard. "We're going to be late, and Titus will not be pleased. One of the other guards will have to bring her back to her barracks."

His partner nodded his agreement. "Let's move it!" he cried to the refugees, waving them back into line. "Hut, two, three, four . . ."

As the guards scampered back to the front of the line, Hopper watched with a frown; something was different. Something was *missing* . . .

Missing from the first guard's belt!

And now the old mouse was smiling up at him. She reached into her apron pocket and offered him the dagger she'd just swiped.

"Nicely done," Hopper whispered, quickly slipping the blade into his coat.

"Good luck," she whispered back. "We're counting on you."

Hopper leaned down and looked her right in the eye. "I won't let you down," he promised.

Then he took Pup's paw and followed the others.

To the hunting ground.

# Chapter Twenty-Five

THE ARENA WAS MOSTLY a barren wasteland, dotted with a few random human objects—an old shoe; an empty box; a strange silver-lined cup or mug of some sort.

*Hiding places,* thought Hopper. *To give the hungry cats at least some sense of the thrill of the chase.*

The odds were stacked severely. The cats would win, always.

The colonists, who were at last beginning to see that the accusations Zucker had made back in the barracks were all true, stood in a trembling knot in the center of the arena.

The sickening scent of fear assaulted Hopper.

Including his own.

But he did not freeze. He did not hesitate or deliberate. He grabbed Pup's tiny paw and ran, practically dragging his small brother along in the dirt behind him. He ran for the silver-lined cup, which lay on its side like a manmade metal and plastic cave.

"Get in!" he cried, lifting Pup and tossing him inside. "Now stay here and be still!" Dread filled Hopper as he realized that those were the very same words he'd said to Pinkie when he'd forced her to hide behind the gravel mound when Zucker's soldiers ambushed Firren and the Mūs contingent.

And he hadn't laid eyes on Pinkie since.

"Hopper, I'm scared!" cried Pup, his eyes shining with tears, his whiskers quivering.

"I know, Pup, but you have to be brave. I won't let them hurt you, I promise."

Even as Pup reached out and gave his paw a trusting squeeze, Hopper hoped he could fulfill that promise. The knot of doubt strangling his throat only amplified his own fear.

When the other refugees—including the ones from other barracks who hadn't heard Zucker's explanation—saw what Hopper had done, they, too, began to seek shelter for themselves. The father rat carried all four of his babies over to the metal-lined cup, and Hopper helped him lift them into it to cuddle up against Pup. The tiny mice trembled in terror, and as Hopper watched, unable to help, his veneer of courage began to crack.

"What's going to happen?" asked a chipmunk, his protruding teeth beginning to chatter. "What's going on!"

All eyes fell on Hopper. He was going to have to tell them the truth. The cats would arrive soon, and there simply weren't enough places for everyone to hide.

"We are being sacrificed," he announced dully. "Titus purchases peace from the queen with our lives."

A murmur of disbelief rippled through the arena, and that soon turned to anger and fear.

"Is there any way out?" asked the father rat.

"Can we fight?" asked his mate.

"We can fight," said Hopper, drawing the dagger from his coat. "All of you, look around . . . see if you can find anything you might use to defend yourself. Anything that might serve as a weapon."

The rodents did as they were told, scurrying about in a frenzy, plucking up stones and sticks to use in battle.

And then . . . a bell rang.

Tolling, echoing . . . a death knell.

"The cats," Hopper whispered, raising the blade.

From a shadowy corner of the arena a door slid open.

A hot gust of feline scent polluted the air, mingling with the rodents' own terror. There were so many of them! Hopper hadn't imagined there would be such numbers. And each of them knew, judging by their smug expressions, that victory was already theirs. The slaughter was guaranteed. The rodents in the arena were no match for these beasts.

Every small creature there was about to die. Including Hopper.

He recognized one as the gray female he and Zucker had ridden the day they first visited the camps.

His glittering black eyes met her upturned glowing ones—he'd petted her, thanked her for the ride, and she'd nuzzled against him—but that was then and this was a different time, a different place, a different purpose. Her teeth glistened, her eyes shone, and Hopper saw no flicker of familiarity or compassion in those yellow-green slits.

The gray cat reached out with one huge paw and swung it at him.

Hopper went toppling sideways, head over haunches. His vision blurred, his mind fogged.

In an instant the area filled with the spitting and hissing of the ferals and the squeals of fighting rodents.

The noise of the assault was a brutal cacophony of screaming, wailing, sputtering.

Hopper tried to get to his feet, but the universe was spinning. He could not get his bearings. Where was the silver-lined cup?

"Pup!" he called, but he was not sure if the word took the form of sound.

He blinked to clear the haze that veiled his eyes, but his head was heavy and his limbs were like lead.

The arena went in and out of focus: *tails and ears and teeth and claws . . .*

And then—was he dreaming?—a snatch of gold! A flash of motion robed in sparkling golden cloth. Pinkie!

A tiny explosion of white—a crisp tunic with red-and-blue stripes!

And he heard it—the horn fashioned of bone,

blaring boldly, proudly announcing that the ally had arrived!

"*Aye, aye, aye! Aye, aye, aye!*" It was a war cry, but it was the most beautiful sound Hopper had ever heard. Rangers began dropping into the hunting ground from above. Hopper looked up and saw dozens of tiny holes had been dug in the upper walls and ceiling. He gaped at the strange and beautiful sight—it seemed to be raining Ranger rats.

"Hopper! Hopper, can you hear me?" The familiar voice echoed across the cavernous space like thunder.

"Firren! You're here!" Hopper cried as she appeared in front of him and helped him to his feet.

"Are you hurt?" she asked.

He shook his head.

"Can you fight?"

"I can fight!" In the distance he saw Pinkie barreling toward a fat calico who was about to gobble a young rat. Filled with a sense of heartaching pride, he watched as she raised her sword and plunged it into the villain's furry shoulder.

The cat howled and dropped the rat, who bit the calico's paw.

Hopper smiled. *Atta girl, Pinkie!* he thought.

"Listen to me," said Firren, picking up Hopper's dagger from the dust. "The Rangers and Pinkie and I are taking over here. The Mūs army is on its way to the camps. Some of my Rangers went ahead and got word of our impending rescue to the refugees. Wasn't easy, since Titus seems to have tripled his security."

Hot guilt nearly paralyzed Hopper. "That's my fault—" he began, but Firren interrupted with a stern look.

"Doesn't matter now, Hopper. The important thing is that the refugees are armed and waiting, ready to fight!"

"You got Zucker's message, then?"

"Yes. He left a warning in the runes that Titus was expecting us."

Hopper smiled at his friend's cunning. "And you know he was never a traitor?"

Firren nodded. Then she looked around. "Where is he?"

"General Cassius has him in the camp."

Firren scowled. "We will see to his safety once we have earned a victory here." She held out the dagger for Hopper to take. "There is nothing we can do to help Zucker right now."

Hopper knew she was right. And besides, this is how Zucker would want it to be done. He would want them to save these innocents first and aid him later.

With a heavy heart he nodded.

"Good," said Firren. "Now we fight."

Together they entered the fray.

# CHAPTER TWENTY-SIX

THEY WERE ALL DEAD.

All but one.

The hunting ground was littered with the hulking bodies of the ferals. Sadly, two of the refugees had been lost to the violent appetites of the quicker cats, and more than a few were injured.

Hopper, rattled and scraped up but unhurt, had lost track of Pinkie in the dust and devastation of the skirmish. But he spotted her now in her elegant golden cape.

She lay still and silent beside the old shoe.

From across the arena he rasped her name ... *Pinkie* ... but she did not flinch. He would run to her if not for the fact that the battle was not quite over.

Only one slinking, hideous beast of a cat remained on his feet, circling the refugees.

Cyclops.

His orange fur was clotted with blood where he'd been stabbed by Firren's rebels, or scratched, bitten, and stoned by the rodents he had stalked.

Stalked and *caught*, Hopper noted; a tuft of sand-colored chipmunk fur still clung to the cat's mouth.

It was clear that Cyclops had been driven mad by fury and pain, and clearer still that he held Hopper and the Rangers all captive; they were hostages in the hunting ground littered with the bodies of his brethren.

They could not move past him; they could not approach him. He was wild, roaring, spitting, flashing fangs and claws.

Cyclops shrieked, an ear-splitting *meeeeoooooowwww* that seemed to cause the walls to shudder. He raced faster now, circling the group and forcing the Rangers to scatter away from his thundering paws to avoid being trampled.

Hopper and Firren stood in front of the recoiling refugees, struggling to determine their next action.

When at last Clops ceased his crazed spinning, he stumbled, then staggered toward the silver-lined cup. His tail slammed into it and the cup bucked upward, then rolled, spilling its precious contents of Pup and the baby rats into the dirt.

Clops stood above the small creatures, wheezing as a slimy dribble of drool spilled from his mouth.

The mother rat cried out. The father ran to throw his body over those of the innocents, Pup included, but the hissing Cyclops had steadied himself and slapped him away with a bloodied paw.

The rat flew across the arena and landed with a dull thud. His babies wailed in terror.

Hopper told himself to run. Pup was exposed. Unprotected.

He took a step, but one of the refugees grabbed his arm and held him back.

Because a golden blur was sprinting now, away from the shoe, across the arena. The hood had flown back, and Pinkie's face with the unmistakable white circle of fur around the eye was plainly visible.

She ran screaming with her sword grasped in both paws, high above her head.

Cyclops's bloody paws went to his missing eye, and he cried out, "Nooooo!"

But Pinkie sprung up from the dirt floor and soared, her sword poised and ready as she rocketed through the air toward the cat's broad chest. The blade pierced the matted fur and the flesh beneath it, plunging deeply into Cyclops's heart.

Pinkie released her grasp and fell to the ground but landed firmly on her feet. Above her head her sword remained stuck in the cat's breast.

Cyclops blinked his only eye, only once. He let out a gurgling whimper that ended in a growl.

And he fell over dead.

The sound of his huge body slamming into the dirt echoed through the hunting ground.

For a long moment no one moved. No one breathed. And then Firren stepped forward and raised her sword in the air.

"Victory!" she cried. The rodents whooped and cheered and cried out for joy. Some fell to their knees and sent up prayers of gratitude to La Rocha.

Some merely collapsed from relief.

But Hopper ran. He broke free from the reveling

pack and ran to where Pup still sat, staring up toward where the cat's face had been. He was quaking with fear but, other than that, could not seem to move. He was in shock.

"Pup . . . ," Hopper cried, embracing his brother. "Are you all right?"

"Of course he's all right, you useless fool," Pinkie snarled.

Hopper looked at Pinkie, nearly ready to retort, when he caught sight of Firren, lingering near the upturned silver-lined cup—the hiding spot that had saved her life so long ago.

He wanted to go to her, offer her some comfort, but before he could do that, there was a clattering commotion as the surviving refugees began to charge the wooden door that led out of the arena; a second later it was pried open and they prepared to scatter.

"Wait!" cried Hopper. "Where are you going?"

"We're escaping," said the young father. "We're going to leave this place and take our chances in the tunnels."

"And what of the others?" Hopper demanded. "Your fellow refugees who are still being held at the mercy of Titus and Felina? Will you simply leave them there in the camps to rot? Or to be sacrificed later on?" He raised his arms in a gesture of invitation. "Fight with us! Make a stand. The tunnels will provide. Broken glass, heavy stones . . . anything you can carry can be a weapon. We have a chance to defeat this evil regime, and that chance only increases with each one of you who chooses to join us."

The rodents exchanged doubtful glances; a murmur went through the group as they debated in whispers. Hopper knew what they were doing; they were weighing their options, testing their mettle.

His mind swirled with thoughts of Zucker, who was still being held at the evil hand of General Cassius. It was bad enough that the royal army knew the rebels were planning to attack the camp, but if Titus's guards had somehow gotten word of the siege at the hunting ground, who could say what action they might take? Hopper wanted nothing more than to help his friend and to free the other refugees. He would go to their rescue alone if he had to.

He only wished he wouldn't have to.

At last the powerful-looking squirrel who had challenged Zucker's authority back in the barracks stepped forward. "You're right. We can't just run. It is our duty to fight, and so we will." He inclined his head to Hopper in deference. "If you will lead us, we will follow."

Hopper nodded. "Excellent," he said, and marched toward the door.

Firren joined him, trailed by the Rangers. Pinkie

followed, cradling Pup in her arms. When the refugees gathered behind, it was quite a tired and ragtag little army they formed.

But it was an army. And that was the important thing.

"We march!" cried Hopper.

Determined, they set out for the camps.

The group halted a short distance from the fence that encircled the camp; the quiet of the grounds, unnerving. Inside, Hopper could see that because he'd so stupidly warned Titus of the rebel raid, the number of active guards had been doubled, their ranks reinforced with members of the royal army.

Outside the fence, however, a steadfast legion of Mūs soldiers had assembled; silent and stealthy as smoke, they waited patiently in the shadows.

Pinkie handed Pup to a chipmunk. "I'll prep them," she muttered, and stalked off.

"Do you think they've heard about the hunt?" Hopper whispered to Firren.

"Doesn't look like it," Firren said. "But it won't be long before they do."

Hopper turned to see Captain Garfield and Pritchard approaching. Hope burst in Hopper's chest. Maybe the prince had escaped Cassius and sent for them. "Did Zucker summon you?" he asked.

Pritchard shook his head. "That's the problem. We received this peculiar missive, saying that Prince Zucker was being held captive."

Hopper quickly explained what had transpired before he and the other refugees were marched off to the hunting ground. "I don't know where Cassius took him," he ended, his voice a desperate squeak.

"That's just the point," said Garfield. "We do."

The captain held out a scrap of paper to Hopper. Hopper thought he recognized the scrawling, but at the moment he just couldn't recall where he had seen it before. He read the message:

*ZUCKER IS BEING HELD IN THE*
*SOUTHERNMOST BARRACKS.*
*TITUS HAS YET TO BE ALERTED.*

Hopper's eyes snapped up from the missive. "Who brought this to you?"

Pritchard shrugged. "Just a small beggar mouse. He wore a hood and kept his face averted, speaking not at all. Simply handed us this note and scurried off."

"So what are we waiting for?" Firren was already heading south along the fence. "Let's free the prince and get this party started. I'll just slip in through one of our easements and—"

"No," said Hopper, pointing to her bloody tunic with the distinctive red markings. "They'll spot you a mile away." He indicated his own attire—the peasant's clothing he'd put on that morning, back at the palace. "I look like just another refugee. I'll be the one to go in first."

Firren hesitated only a moment, then nodded.

"I'll set Zucker free, and then Firren, you lead the Rangers, the Mūs soldiers, and Zucker's troops in a full-scale assault. But I'll need a signal to let you know when it's time to begin the attack."

Smiling, Firren removed the hollow chunk of bone from where it hung around her neck and handed it to him. Hopper was touched at such a show of trust. And respect.

Reverently, bravely, he took the horn. Then, without another word, he slid into one of the Rangers' secret entrances and headed for the south barracks.

# CHAPTER TWENTY-SEVEN

HOPPER'S BLOOD THRUMMED THROUGH his veins as he crept across the camp, eluding more guards than he cared to count.

As he approached the barracks where Zucker was imprisoned, Hopper saw two sentinels. In an instant he flung himself under a cart loaded with chunks of ripe fruit. He held his breath and listened as they advanced toward the cart, complaining about the rebel insurgence and helping themselves to the fruit.

The seconds ticked by, and still they gorged themselves. He would have to distract them if he was going to get inside that dormitory.

But how?

It came to him suddenly and vividly. He would do what Zucker did that very first day when they'd had to hide from Firren in the tunnel. Strange how Hopper had once feared the graceful warrior with whom he was now fighting right alongside.

Quietly he plucked a pebble from the dirt and tossed it in the opposite direction of the dormitory door, just as Zucker had done. The stone landed with a dull *thunk* several yards away.

"Did you hear that?" one of them asked.

"Better go check on it."

The sentinels hurried off, and Hopper darted from

his hiding place for the barracks. He leaped in through a half-open window.

Zucker was seated on the splintery floor, bound and gagged and propped against the wall. He looked up when Hopper scampered in through the window, and his eyes seemed to sparkle with relief.

It took only moments for Hopper to chew through the ropes that secured Zucker's paws. Then he tore off the gag.

"Hey there, kid," said Zucker, leaping to his feet. "Glad you could make it."

"Well, you know me," Hopper replied, beaming. "I just hate to miss a good rebel attack."

"Ready to cause a little trouble, kid?"

"I was born ready, Zuck-meister."

Together they burst out the barracks door and strode to the middle of the camp. Hopper raised the signal horn and blew, the sound ripping through the charged stillness of the camp. Hopper's declaration of war.

The Mūs army led by General DeKalb poured into the hidden portals, chanting. A hundred voices became one voice, echoing through the camp.

Zucker's troops arrived bringing the might of their military training, while Firren and her Rangers dominated the enemy with grace, speed, and ruthlessness. The refugees who could fight did; the human trinkets and gadgets made a fine arsenal against Titus's soldiers. Several of the camp's buildings had been set aflame, throwing off heat, sparks, and smoke.

Hopper sprung along at Zucker's heels, fighting as proudly and as skillfully as the prince's soldiers. Zucker moved like lightning, confidently and with great purpose, his fight an act of penance for Titus's sinister treaty.

Suddenly the prince froze in his tracks, his eyes focusing on the guardhouse by the main gate. His whiskers began to twitch. He sniffed the air.

"What is it?" Hopper shouted above the din of clanging metal and howling voices. "What scent are you catching?"

Zucker's eyes blazed. "Fear," he snarled. "I smell fear."

Zucker took off quickly, and Hopper shadowed his every move, avoiding the burning barracks and flames that lit the darkness until at last they reached the guardhouse. Zucker flung open the door, nearly ripping it right off its hinges.

Hopper gasped. Inside, General Cassius cowered on the floor in the relative safety of the wooden shelter while war waged outside.

Hopper's fur stood on end as a guttural growl emerged from Zucker.

"Spare me, good prince!" the general begged, covering his face with his paws. "Please. Let me go."

Muscles tensed, teeth bared, Zucker loomed above his enemy. The sword in his grasp shone like a promise. Hopper could only guess what the prince was thinking—if he plunged that sword into Cassius's breast, he would be more than justified.

He would be right.

Zucker raised the sword above his head. "For my friend," he whispered.

Hopper held his breath, gaping. But the prince did not strike. Not yet. Above his head he swung the sword in tiny circles, the blade catching the glow of the fire, throwing off shadows.

"Please!" Cassius cried. "Spare me!"

"Spare you? From what? Justice?"

Cassius whimpered. "From all of it. The blade. The fire." He flicked his panicked eyes to the flames licking closer and closer to the outer walls of the guardhouse. "Oh, it's like hell out there. Surely this is hell."

"Well." Zucker snorted, sword still poised aloft. "Then I guess you're exactly where you belong."

Hopper eyed the snapping tongues of the

encroaching flames. He could feel the heat as the blaze leaped and danced, drawing nearer. He, like Cassius, understood that one swipe of Zucker's sword, one thrust with the steely weight of it, would end the general for good.

"It is my right to avenge him," Zucker said, his voice trembling.

"Who, Zucker?" Hopper squeaked. "Avenge *who*?"

"Your father!"

Hopper stumbled backward, the words hitting him like a feral's swipe. Cassius had killed Dodger.

When the prince spoke again, Hopper wasn't sure if he was speaking to him or to the quivering general on the guardhouse floor. Perhaps he was talking to himself. Or maybe, just maybe, he was speaking to the past, to someone he used to know.

"I can end it all right now. With one fell swoop I can quell the pain I've been carrying. I can repay hatred with hatred."

*Hatred?*

Hopper jumped; the word—*hatred*—had seemed to come out of the smoke, out of the blue-hot core of the fire itself. Had it been an actual voice or just the roar of the fire? Was it a whisper from deep within a dream? Or was it real?

Hopper couldn't say, but he knew with absolute certainty that he had heard it.

And Zucker had heard it too. He lowered his sword

ever so slightly and pricked up his ears, listening in disbelief to see if the voice would come again.

And it did. Low and steady, words rippling through smoke. Close and far away at once. A voice, but whose?

*It was never supposed to be about hatred.*

Hopper's eyes darted this way and that, but through the billowing blackness it was impossible to see anything beyond Zucker in the guardhouse doorway and Cassius huddled on the floor.

*It was never supposed to be about hatred.* The words repeated, igniting in Hopper's ears, then melting into the fire.

"Hatred," Zucker repeated, his shoulders sagging with shame. "Dodger had no use for that emotion. And neither do I."

Hopper watched as the prince slowly lowered his sword and stepped out of the doorway.

The general was still curled in a trembling ball on the floor. When Zucker addressed him, his voice was little more than a rumble from his throat. "I'd tell you to run, Cassius, but I'm pretty sure you don't have the guts."

The prince turned his back on the coward, just as the first flames began to nip at the old, dry wood of the guardhouse.

# Chapter Twenty-Eight

It was over.

Titus's guards had fled. The rebels had triumphed.

Zucker directed his troops to see to the wounded and put out the fires. Hopper scanned the area for Firren; he spotted her leaning against the fence on the north side of the camp.

Zucker saw her too.

Hopper couldn't believe how suddenly shy Firren looked, glancing in their direction and quickly averting her eyes.

"Look who it is," he whispered to Zucker.

"Think she saw me?" The prince's voice wavered as his paw smoothed the fur between his ears.

"Doesn't matter if she *saw* you." Hopper grinned. "She can *smell* you, remember?"

"Yeah, kid." Zucker smiled. "I remember."

Now Firren took a deep breath, squared her dainty shoulders, and came to join them in the middle of the camp.

"Prince."

"Rebel."

"We meet again."

"We sure do."

Hopper looked from one to the other and decided they needed a moment to talk in private. With a little nod he excused himself and made his way to the camp's main mess hall, where all the refugees, including the ones from the hunt, had assembled.

Pinkie had collected Pup from the chipmunk and was attempting to soothe him. Hopper approached his siblings and declared without preamble, "I'll take Pup back to the palace with me."

"What palace?" Pinkie asked. "That Atlantian monstrosity? Pup goes there over my dead body. He's coming with me, to live among the Mūs. After all, that's what we are. Mūs. Half, anyway."

"No," said Hopper. "We should stay with Zucker. We have so much to do now that we've exposed Titus's lies. Pup will love living in Atlantia."

"You go play royal sidekick," said Pinkie, stroking Pup's still-quivering whiskers. "But I'm going down under to lead our tribe. And I'm taking Pup with me."

By now several members of the Mūs army had made their way over to Pinkie. They were an intimidating bunch—small but powerful and, evidently, unwaveringly loyal to Pinkie. They lined up before her, awaiting her orders.

"We go now," she boomed, throwing her head back proudly. "To proclaim to our village this glorious victory over Titus. Sage and Temperance and Christoph will have much to plan, and I intend to guide them in it."

"As you say, Chosen One," said the highest ranking of the Mūs soldiers. "We serve at your pleasure."

At the soldier's use of the title "Chosen One," Pinkie shot Hopper a wicked grin. *Take that!*

"Please, Pinkie," said Hopper, regretting the desperate catch in his voice. "Let Pup stay with me. You will see him again, I promise. Just, please, let me be his guardian."

Pinkie curled her lip. "Why don't we let Pup decide?" she suggested. "Pup, little one, would you rather go back to Atlantia—where they feed innocent rodents to vicious feral cats—or come live among your family in the Mūs village with me?"

Hopper dropped his head. With that kind of pitch he knew exactly who his brother would choose. He would go with the sibling who had once called him "runt" and "weakling." He would go with the one who was wrapped in a robe of gold.

And all because Titus had made an unforgivable pact.

"I want to go with Pinkie," Pup whispered. "I don't like it here, Hopper. Please understand."

Hopper nodded, but he could not raise his eyes to meet his brother's face, or worse, the smug look he knew would be plastered across Pinkie's.

"Take care of him, Pinkie," Hopper said. He kept his gaze on the ground, but his words were firm. Not a favor, a command.

"Of course," said Pinkie.

Then the Mūs officer clicked his heels and barked, "Hut, hut . . . march!"

With Pup in her arms Pinkie led her soldiers out of the camp and into the tunnels.

And out of Hopper's life.

He felt the emptiness like a hole in his heart. All hope left him. He'd lost what he loved the most—again! How many times could one's joy be taken, stolen, destroyed?

Hopper crumbled to his knees in the bloody dirt and wept.

*Abandoned. Alone.*

*Again.*

Again!

He had fought for everything, and he had won nothing.

But Pinkie . . . Pinkie had triumphed over all of it.

Hopper had no idea how long he crouched there, crying.

Forever would have been fine with him. But that was not to be.

Because someone was lifting him gently . . . picking him up from the dusty, tear-splattered earth where he knelt.

"Let's go, kid."

"Zucker?"

The prince nodded. "We have to get out of here," he said firmly. "Now."

"Why? It's over."

"It's not over, not yet. The Rangers bring word from Atlantia. There's unfinished business to see to there in the city, and I can't do it without the Chosen One."

Carefully Zucker settled Hopper over his shoulder. It made Hopper think of the soldiers carrying the wounded prince back from the rescue mission.

"Where's Firren?"

"She went ahead to start the fight." Zucker chuckled. "Typical, right?"

Hopper answered with a long, sad sigh.

As they wound upward through the tunnels back toward Atlantia, Hopper was aware of a great many rodents hurrying past in all directions.

"What's happening?" Hopper asked. He was happy to feel a mild twinge of curiosity; it was a small start toward dispelling his heartache.

"It's an exodus, kid. And they're not just fleeing the camp," Zucker explained. "They're fleeing Atlantia, too."

"Really?" Hopper wriggled down from the prince's shoulder and fell into a brisk step beside him. "Why?"

"It's an uproar. Felina is enraged, which pretty much puts an end to the so-called peace accord. The Atlantian citizens know they aren't guaranteed safety anymore, so they're no longer willing to stay. It's out of control. There's looting in the marketplace, and some of the angrier ones are attempting to storm the palace."

The palace! Hopper gasped as the question only just occurred to him. "What's going to happen to Titus?"

Zucker grinned. "He's been secured."

Atlantia was visible now. The gate once so poorly minded by Cyclops swung wide. Zucker took Hopper's hand as they shouldered in against the flood of rats and mice who crowded out of the city, carrying bundles and bags and boxes stuffed full of their possessions. As they made their way through the city, Hopper was sickened to see broken windows, broken-down doors, and smoldering remains of small fires.

Zucker explained that Titus's army had tried to lay siege to their own city and hold the citizens of Atlantia hostage. It was unclear whether Titus himself had called for or even approved such violent actions, but however it had come to happen, the result was that the rodents of Atlantia had risen up and rebelled. Ultimately Titus's army had beaten a quick retreat.

As they tramped through the once-pleasant neighborhoods, Zucker and Hopper dodged the flow of rodents who had but one collective goal—to leave Atlantia behind them before Titus could rally and find a way to sacrifice *them* to Felina in an attempt to win back his own freedom. Their running feet and shouts and cries of fear and anguish created a din that echoed out of the city and into the dark tunnels toward which they raced.

But there was something else, some other sound reaching Hopper's ears now. He pricked them up and listened.

Music?

Singing!

No . . .

Chirping!

As they rounded the bend that put them in view of the palace, Hopper stopped stock-still and stared. The once-exquisite palace seemed to be engulfed in some dark, writhing shadow. A cloak of movement and sound.

A swarm!

Zucker smiled. "Crickets, kid. I told you they could do some damage if their numbers were large enough."

Hopper could only gape at the scene before him. The entire royal structure was covered, thick with who knew how many thousands of insects—bugs! Every door, every window, every possible escape route was sealed tight beneath a winged veil of chirping crickets. If Titus and his advisors were imprisoned inside, they surely would not be coming out anytime soon.

"Where did they come from?" Hopper breathed. "How did they know?"

"Firren enlisted them," Zucker explained. "She

remembered what you told her about their ability to swarm. So I suppose you're partially to thank for this."

A horrible thought struck Hopper. "Marcy!" he cried.

"She's fine," Zucker assured him. "In fact, she came with my soldiers to fight in the camps. She's a tough little rat, I'll tell you."

Hopper relaxed, listening to the surprisingly happy song of the crickets. From a long way off, the smell of fading smoke from the fire in the camp singed the air, but that, too, brought Hopper a sense of joy and relief. The camps were liberated, the guards defeated.

Titus had been overthrown.

Hopper thought of the night he and the emperor had stood together high above Atlantia, and Titus had called him the Promised One and ruffled the fur between his ears. It had been plain that the emperor was not a rat used to showing affection, but there on that ledge overlooking the city, Hopper had sensed a clumsy gentleness that made him wonder if perhaps there'd been a time when Titus had been different. His words had been kind, his tone genuine, almost longing. It was as though the very emperor who'd been the architect of the evil—in that moment, at least—truly wished it could be different.

Hopper looked up at Zucker with wonder in his eyes, and as always, the prince seemed able to read his thoughts.

"We set it all to rights, kid. We made the tunnels safe—for real this time—and when we can, we will rebuild the city."

Hopper could feel the magnitude of the task settle over him. It was exhausting even to think about. But he knew that it would be done.

And he would be a part of it. He had to be.

Now someone was clearing his throat behind them. Hopper and Zucker turned to see a chubby Mūs soldier.

"I am to deliver this to you and await your prompt reply." The military mouse handed Hopper a scrap of paper that he recognized immediately. It was from the yellowed sheaf that made up part of the Sacred Book he'd seen in the locomotive in the Mūs village.

*Chosen One,*
*There is still so much to be done. Have faith and*
*be strong, for I shall come for you.*

And it was signed:

*La Rocha*

Hopper read the note, folded it, and slipped it into the pocket of his tunic.

"You may tell him that I will eagerly await his arrival."

The soldier saluted, then bowed.

As Hopper watched the soldier take his leave, it occurred to him that the missive that had been delivered to Garfield by the beggar mouse had been written on that very same sort of paper. He'd been too distracted by the imminent battle to make the connection then, but now he couldn't believe he'd missed it. Did the beggar mouse serve La Rocha in some way? Was he working on the mystic's behalf as some sort of Mūs spy? Or was it more likely that there were scraps of that brittle yellow paper fluttering all throughout the tunnels with the rest of the garbage?

Probably. And besides, Hopper just didn't have the energy to contemplate such a coincidence right now. He was simply too exhausted.

"What was that all about?" Zucker asked, motioning after the departing soldier.

"It was about the future," Hopper replied with a yawn. "It was about fulfilling the prophecy and making things right."

"Oh, is that all?" Grinning, Zucker reached out to ruffle the fur between Hopper's ears, then stopped himself, opting instead to offer his paw to shake. "Well, you let me know if I can help you out with that . . . Hopper."

Hopper smiled sleepily as he shook paws with the prince. Then it hit him.

"Hey! You called me Hopper."

Zucker's eyes twinkled. "It's your name, isn't it? Or maybe you prefer Chosen One?"

"That's not what I meant. It's just that, well, you used to call me—"

"I know what I used to call ya." Zucker chuckled, but his face was serious. He squared his shoulders, clicked his heels, and snapped Hopper a crisp salute.

Hopper flushed and saluted right back.

Then the prince excused himself to enter the palace; the crickets had orders from Firren that he was the only one to be allowed in until further notice.

Hopper was perfectly content to wait on the broad marble stairs.

He sat down and closed his eyes. Lulled by the cricket song, he must have dozed off for a moment, because he had a fleeting dream of the old cage in Keep's shop. The aspen curls were crisp and clean beneath him, Pinkie and Pup were sleeping comfortably, and their mother beamed with joy over her newborn litter.

And again there was the presence of that kind and gentle but powerful stranger, the second warmth, the second heartbeat. The goodness. The love.

Something jolted him awake. Not a sound or a touch but a feeling.

He opened his eyes and jerked upright, his eyes scanning the steps of the palace and the sidewalk below them.

There! Motion!

Hopper caught only a glimpse . . . a flash of gray-brown fur and a tail, darting away to disappear around the corner.

Friend? Foe? Stranger? He could not tell. He stood but could not bring himself to chase whoever it was that had come and gone so quickly. He felt no threat, no fear. Just a tingle of wonder and the lingering warmth of his dream.

Above him, he knew, there was a world of pet shops and sidewalks and all manner of human mystery.

Beneath him the remains of the refugee camp smoldered to embers.

Behind him a swarm of crickets held an emperor captive.

And before him . . .

Well, Hopper did not know precisely *what* lay before him now.

Alone on the grand steps of the Atlantian palace, Hopper gazed out over the abandoned city. He raised his chin and opened his arms and spoke to no one . . . and to everyone.

"I will make it right," he said in a clear, steady voice. "I promise to be steadfast and unfailing and worthy. And above all, I vow to make things right."

How? The little mouse could not imagine.

But he did know that from this moment on, he would do all in his power to see it through.

He would see it through and make it right.

# EPILOGUE

IT WAS HOURS BEFORE Zucker arrived at the entrance to Atlantia; it was well past dinnertime, and he was hungry, exhausted, and in a daze of confusion.

Cyclops opened the gate wordlessly. Zucker took in the bloody clump of bandage the cat pressed to his missing eye and walked past without comment.

He went directly to his father's audience chamber, where the emperor was meeting with his most trusted advisors and the elegant Queen Felina. Her jeweled collar twinkled as she inclined her head to the young prince.

Zucker bowed to Titus. "I beg a word, Father."

"Now?" Titus looked down his disfigured snout at his son. "I am engaged in royal business at present. You will have to wait."

Zucker considered pressing the issue, but he knew Titus would never relent. To show any deference to his only child might make him appear weak to his ally, the feline queen.

"All right," he said stiffly. "Later, then."

Titus gave Zucker a fierce look. "You have forgotten

to express your respect to our royal guest!" he barked, eyes flashing as he motioned to the white cat.

She was licking her chops, looking smug and satisfied.

Obediently Zucker gave the visitor his most gracious bow. "Good evening, Your Highness," he said. "You are looking very"—*well fed,* he realized, with a stab of panic—"lovely."

"Thank you," Felina purred. "My soldiers and I have just come from a most wonderful"—she smiled slyly—"banquet, I suppose you might say, especially arranged by your royal father. I enjoyed the most wonderful meal. It was positively . . . queenly."

"Well, that is suitable," said Zucker.

"You have no idea," the cat murmured.

"If you will excuse me, I am off to the royal apartments. I wish to speak with my mother, Empress Conselyea."

Titus cleared his throat and shifted a look at the large white cat. "As it happens, your mother is not about at the moment."

Zucker's whole body tightened, his senses on alert. "Not about?" he repeated.

Titus shook his head. "She has only just this morning been dispatched with the newest wave of colonists. She decided that, as their empress, she wished to lead them in their efforts to establish a new village to the east of Atlantia."

Zucker's heart stopped beating. "What did you say?"

"I said that your noble mother has taken it upon herself to go off and be a part of the worthy and ambitious colonization of the tunnels."

Felina flicked her snowy tail. "It was, shall we say, quite an enormous *sacrifice* for her." She sighed contentedly. "Personally, I think allowing Conselyea to become a colonist was a positively delicious idea."

It was as though all the blood drained from Zucker. He felt hollow, sick. Empty of everything but a sudden unquenchable rage.

His paw went to his sword. The sound of Felina's rumbling purr thundered in his ears as her words settled in his guts.

And he knew . . .

*He knew.*

Dodger and Firren had been telling the truth. The truth about the treaty and the hunt and the evil deceit being perpetrated by Zucker's own father, the emperor.

But even Dodger could have never imagined just how malicious Titus truly was.

Now, as his eyes darted from one malevolent monarch to the other, Zucker wondered:

Could he kill them both right now?

Was he quick enough, furious enough, to impale his father with his sword, then without so much as a second's hesitation, swing the blade and slice the queen's tongue right out of her mouth? Could he accomplish both of these gory deeds before his father's guards even realized his intentions and moved to restrain him?

Could he avenge his kind and gentle and utterly unsuspecting mother, who had been sent to a violent doom to satisfy the wretched self-serving agenda of a rat emperor and the voracious appetite of a heartless feline queen?

His heart sank.

*No.*

He was outnumbered. Outsized and outweighed. He would be dead on the floor before the tip of his sword even found his father's chest.

Besides, he was too numb with heartache, too stunned by the loss, to even find the strength to lift his weapon.

And furthermore, if he did attempt to assassinate these beasts and the guards killed him right here, right now, he would be surrendering any chance he might have to align with the rebels Firren and Dodger and put an end to this evil.

He could not bring back his mother.

But he could stay alive to fight in her honor. He could prevent this kind of atrocity from happening again. And again . . . and again.

"She went forth with such purpose," Titus reported with a sigh. "So regal was she, leading her subjects into the promise of a new and wonderful world." With a shaking hand the emperor covered his heart. . . .

Felina belched.

*Keep it together, Zuck,* the prince willed himself silently. *If he lies, you have to lie harder. Let him think you believe him. Let him think he's won.*

*But he hasn't. He won't.*

Zucker squared his shoulders and managed to smile. "Well, then I am proud and wish her well," he said. "Perhaps one day I shall visit her in her thriving new colony?"

"Perhaps," said Titus, his eyes blank. "But then your place is here, not out in the tunnels, isn't it?"

*If you only knew,* Zucker thought. *If you only knew . . .*

He bowed and left the throne room.

A war had begun. Somehow Zucker and his new friends were going to have to win it.

Deep in his heart, he knew that they would.

# ACKNOWLEDGMENTS

(MOUSE) HEARTFELT THANKS TO Ruta Rimas, who truly made this book possible. With unfailing instincts and a supercreative spark, she's the kind of editor writers wish for. She has been such a huge part of Hopper's story. He and I are both so lucky to have her.

I'm also fortunate to have the world's two greatest agents, Sue Cohen and Madeleine Morel, getting the job done. Thanks for taking care of business and for respecting my tendencies to panic, forget, take on too much, and never read all the way to the bottom of an e-mail.

# What happens next for Hopper and the rats of the tunnels?

Find out in this sneak peak
of *Hopper's Destiny*!

IT WAS NOT CRISP, cozy aspen curls he felt beneath him.

It was the cold, hard cement of the pet-shop floor that pressed against the fur of his belly.

Everything hurt—his bones, his teeth, his tail. He was aware of a frenzied scuffle going on around him—sweeping sounds, and Keep's heavy feet, his angry voice.

Pup opened his eyes.

The world from this vantage point was a flat, dusty expanse of floor dotted with the lifeless bodies of his cagemates. His stomach turned with grief and disgust as he blinked away the blur and searched for his siblings.

"Hopper?" he called. "Pinkie?" But his trembling voice was lost in the windy noise of straw against cement and the pattering of rain on the sidewalk outside the open door. Of course Pup did not know the names for straw and rain. He knew nothing of human objects and life outside his cage. But he did know this: he was in trouble.

"Hopper . . . Pinkie!" He tried again to holler, but his words were no louder than passing thoughts.

With great effort he lifted his head and scanned the shop. There! His brother and sister, scrambling down the cord that grew out of the money machine like an electrical tail!

*They're coming to get me,* he thought, relief overtaking him. *Hopper will save me.*

Pup closed his eyes and waited. The vibrations of Keep's tromping feet shook the floor, and damp air swirled in from the stormy world outside the door.

The door . . . toward which Pinkie and Hopper were running.

"No!" Pup cried out. "Wait for me."

He tried to lift himself onto his paws, but his fall—a terrifying drop through space, which he was only now beginning to remember—had left him far too sore. He could barely move at all, let alone with enough speed to catch up to his siblings.

Eyes wide with disbelief, he watched as the broom chased Hopper and Pinkie toward the door.

And then, with a bang, it slammed behind them, trapping them, Pup realized, forever out, while he was stuck here, forever in.

However long forever might be he could not begin to guess.

A flicker of motion caught his tear-filled eyes, and he turned toward it. A cagemate, left for dead beside a torn scrap of plaid fabric, had begun to stir. But Keep spotted the movement as well. Pup made to shout a warning, but the stiff bristles of the broom came down hard with a loud slap. Pup could almost feel the impact on his own shivering body as the updraft caused by the swinging broom sent the scrap of fabric fluttering into the air. It hovered briefly, like a checkered kite, then drifted downward to land once again on the dirty floor, this time within paw's reach of Pup.

"Gotcha!" gloated Keep as he shook his broom clean.

Pup gasped, his breath strangling in his throat as he bit back a whimper of terror.

"Nasty little varmints ripped my shirt," Keep muttered, frowning at the piece of fabric. He grabbed a dustpan from the counter and swept the squashed cagemate into it. Then he stamped across the room and bent down, using his boot to kick another unconscious mouse into the rusted dustpan.

Pup felt his blood freeze. Keep was cleaning up. . . . Mouse after mouse was being flattened, then swept or shoveled into the metal receptacle. Unless he could find a way to conceal himself, he would be next.

Muscles aching, he reached his tiny paw toward the fabric scrap. His claws closed around the frayed edge and he tugged it over himself, just as Keep turned to scan the area of the floor where Pup lay.

"That's all of 'em," the human grumbled, heading

for the back exit with his tray full of corpses.

*Not all of 'em,* thought Pup, quivering beneath the fabric. His brain spun as he tried to formulate a plan. But nothing of his life in the comfy cage had prepared him for a moment like this. He was alone and afraid, with only a torn piece of cheap material to protect him.

His siblings had escaped.

No—they'd gone and left him, without so much as a backward glance.

It was an image Pup would never forget, their two tails disappearing through the sliver of open space between the door and the rain. Part of him understood that they'd been running for their lives and had probably believed him already dead, but another part of him hurt, smarting to the depths of his soul. He'd been abandoned by the only two mice he'd ever trusted. The only two mice who had ever protected him.

As he huddled there beneath the plaid tatter, a small seedling of emotion began to take root. Pup could not identify the feeling, of course; it was as new to him as snakes and brooms and rainstorms. But he knew it did not feel good.

It made his claws clench and his teeth grind and the back of his neck sweat.

Had he been more worldly or educated, he would have known exactly what to call the sensation. But he was neither of those things. He was innocent, and naturally sweet, and until now he'd never had a reason to feel this miserable, gut-searing, heart-chilling *thing* he could not name. He understood only that he did not like the feeling at all.

And so he fought it, let it go, hoping it would never return.

But it would return. It would come for him again, though he could not imagine now how or when or even why. It would visit him in a place and circumstance he was still too inexperienced even to dream of, this biting, clawing feeling that filled him with such darkness. This thing he did not know enough to call anger, which had already given way to fear.

Because it was that moment when the door to the shop slammed open, letting in the noise, the damp, the rain.

And the boy.

The boy with his terrible, vicious, hungry snake.

"You again," snarled Keep, returning with his empty dustpan. "What do you want this time?"

"Same thing I wanted last time," the boy said. "Breakfast for my buddy. I only got two blocks away when I remembered he ain't eaten since yesterday. He can't wait for me to find another pet store, or trap some scrawny subway rat. He needs a meal now."

Keep snorted. "Well, that's too bad, because his breakfast just escaped. Every last hair of it."

Pup peered up at the despicable boy and the repugnant reptile that squirmed on his shoulders. Fangs curved out of its open mouth as its eyes darted around the shop.

Keep walked to the door, but before he could push it closed against the splashing rain, a gust of wet wind blew in, lifting the plaid scrap into the air once again and revealing Pup, curled on the floor.

"There's one," said the boy, pointing a bony finger.

Pup forced himself to lay still, allowing his eyes to open only into the tiniest of slits, through which to watch this sickening transaction.

"It's dead," said Keep.

"So what? Bo don't mind—do ya, boy?"

The snake answered with a hiss. Dead breakfast was better than no breakfast, it would seem.

"Still gotta charge ya," said Keep, ever the savvy businessman, "even if the beast's deceased."

"Half price," said the boy. "It's dead *and* puny." He dug into his pocket and fished out some coins.

"Fair enough," grumbled Keep. "Dead rodents only stink up the joint anyway. Go ahead. Take it."

The boy reached down and scooped up the presumed-dead Pup, who closed his eyes tight and held his breath. He almost wished he *were* dead.

Satisfied with their purchase, the boy and his snake ventured back out into the rain. Listening to the sound of his captor's sneakers slap the wet sidewalk,

Pup kept his body still and his eyes squeezed shut.

If only he had opened them.

If he had, he might have been able to peer through the slender space between the boy's fingers and see his brother and sister in the shadow of a trash barrel, fighting over a discarded piece of hot dog. He might have seen them lunge at each other, then roll toward the rushing water in the gutter.

He might even have seen the raging current sweep them away, to disappear from the Brooklyn outdoors forever.

Or perhaps not forever . . .

But Pup saw nothing except the inside of his own eyelids, pretending for all he was worth to be a lifeless knot of fur in the boy's clammy palm.

He would be dead soon anyway.

He might as well get used to it.

Pup had no idea how long he was clenched inside the boy's fist. They seemed to be traveling a great distance, the boy walking, the snake wriggling. At some point the boy stopped moving and stood still, only to continue to be propelled—not forward, but downward, smoothly. This seemed to trouble the snake, who (Pup could sense from inside the dark cocoon of the boy's curled fingers) grew tense around the boy's neck.

"It's okay, Bo. It's only an escalator. We'll be on the train in no time."

*Train,* Pup thought. Another word he'd never heard, another concept entirely foreign to him. But the idea of it, whatever it was, managed to soothe the snake.

Then the boy was walking again. Wherever the escalator had deposited them was a place without rain, because the spattering sound had stopped and the occasional drop that dribbled in between the boy's fingers had ceased.

Pup could smell humans—more than he'd ever smelled before, more than there had even been at any one time in Keep's cramped shop—and he could hear their gasps and cries of fear at the sight of Bo, writhing around the boy's neck.

The boy stopped walking, and suddenly Pup's delicate ears were assaulted with a loud growling noise that made his heart thump. The growl was followed by a kind of whistling shriek, as if some enormous beast had just exhaled.

"Best thing about riding the subway with you, Bo," said the boy with a chuckle, "is I get the whole car to myself."

Pup sensed the boy sitting, and then more movement, fast and sleek.

"Okay," said the boy. "Let's get you fed. One dead runt coming up."

The boy uncurled his fist, and Pup felt a chill as he was exposed to the air. Using his other hand, the boy pinched Pup's tail and lifted him up so that he was dangling, presumably, just above those lethal fangs.

"Open wide," the boy told Bo.

Pup was so seized with panic that he forgot to play dead; he opened his eyes and found himself bathed in a sickly greenish light, face-to-face with the diabolical boy.

Startled, the boy let out a shriek, releasing his grip and flinging Pup across the train car.

Bo hissed, furious at having been deprived of his breakfast a second time.

*Thwumpff.*

Pup landed on the seat opposite the boy's. He quickly scrambled to the edge and dove to the floor, keeping to the cavern beneath the long row of seats, where the boy could not see nor reach.

And he ran.

For a mouse his size, it was a lengthy run indeed. He could hear the wet soles of the boy's sneakers squeaking on the floor as he clambered around the car, searching out his undead prey.

"There he is!" the boy cried. "We got him cornered."

But just as the boy reached out to snatch Pup, the train came to a sudden, screeching halt. Boy and snake were flung forward, stumbling.

To Pup's delight, his pursuer fell hard, face-first onto the dirty floor.

The boy groaned; the snake squirmed.

Pup pressed himself up against the shiny metal door.

A mad hissing filled the car as the snake unlooped his scaly self from the fallen boy's shoulders and began to slither toward Pup.

But the whistling shriek of breath came again, and behind Pup the doors jerked wide, knocking the trembling mouse off balance.

Pup teetered on the edge of the subway car only long enough to see Bo's fanged mouth open.

And then he fell.

Out of the car and into the darkness.